Fear Ain't All That

Fear Ain't All That

Clint Adams

Copyright © 2005 Clint Adams

All Rights Reserved

ISBN 0-9768375-0-1

Published 2005

Credo *Italia*
2005

I dedicate this book to my mother,
with love and gratitude,
for having given me a most extraordinary life

ACKNOWLEDGMENTS

Thank you, Carla Perez, for your unending support and encouragement. We were meant to meet for many, many reasons, and I'm grateful for each and every one of them. From the years when I wrote the MIGUELITO children's stories to the present, thank you for cheering me on, thank you for pushing me to continue. You, your husband Virg, your daughters, and your son are rare treasures. Thanks to you all for making me feel like family.

Thank you, Diane Christiansen, for our twenty-five year friendship. You helped me when I needed it most; without you this project never would have been completed. Thanks, also, to your daughter Dominique, the wisest fourteen-year old I've ever met. You both have many reasons to be proud of each other; I think you're both heck'a cool.

Thank you, Samantha, for giving me so much joy. I will be grateful to you forever for always being a miracle in my life.

Thank you, Lindsay Yeazell. Both you, and your husband Jerry, are saints for listening to me go on and on and on about this book…and my cat.

Thank you, Angela Adair-Hoy, for saying "yes." Thanks to the editors and literary agents of the past who had told me "no" – you were meant to.

Thank you, Frank Greco, for your contributions, and for "getting it" so completely. No one has ever validated my efforts as much as you.

Thank you, Rose Hilliard at Time Warner, Inc., and Anne Hawkins of Hawkins & Associates, Inc. You both motivated me and inspired me to turn MIGUELITO into FEAR AIN'T ALL THAT.

Thank you, Sheryl Crow. Meeting you was an experience I'll never forget; your remarkable positive attitude influenced me more than you will ever know.

Thank you, Henry Riojas. I will always remember you and I in Circuit City together; I've never seen anybody negotiate better than you. If heaven is as good as it's cracked up to be, I'm sure you're now having the time of your life.

Thank you, Lynn Anderson and the Epidermolysis Bullosa Medical Research Foundation, Alfred Lane, M.D., Joseph McGuire, M.D., Eugene A. Bauer, M.D., Elliott Krane, M.D., the Stanford University School of Medicine, Graciela Torres, and Lexie Nall, Ph.D.

Fear Ain't All That

CHAPTER ONE

"Mom, do you think Aunt Shirley changed her hair again?" I asked.

"My goodness, Miguel, I certainly hope not. I think she changes hairstyles as often as she changes clothes."

"I kind of like that she does that. It always makes me wonder what she's going to look like next."

"Well, try not to say anything rude when you see her."

"I won't, Mom." As soon as I was picturing my aunt with short-spiked orange and black hair, I noticed that Mom had missed the turn to go to south on Highway 101. "Mom, we should have stayed straight, to get to the airport."

"Oh, I know. This will take us there just the same."

"But the airport's right off 101."

"280 connects to 101 in San Bruno, Miguel. We'll be there in plenty of time. Her flight might even be a little bit late. Not to worry."

"It just seems like 280 takes us more out of the way."

"There are just too many accidents on 101. Remember how those two people died in that horrible pile up last week? That was awful. Highway 101 is much too dangerous. Is your seat belt fastened? Make sure your door is locked."

Mom always reminded me to lock my door whenever I was in a car. She said that if your car door is locked, your body won't drag on the ground if you're thrown out during an accident. Mom's real good at thinking about things other people forget.

In just about an hour we were going to see Aunt Shirley for the first time in over a year. Aunt Shirley is my mom's sister, but they're definitely like night and day. Sometimes it's hard to think they're related at all. They don't even look the same. Mom's thirty-six, tall, with blond hair and blue eyes. Aunt Shirley is twenty-nine, with brown hair most of the time, and is about five three. But the absolute major difference is the way they live their lives.

My mom always used to say that Aunt Shirley is unique and one of a kind. And I guess that's true. She isn't just different from Mom, she's different from anyone I've ever known. Aunt Shirley's the only person who ever told me I was going to survive.

"Drink your water, Miguel. It's a warm day and you don't want to become dehydrated."

"How long is Aunt Shirley going to stay with us, Mom?"

"It could be for a while. She thinks she'll be moving to Berkeley soon, but we'll see. I don't know how she got it in her head that she'd be able to buy that house. I admire her efforts though. It'll be fun having her with us."

"Yeah. She's heck'a cool." But Aunt Shirley is way more than cool, and her moving to the Bay Area is something I always dreamed would happen. Mom warned me not to get too excited, but I couldn't help it. It was the middle of June, school was over, and Aunt Shirley and I were going to have lots of time to spend together. I couldn't wait. What would she teach me next? What new place would she take me to? Would she remind me of all her ways to make myself well? I hoped so.

Aunt Shirley said that Boston is like the east coast version of San Francisco, but San Francisco is still better. I was glad she thought that, so that way she wouldn't want to go back to Boston anymore since they're kind of the same. Plus, I don't think Boston has any cool things like the Exploratorium or the model of the bay that has its own wave-making machine.

"How long does it take to get a doctor degree again?" I asked Mom.

"*Doctoral* degree. It should take her a few years to complete. Shirley is very goal-oriented. I don't imagine she'll take more time than is required. Did you bring your cap with you?" Mom asked as we got closer to the short-term parking at the airport.

"Yes, Mom," I said as I put my Giants cap on. Mainly I did that to cover some of the mask bandage I have to wear on my face. My skin has to be protected all the time because that's what my disease is, a skin disease. It's called Epidermolysis Bullosa, and that means that the skin blisters. I think Epidermolysis and Bullosa are Latin words, but that's what it's called in America too. The exact kind I have is called recessive dystrophic Epidermolysis Bullosa, and way too bad for me, that's the worst kind. The main thing about E.B. is that I always have to be real careful, and because of my mom, I learned how to be extra cautious about everything I do. Mom's totally protective of me because she loves me so much. I love her too.

We found a parking space and had plenty of time to spare, even after taking the wrong freeway. Before we got out of the car, Mom, like she always did, looked into the car mirror to fix up her face. It never looked that messed up to begin with, but it was just her habit to do a few things to it just to make sure. One thing she always did was comb her eyebrows up because that's what she saw Cindy Crawford do once before in a fashion show at Fort Mason. Next was her hair that she fluffed up, and the way she did it actually made it look more messy. So, it was like it was the opposite of combing. "I'll open your door," she said.

"No. I can do it. Let me do it." Sometimes I struggled a little bit, but it made me feel good to make the door handle open even though I don't really have fingers anymore. "I can, let me," I told Mom. I didn't like it when she'd watch me do it my way because then I get real nervous. Our car had like a hook that you've got to get your finger into to pull the door open. My way was to use both hands pressed together with a pen in between them. Then, most of the time, I could pull the hook towards me and get the door open. "Wait, I can do it." This time it was taking extra long. Mom was staring at me, waiting. She was looking around to see if other people were looking at us. That made me even more nervous.

I tried a lot of times, but either the pen was slipping too much, or it was just too skinny to try to grab onto the hook. I couldn't do it.

I looked at Mom, and without saying anything she just opened the door from the outside and I got out. When she opened it, the look on her face was like she felt sorry for me. But I was hoping that she was glad for me that I at least tried to do it on my own. The minute we started walking to the terminal she said, "Why don't you lead the way to the gate. You're so much better at figuring out those monitors than I am." It didn't happen very often, but I really liked it when Mom believed in me and what I can do.

To be honest, there were so many screens and they all looked alike. They all said *Arrivals,* but I wanted to show Mom that I knew what I was doing. I wanted to look extra confident even if I really wasn't. Some of the flights were in red, some in blue, some in green. It was real pretty the way they did it, but what did all those colors mean? I didn't get it. Then I saw the word Boston, and I knew it had to be Aunt Shirley's flight. Right next to the flight number was the word "LATE" in bold, big letters. "Mom, it's late. What time is it now?"

"It's almost two-thirty."

"Well, this says the flight's not coming in until four-twenty-three." That meant that we'd have to hang around the airport for another two hours.

3

And, hanging out anywhere meant that there would be more people to stare at me. Aunt Shirley had always told me that people stared because they were curious, that's all. Whenever I didn't feel like explaining to them I'd say, "*The Mummy's* my favorite movie, and I'm just trying out my costume before Halloween gets here." I never said that in front of Mom though. She'd freak. Just because I always have to wear bandages all over my body most of the time she still never liked me calling myself a mummy. Not even as a joke. "Those bandages are protecting your skin. They're keeping you healthy. And there's nothing funny about that," she had always told me.

Not looking too discouraged about having to wait more time than she thought, Mom took me to a close by gift shop. Finding magazines to read is something we both liked to do. In the gift shop the customers were too busy looking for the thing they were going to buy, but the girl at the counter was the first one to stare at me. It's like I had just arrived at the airport on a flight from another planet. Was I imagining this? Is this what she was thinking? Or was she thinking, "Does that boy have E.B.? I wonder what that must be like?"

Then some businessman paid for a Milky Way and the girl stopped looking. So did I as soon as I saw a People magazine with Britney Spears on the cover. I like her a lot, but not as much as Christina Aguilera or Ricky Martin. It was always my dream to go to one of their concerts. The last time I saw Aunt Shirley she even made me put that on my *To Do* list. That's a list she made up for me to write in every day. She had told me that as long as I have things I have to do, the longer I will be around. "It's only the people who forget about all the things they have left to do, all the things they want to do, are the ones who die too early," Aunt Shirley had said.

Wow. I wondered if she was going to get pissed at me for not writing in my list lately. And lots of the things I had already written down I hadn't done yet. Was she going to ask me about that? Probably. Bummer. She even told me that every time I had to go to the hospital for treatment was because my list wasn't full enough. "When your mind stops working your body takes over," she always told me.

Eventually Mom and I walked out of the gift shop, but we hadn't bought anything. We couldn't go right up to the flight gate because we didn't have a ticket, so we waited inside one of the restaurants. It was a place that had crabs. I guess mostly just tourists ate there because that's what they think San Francisco people eat all the time, crabs and Rice-a-Roni. As long as I could eat Jell-O, or cheese, or something soft I was fine.

Where we sat was right at the window, and both my mom and I were real quiet. I just looked out at all the different planes. "Mom, how come that airline is called Virgin?"

Mom looked kind of surprised, and it took her extra long to answer me. "Miguel, I'm not sure. Because it's owned by the same man who owns the Virgin Superstore on Market Street. He wanted the names to correspond."

That answer totally wasn't good enough for me. I knew what a virgin was, but that answer wasn't logical and didn't make too much sense. What's up with that? Oh well. "Can we go to someplace way different for vacation this time?"

"Where? Where would you like to go?"

"I don't know. How about Africa? So we can see all those kinds of animals close up that are just in zoos."

"Oh, Miguel. I'm not so sure about Africa. I think that may be too dangerous. Did you know that nearly twenty-five million people have died there from AIDS? Just in the central and southern portions alone."

"But that doesn't mean we would get AIDS by visiting there."

"How about thinking of somewhere else? I'm sure there are many more fascinating places that are far less risky to visit."

"Well, what about Peru? To see those cool Inca pyramids that are way high up in the mountains?"

"I'm not so sure that's such a good idea either. South America seems so prone to massive earthquakes. Who's to say they won't have another at exactly the same time we're there."

After Mom said that I told her I'd think about more places, but I didn't. I figured that whatever else I would come up with Mom would have another reason for us not to go there. I just looked out at the planes and didn't think about too much at all. Then I remembered about what Aunt Shirley always kept telling me about the *f*-word. She said that that was the dirtiest word ever invented, the absolute worst word in our vocabulary. She said God didn't invent that word, people did, and it never should have ever existed in the first place.

There was another *f*-word God did invent though, a word called faith. It's the opposite of the other one. Aunt Shirley told me that I would never get well, ever, until I can get rid of the first *f*-word completely, a word called fear. "It's a killer," she used to tell me.

After remembering what Aunt Shirley taught me about the two *f*-words, I looked over at Mom. She always, always looked afraid of something. "What are you thinking about, Mom?" I asked.

"Shirley. She's going to be so disappointed when she doesn't get that house. We'll have to think of something fun to do to cheer her up."

"How do you know for sure she won't get that house?"

"She just won't. She'll never be able to qualify for a loan. You have to have lots of money in the bank in order to buy a house these days. Especially in the Bay Area."

When I watched Aunt Shirley coming towards us I couldn't believe it. She looked just the same as always, except for her new hair. It was red this time, and it looked like she forgot to fix it up after she fell asleep on her plane pillow. Half of her shirt was tucked back into her pants, and the other half wasn't. I noticed her first. "Mom, there she is. Hey, Aunt Shirley! Over here!"

"Not so loud, Miguel. She'll see us."

Aunt Shirley started running over to us. She was more excited than we were. She almost knocked over a man on her way to get to us, but it looked like she didn't care. And, one of the paper bags she was carrying fell, tore, and some of her clothes spilled out onto the ground. "Shit," she yelled out. But soon she was right in front of us. She hugged me right away, and it felt so good.

"Not too tight, Shirley."

"Hey, Sharon. Don't start with me. Get over here." Then Aunt Shirley hugged Mom real, real tight. No one else ever hugged Mom like that. I wondered if Mom liked it as much as I did. Mom and Aunt Shirley love each other a lot. They're like the way my brother Jorge and I were before he died. Kind of like twins, but not really.

"I can't believe I'm here. I can't believe I live here now. It's so great to see you two," Aunt Shirley said.

"Guess what, Aunt Shirley? Mom drove us all the way here. We didn't have to take a limo."

"Get out! Well, good for you, girl."

"It's no big deal. Stop," Mom said.

"Sure it is, Sharon. Little steps. That's what they are…little steps." Aunt Shirley was talking about Mom and her fears, and how she needed to finally get rid of them. I knew I was next. Was she going to ask how I was doing? That was always the first thing she wanted to know, if I've gotten rid of all my fears yet. "And, Mr. Miguelito man, what's up with you? How's your *To Do* list coming?" I just knew she was going to ask me that. "Are you remembering to say 'I will' instead of 'I want'? You're the one who makes things happen…not some other goomer. Don't forget it, bub."

"Well, sometimes," I said, in sort of a wimpy voice.

"Uh oh. I have the feeling sometimes means never." Aunt Shirley had an impatient and determined look on her face. She turned right over to Mom and said, "Let's hit the road, sis. I can see I've got some work to do here."

Faster than usual we all walked to get Aunt Shirley's luggage, ran to our car, left the airport, and drove home. Mom and I were too afraid to interrupt Aunt Shirley who was talking the whole time, but we didn't seem to mind. We were glad she was with us. I had the feeling Aunt Shirley's visit was somehow way more important this time. I had no idea though I was going to learn something from her that would change my life forever.

CHAPTER TWO

My mom told me that Yoko Ono lived in our building, on the very top floor. She's supposed to be somebody famous, but I didn't really know what for. I saw her once in the elevator with her glasses off, and I liked that she didn't glare at me the way most everybody did.

To me, our apartment was definitely the coolest. The best part about it was all the awesome places to see from out of the windows. Every day I looked for something new, something I had never seen before. Being in front of each window made me feel like I was in another world. Some places I'd make up from the map in my head, but other ones were real. My favorite real place was the Campanile building across the bay at UC Berkeley. I looked at it all the time since I found out Aunt Shirley was going to go there.

Whenever I wanted to feel good I took my binoculars out of its case and pointed them to the East Bay. It took a while, but when I focused it just right I could see the massive gray bricks that the Campanile's built with. I always wished I could hear the bells ring from it, but that's too much to ask for from binoculars. That way I would know when it's time for class. I thought maybe I'd go there someday, get real smart, and discover a cure for E.B. Then, for sure, that would make me real famous and people would talk about me in a real good way. But, even better, it's a way I could keep myself alive, instead of waiting for someone else to do it for me.

After the tall Campanile building, my next favorite thing to look at from my window was the Golden Gate Bridge. It's really not gold though. That would be way too expensive and people would try to steal parts of it. The real color it's painted is brownish-red and it's not even shiny. I'm so glad the terrorists didn't bomb it like they were supposed to. That would have been totally bad. Plus, how would I get to Sausalito? Sometimes I heard people call the Golden Gate Bridge the "Gateway of the West." I never thought it really was though because most people probably come in from the airport.

Khadijah said she's from New York, but her name's from Egypt. She was my new at-home nurse who I just met, Khadijah Parker. After she got done talking to Mom in the kitchen she came back into my room by herself and said, "It sounds like both of us have names no one can pronounce."

"I know. You mean my mom didn't know how to say your name right?" I asked.

"No. Not really, Mig-hiul-ito."

"You know what? That's still not right. Why don't you just say Mikey. That's what Miguelito's close to in English, Mikey."

"Are you sure?"

"Yeah. I get that all the time. People just never seem to get it right. I don't care, Khadijah. Just say Mikey."

"OK. As long as you're comfortable with that."

We both looked at each other at the same time not knowing what to say next, so then I took my turn and asked, "So do you know a lot about E.B.?"

"Well, yes. I've never worked with anyone who has E.B., but I've been trained very well. I know that it's an inherited disease. You'll be requiring daily care, and your mother told me that I'll be needing to dress you every morning."

"That's right. You know what I tell strangers what E.B. is? The easiest way to make them understand?"

"What?"

"I tell them, 'Did you know that there's a kind of glue that holds the layers of skin together? Well, I don't have that. My body doesn't make it. So that's why I have to be extra careful all the time. It's the same way on my insides too. I can only eat certain things. Like no potato chips, no cookies. That would be like cutting the inside of my stomach with razor blades.' After I tell them all that they get kind of grossed out and don't ask me anything else."

Khadijah liked my story. I didn't know if she got weirded out by what I just said, but she walked right over to the huge bay window in my room to check out the bay. "Wow, you must have the best view in the whole building. This is incredible. Gosh, you can see the entire East Bay from here. That's where I live."

"Where?"

"Berkeley."

"No kidding? Wow, that's amazing. You know what? You didn't get to meet my Aunt Shirley because she just went for a run through Crissy Field. But she's moving there real soon, to Berkeley. And she's going to go to school there too. Do you go to school at Berkeley? Or do you just live there?"

"Yes, I go to Cal. I'm in their dance program. I want to be a professional dancer someday. What's your aunt studying?"

"Acting. I mean, the kind of acting that's not really acting." I couldn't think of the right word right away, then I remembered. Drama, but not the acting part. She's getting her doctor degree there. You know, the kind that's not a hospital doctor. She just wants to write plays but not be in them."

"Are you serious? I can't believe this. The dance program is part of the drama school there."

"Well, she'll be back in about an hour. You'll get to meet her. She'll be pretty sweaty though, if that's OK. But she's way cool."

"Oh, sure. I can't wait."

Having Khadijah as my newest at-home nurse made me feel like something special was going on, mainly because I found out she's kind of connected to my favorite person, Aunt Shirley. Maybe they'd become friends. Maybe we could all be friends. I should have known Khadijah was a dancer from the start. Her black, curly hair was kind of big, and her chest was too. She definitely looked like she could be in the videos on MTV. Not like the Destiny's Child or TLC videos, but more like the Janet Jackson ones. She's real pretty like Janet Jackson, even though her really tiny nose is more like LaToya's or Michael's.

Out of nowhere it was nobody's turn to say anything. Khadijah was still standing at my bay window and it got real quiet again. Then as soon as she turned to see the picture on my special glass table near my bed she asked, "Who's this?"

I was caught off guard, and all of the sudden I didn't really feel like talking about anything personal. But she asked about it again. "A friend of yours?"

"Um, he was...I mean, he's my brother," I answered.

"Oh, your mother didn't mention that you have a brother. Where's he? Does he live with your father?"

"Well, no. Um, he's dead. Jorge had E.B. too."

"Oh, wow. I'm so sorry, Mikey." She looked totally embarrassed for asking about Jorge in the picture.

"It's OK. I like to have that picture there so I can look at it a lot. I want to remember him every day. He'd probably like it that you asked about him, even though he doesn't know who you are. He'd definitely think you were real cute, you know, 'cause you look like a movie star."

"A movie star? Oh, my. Well then, I'm flattered. He's pretty cute too."

"Oh, he'd *really* like to hear you say that. Jorge never had a chance to have any girlfriends. He probably would have if he'd have lived longer. I miss him a lot. He was my best friend. He was smart too, he taught me lots of important things."

"That's great that he was able to do that...be your brother *and* your teacher."

"Yeah, it definitely was. I know I don't know you too well, but I'll show you how smart he was. He gave me something real special right before he died. It's kind of private. I keep it under my mattress so it won't ever get wrinkled." With all my strength I reached for it, but it was farther back than I thought. "Can you help me? Maybe you can lift this corner part up, so I can get to it."

"Sure. No problem."

"In case you didn't know my hands are what they call, 'mittened.' All the skin has grown over my fingers, so it's like they're not there anymore. The only time when it's the most uncool is whenever I've got to use the keyboard on my computer. But I got over it."

"What are you two up to?" my mom interrupted, as she stood in the doorway staring.

Khadijah began answering. "Mikey was going to—"

"We were just adjusting the mattress. It's good to do that once in a while, so it won't wear out in the wrong places," I answered quickly, as I immediately let go of what I was grabbing for.

"Well, that certainly is efficient of you both. How are things going? Is Miguel filling you in on everything you need to know?"

"Yes, Ma'am. He's been great."

"Yes. I think Miguel knows more about E.B. than most medical experts."

"Mom, guess what? Khadijah's goes to Berkeley, just like Aunt Shirley. And, not only that, they're in the same compartment."

"*De*-partment. Really?"

"Yeah, whatever. Can you believe it?"

"Well, that truly is a coincidence. Isn't it?" my mom said, while looking a little shocked.

"Khadijah, when you meet Aunt Shirley she'll tell you that it's not a coincidence. She'll say there's a reason why you two are in the same department. Aunt Shirley says there's reasons for everything."

"Miguel, don't confuse Khadijah about your Aunt Shirley. You'll be able to meet her soon. I know you'll get along just fine. Maybe you'll be able to help her along. She's starting up there this fall."

"Oh, of course. I can't wait to meet her," Khadijah said.

As Khadijah and I were making tuna sandwiches in the kitchen, Aunt Shirley almost broke the front door down with her pounding. Mom had gone to Union Square to do some shopping, and she wasn't coming back until a lot later in the afternoon. "Oh my God. These hills are killers. Whew!" Aunt Shirley yelled out as she opened our front door after realizing that she had her own key.

I ran into the living room and greeted her immediately, "Hey, Aunt Shirley, guess what? Come in here, Khadijah." Khadijah walked in, and I introduced them both.

"You ran up Nob Hill?" Khadijah asked.

"You better believe it. I first ran from here, down Jones Street, through Fort Mason to Crissy Field, then to the Bridge, and back up again. But I tell you, there's nothing like a good challenge first thing in the morning. That makes the rest of the day a piece of cake. Even if it does leave you a little breathless...running uphill."

"Aunt Shirley, Khadijah's in the drama department at Berkeley. I mean, the dance department, they're the same."

"Get outta here. Well then, let's get right to it. Spill the beans."

"What do you mean?" Khadijah asked.

"We were meant to tell each other something, or learn something from each other. Or maybe our meeting has something to do with this guy right here. I guess we'll find out sooner or later."

I knew Aunt Shirley would say that they were meant to meet. Right off Khadijah looked confused and kind of afraid. But all three of us ended up hanging out for a while until it was time for Khadijah to head back home to the East Bay. She seemed to fit right in, and I was so glad she was my new nurse. The classes she was taking that summer were at different times from when she needed to take care of me in the city, so everything was totally convenient.

The weather outside was real sunny, but not too warm. It was just right. More like in-between weather. No more rain, but just before the foggy summer. And way before the earthquake weather that happens during Indian summer. Maybe the nice weather made Mom extra happy because when she came home she was smiling all the time. She was really happy to see Aunt Shirley there. Mom looked full instead of empty. Seeing Mom so happy made me feel the same way.

"Shirley, is there any way you could stay here with us while you attend your classes? You're more than welcome to stay as long as you want."

"Yeah. That way you could just take BART to get there. No biggie," I said.

"BART? What the...? Is that your *T*?" she asked.

"Yes. It's the same as the *T*."

I definitely didn't know what the *T* was. A dirty word they had to spell instead of saying out loud? Whatever. I didn't want to look dumb, so I just asked, "Are you going to, Aunt Shirley?"

"What are you talking about, guys? You know I'm buying that house in the hills. Escrow closes in about two weeks now. I can't wait for you both to spend lots of time with me there."

Mom's face turned to me and looked real skeptical, like right when those call-in psychic infomercials come on TV and Mom always says, "I can't believe people believe in this nonsense."

"You're for sure going to move there then?" I asked.

"Oh, yes. Absolutely. I can't wait. It's going to be my own private haven."

"Well, what about the financing? Has that come through yet?" Mom asked.

"No."

"What's your FICO score? How much is the down payment? Were you able to come up with that?"

"No."

"Did someone tell you you'll be able to get the financing? A mortgage broker?"

"Not yet."

"I don't understand then. Why don't you just plan on staying here with us until you're able to—"

"Oh. Thank you. But I *am* buying that house. I've worked hard to make it happen, and it will."

"What exactly makes you think you can though?"

"Because I believe."

"You believe what?"

"I believe I can make this happen. By believing it will happen...it will. I believe the financing will come through exactly when it's supposed to. I have no reason to believe I won't be moving into that house. None. I have no fear whatsoever. And what do I have instead, folks? I have absolute faith it will all come about."

"Oh, my. Fear. 'Have no fear.' That's your beloved credo."

As usual Mom and Aunt Shirley talked again about a subject that always came up, fear vs. faith, so I went into my room to check my e-mail. When I was there I wasn't sure if they were done or not because I couldn't hear anything. They've had this talk about a million times before and I always got real tired of listening to it. It was the one topic that usually got Aunt Shirley really fired up, you know, pissed.

By the time I had deleted my last junk message about trampy teen vixens, Aunt Shirley came up to me at my desk. She looked real calm, but it was like she was just forcing her face to be that way. It didn't look natural at all. She said, "Miguelito, I've decided that it's better for me to stay in the East Bay until my house is ready."

"Why? You don't like it here? Is it me?"

"Of course not. I love you. This has nothing to do with you. It's just better this way."

"So then it's Mom. Is it because of the fight you just had?"

"No. We weren't having a fight. We're just completely different. I love your mother a lot. She's my sister. I'd do anything for her."

"I don't really get it then. If you stay here with us it doesn't cost anything."

"I just have to go. It's not...really good for me to be here. I have to protect myself."

"From E.B.? You know it's not contagious, right?"

"I know that, you jughead. I told you, this has nothing to do with you. I love you more than sugar, and you'll visit me often in Berkeley. We'll have a terrific time. Keep that one in your head, doll."

"OK. Yeah, that'll be good."

Then Aunt Shirley's eyes were trying to tell me something, and I had to wonder what until she said, "Someday you'll know exactly why I've had to leave. I know it'll all be so clear to you, you'll see. And when it does your whole life will change. Someday."

Even though Aunt Shirley told me I would know someday, I already did. The minute she walked out of my room all I could think about was something I heard a couple of months before. "You've got to destroy all the fears you've learned...," Aunt Shirley told me out loud. Then her eyes said, "...or you'll never survive."

CHAPTER THREE

"Wait a minute. How do you say it again?" Mom's new boyfriend asked. His name's Hunt Manly and he's some kind of movie-person from L.A. I didn't know if he was for real or not, but I acted like he was because he's Mom's friend.

"It's Mee-gehl-eee-toe. Or, you can call me Mee-gehl."

"Meee-guhl-eee-noe."

"No. That's still not right. But, I don't care. Just say Mikey. That's cool."

I could tell he tried his best, so that's OK. This was the first time I met this guy my mom was going out with. They'd been together two or three months already, but for some reason I'd never met him before. Mom wanted the night to be special so the boyfriend decided we'd all have dinner at the Fairmont Hotel. It's only a block from our apartment, directly through Huntington Park. Mom was still getting ready in her room, so Hunt and I were alone in the living room talking.

He looked kind of like an actor-type 'cause he had gel in his hair. San Francisco people don't do that. And since he looked that way I figured that's how he got his name. "Is your name real?" I asked.

"Is it *real?* Of course."

"I just meant that it sounds like a made-up name. No offense. You know, like somebody from *The Young & the Restless.*"

"I know. I've heard that before. And, I guess you could say that Mih-gweleee-no sounds like a name straight out of some Mayan village in the Yucatan," he said with a hard look right back at me. At first I was going to apologize because I didn't mean to insult him, but then, after what he said, I didn't care.

"How much longer, Sharon?" the guy shouted towards Mom's room.

"I'm nearly ready, Hunt. Two more minutes."

The boyfriend and I didn't say anything during those two minutes that turned into ten. Then, just trying to be friendly, I said, "You probably

15

already know they filmed *Hotel* at the Fairmont. That's a really cool TV program because they show so much of the city in it. Except when they did all that I wasn't born yet. But at least I can watch it now on SoapNet."

"Well, they didn't actually film it there. I'm sure they just shot exteriors and some second-team stuff."

"Oh, yeah. That's right." I didn't know what that meant. I didn't even know TV people were on teams. "But there was lots of other stuff that was filmed here in the city. Do get to be with a lot of famous actors?"

"I don't really get to know them. They *work* for me. I'm their boss. I'm a producer. Sharon, do you think you can you speed it up a little?"

Mom walked out, and from that moment on the boyfriend really didn't listen to mostly anything I had to say. He was totally focused on Mom. And Mom was focused on him. As we left our building he and Mom walked in front of me, and I walked behind. The boyfriend made a weird look to my mom after they walked by one of the regular homeless people in the park. "Hey, Charlie. What's up?" I said as I passed by.

"Are you staying out of trouble, young man?" Charlie asked.

I nodded yes, and didn't really answer more because I didn't want the boyfriend to give me that same weird look he gave to Charlie.

"Mom, can I have the dim sum? That should be OK, right?" I usually couldn't eat the kind of food everybody else got to eat, but I thought dim sum would be perfect. Not spicy. Not sharp. Easy to digest. Just perfect.

"It should. Just make sure not to dip them in the sauce," she answered.

We were at a restaurant in the Fairmont I had never been to before, the Tonga Room. It was way cool, but I didn't get it. The whole place looked like *Gilligan's Island* but without Gilligan, Ginger, Mr. Howell, or anyone else from the show. And, there were tons of strange sounds too. "How come this place has so many weird noises?" I asked.

"Ambience. Rainstorms and hurricanes are common in Polynesia," the guy said. He answered my question by not looking at me. He was looking at his menu when he spoke to me. I guess he thought I must have been invisible.

"I think this is all heck'a cool though. I've never seen outdoor palm trees inside before, and that pond too. Wow. I hope there's no birds in those trees up there, or else we'll all end up with bird poop in our dinners."

"Miguel, please. That's disgusting," Mom said.

I mainly said the thing about the bird poop to see if anyone was really listening to me.

When the dinners came, all the food smelled pineappley. Yum. I just ate and let Mom and her boyfriend do most of the talking.

"So, when are you coming down again? There's plenty of restaurants we haven't tried yet. And don't forget about all that shopping," the boyfriend said.

"Well, I'm not exactly sure. My sister just came out here, and I want to spend time with her," Mom said.

"Bring her down with you. I'd love to meet her."

"Oh, I think she's too busy right now. She's got a lot on her mind."

"Instead of calling it Los Angeles, Aunt Shirley calls it the city of lost angels. Get it? She kind of hates it. She said she'd never go there even if you paid her a million dollars."

"Miguel, dear. Finish your dim sum," Mom said.

I could tell that I didn't really need to say that to the boyfriend, but I also knew how important it was to tell the truth. Maybe Aunt Shirley was wrong though. Maybe there were good parts about L.A., and about the people who lived there. Maybe the best sides of who the boyfriend really is just didn't show yet.

"Sharon, you know, I'm going to be needing someone who has experience putting together fundraisers soon. For a big event at the Beverly Hilton. And, it's going to be tied into promoting one of my films that's due to come out soon."

"The one about the e-mail slasher?"

"Yes, that one. Do you think you'd be interested in working for us?"

"In L.A.? What's the cause? The event will raise funds for...?"

"I'm not really sure. Something about AIDS or rape. One of those. I forget."

"But, Hunt. Would I have to be there for just a few weeks? Or a few months? About how long?"

"We'd probably need you for several months. You could do some of the work from here I'm sure. You'd be able to meet a lot of celebrities. Lots of important people. It's a good opportunity for us both."

"Well, I'm not so sure I've got the time right now. Miguel and I are right in the middle of planning our fall vacation. And, he has to be near Stanford for treatment. Plus, Shirley and her new home. I know she'll need me to help her decorate. If you truly need someone right now, I'm not sure I'm the one."

"Why don't you bring Mikey down with you. And, as far as your sister goes, I think you and she probably have very different tastes. Mikey, what do

17

you think about that? How would you feel about meeting some of Hollywood's top dogs? Tom Cruise? Ben Affleck? Erik Estrada?"

"Wow. You know those people?" I asked.

"Well, no. Not exactly. But I know people who do."

"Yeah. That would be way cool. Definitely. How about Ricky Martin?"

"Sure. Why not. I'm sure we can track him down."

"Mom, is that OK? Can we go? I don't have any school. And, if I don't get sick I don't have to go back to Stanford for another month."

Mom looked worried, but I bet she was glad to see me so excited about something. She had a grin on her face, and she liked it when I was really happy. I knew she would say yes because if she said no I'd be totally sad. Mom wasn't the kind of person to just say "What the hell?" She had to think about things real hard before she ever said OK to anything.

Finally it was the fourth of July, a day my dad and I always used to celebrate together. I missed him so much. After he and Mom got their divorce two years before, I only got to see him once in a while. My dad's from El Salvador, so that's where my name comes from – it's Spanish. Dad picked it out when I was a baby, and he got real mad at people who couldn't pronounce Miguelito.

Even though I didn't get to see him too much, Dad used to write me letters all the time. I liked that. My mom always used to say that he kind of sounded like Ricky Ricardo. I thought of Dad a lot when I looked out my window to see ships going past the Golden Gate Bridge and out into the ocean. When I got real lonely I pretended I was on one of those ships that was going to El Salvador. And that way I could surprise my dad. He would have been glad to see me for sure. The last time I had seen him was at my apartment on Halloween almost a year ago, three days after my twelfth birthday.

Dad had lots of presents for me on that visit, and they all came from El Salvador. "I know you're going to like this one," my dad had said to me, "but you're going to have to read the directions in Spanish. No problem, right?"

"Right, Dad. No problema," I answered.

"Joe, I'm not so sure that speaking Spanish is such a good idea. It'll confuse Miguel," my mom had said. She called my dad "Joe," but his name is really Joaquin. Mom kind of did that once in a while, turning anything Spanish into something American, just so she could pronounce it right.

Dad gave Mom a weird look, but then quickly asked me, "So, are you going to open it? Or what?"

"Duh yes, Dad." With the way my hands were, I had to tear the paper kind of slow so it wouldn't scratch me. But, when I finally ripped it all off, and lifted up the lid of this huge box I couldn't believe it. "Oh my God!!! Are you for real, Dad? I've been wanting one of these forever." It was an absolutely awesome digital camera. They were a totally new thing then. "Now I can take pictures of everything, and send them all over the world along with my e-mails. Thanks, Dad. This is way cool."

"I want to have lots of pictures of you when you write to me, OK? And you better be smiling in them. Got it?"

Dad knew I didn't like to smile too much because E.B. kind of messed up my teeth pretty bad. They were sort of stained and gross. "Of course, Dad. I'll send you pictures all the time," I had told him. Then I walked over to him at the couch and hugged him. Somehow he knew exactly what I wanted more than anything.

I was going to ask him how to work the camera, but my mom interrupted by asking me, "Now, do you really think you'll be able to manipulate all those complicated mechanisms? It looks so menacing. Maybe there's an easier one for you to use."

"What, Mom?"

"How are you going to push all those buttons? How are you going to focus that lens? I mean, it's a nice camera. But your hands can only do so much."

"But, Mom, I can still do lots of things with my hands. I'll make it work. You'll see."

"Joe, this was a great idea. But I don't really know if it was so practical."

I could almost tell that a fight might happen soon, so I went over to a chair on the other side of the room, sat down, and pretended to read those Spanish directions to myself.

"Sharon, give the kid a chance. Let him try it out. Then, if it doesn't work, I'll get him another."

"I'm just trying to minimize the disappointments in his life. Letting him get excited over something he will never be able to use is a health risk."

"I believe the more opportunities Miguel has, the healthier he'll become."

"But it's not just his health that concerns me. It'll be so awkward for him. I just know he'll become so self-conscious of other people looking at his hands. You see, when he tries using it in public. That's all I'm saying."

"Sharon, I don't get it. Why don't you let Miguel live his life? He's a resourceful kid. What are you so afraid of?"

"Well, I don't know, Joe. My goodness, your rose-colored visions. I just don't want to let Miguel get his hopes up. I'm only thinking of what's best for him. You should do the same."

"There's no way I will ever *not* let Miguel get his hopes up. I won't do that. Miguel is going to survive and live a happy life. I'm certain of it!" My dad yelled out, as he pounded his fist down on one of our glass tables. They've had discussions like this before, so it wasn't ever new for me. But this time Dad looked so determined, so definite, like he had some sort of plan inside his head. Whenever he would visit it was because Mom invited him. She had sole-custody of me, so Dad really had no say in my life. He was just a visitor.

Dad looked over at me sitting across the room, and gently grabbed my mom's arm. He took her into the kitchen so I couldn't hear anything. I just stayed in my chair, glanced at the rest of my presents I got that I really didn't care about, and thought of what my mom and dad could be saying.

Was my mom going to make him take the camera back? What was Dad going to do? Was he going to maybe kidnap me and take me back to El Salvador with him? Was my mom going to make it so I could never see Dad again? Were we all going to have to go back to court another time to see who gets me?

Before long everything got still. My dad came out of the kitchen, but Mom stayed in there. Dad and I never discussed any of the questions that were in my mind, so we couldn't talk about any of the answers either. Maybe I didn't want to know.

Dad came back out and said it was time for him to go. So he and I left my apartment and walked to the elevator outside my front door, and there we waited.

"These elevators sure are taking a long time today," my dad had said.

I was glad it took so long because the longer it took to get to our floor, the more time we had to spend together. "Yeah. Well, maybe somebody's moving today. That happens a lot." We got in and down we went to the garage. *Twenty-Nine, Twenty-Eight, Twenty-Seven, Twenty-Six.* Now the elevator was going too fast for me.

"El Señor Miguelito, you know I'll be back for you someday, right?"

"Really? I thought you had to stay in San Salvador for a while." *Nineteen, Eighteen, Seventeen.*

"Miguel, I promise you. Whatever it takes I'll be back for you. I will work it out somehow so you'll be able to live with me part of the time. Whenever you need me I'll be here for you, to take care of you...always."

When he had said that he held my hand and it didn't hurt. I knew what he just said was special and true. *Eleven, Ten, Nine.* Then, a man and woman slowly got on at the eighth floor. They were dressed up like Regis and Kelly. And they were both carrying microphones which was kind of dumb because on their TV show they never really do that. The Regis-man couldn't stop looking at me. He was a little drunk or high and said, "That costume is far out, kid. You look like you're straight out of a *Frankenstein* flick."

"No. Not *Frankenstein,* more like *The Mummy*, the Kelly-woman, who was also a little high, said to the Regis-man.

Before I could say anything my dad looked at me and made his eyes roll around in a circle. His look to me automatically erased what the man and the lady had just said. I've heard things like that so many times before, that I looked like a mummy, but my dad was never around to do anything about it.

"My son wears these bandages every day of his life. And at age twelve he's learned more than you'll ever know in your lifetime. He's first class." *Lobby*.

"Hey...look, sir. I had no idea," the man said to my dad while looking kind of dumb. Then he said to me, "I'm sorry, kid. I didn't know."

"That's OK. It happens all the time." The elevator doors opened, the two people got out, then the doors closed quickly. *Garage 1, Garage 2, Garage 3*. Dad and I walked over to his rental car without saying anything.

When we got to it we stood there and Dad talked first, "For the rest of my life I will never be more proud of you than I am right now. You amaze me."

"What do you mean, Dad?"

"There won't ever be another boy alive who has what you have. Always remember how special you are. Remember it every day. Remember me telling you this. You are truly good, Miguel. The respect you come up with for others is incredible. You are powerful. I know you have the ability to make yourself well. I'm sure of it."

"I *do?*"

"You crazy burro. Of course you do, you know that. And I'm going to keep writing to you, and I'll be expecting responses too. Responses with pictures taken from your new camera."

"OK. I will, Dad. I'll write to you, and I'll definitely send some pictures. But, when am I going to see you again?"

"Soon, I hope. And I'll always be thinking of you. I love you, Miguelito," Dad said, as he hugged me hard enough so I could feel it, but not enough so it would hurt. I could see him try not to cry, but I could still tell. He got in his car and so did I.

He gave me a ride to where the elevators were, and I said, "I love you too, Dad. And thanks for all my cool presents. Especially for my camera."

"Good-bye, my Miguel," Dad said after he stopped the car. We both got out and hugged each other.

Right before Dad got back in I said "good-bye," but I couldn't see his face. While I got onto the elevator I turned around, pressed *Thirty*, and as the doors were closing I saw Dad say, "M-a-k-e...y-o-u-r-s-e-l-f...w-e-l-l," through the car window.

I wasn't sure why he had said than then, but I shook my head to say "OK."

Many months went by before I ever saw him again.

CHAPTER FOUR

"Am I going to have to be here much longer?" I asked.

"More than likely another week or so, at least," the beginning doctor answered.

"But then I'm going to miss too much school, and get real behind with everything."

"Doctor de Pascual told me that you've had several stays with us here before. You're quite used to it, yes? All the procedures?"

"Yeah. I know about them all, that's for sure."

"So you know by being here you'll be treated very well. From what I can tell everyone here really seems to like you."

"I like everybody here too, especially Lefty."

"Who's that? I'm afraid I've never heard of him."

"Sure you have. Dr. de Pascual. Since his first name is Elefterios, I just call him Lefty. I always have."

"I doubt if he'd let anyone else call him that but you. You must get along with him rather well."

"Yeah, he's way cool. He tries real hard to make it so I won't have to have surgery another time. Are you the one who decides if I have to have it again?"

"No, Dr. de Pascual will make that decision. But remember, right now you're here for observation only, and treatment to your intestines."

Talking to me was one of the beginning doctors in the Dermatology Department. There were always a bunch of new ones coming in. But, this one's OK. I never knew if he was a resident or intern or whatever, so I just called him, "Doctor."

I spent a lot of time at Stanford. It's really called the Lucille Salter Packard Children's Hospital at Stanford University Medical Center. Nobody ever said all that though.

It's the kind of place where a lot of important research gets done. There are tons of laboratories with scientific experiments all over the place there.

23

When they find a cure for E.B. it's probably going to come from one of the doctors at Stanford. I could never tell my Aunt Shirley that though because she had this thing about Stanford. She thought Berkeley was way better. The two schools are rivals, like USC and UCLA, Harvard and Yale, peas and carrots. You know, that kind of stuff.

Aunt Shirley also had a thing against anything private, anything that's not for all the people. Berkeley is a public school and Stanford is private. I'm not really sure what's up with that, but Stanford people always make a big deal that John F. Kennedy and Chelsea Clinton went there. I think Berkeley's most famous student is still Patty Hertz, that girl from the car rental place who got kidnapped.

Anyway, what I always cared about the most was to get better, no matter where I was. No matter who found a cure first. Getting an infection on the skin in my lower intestines never happened before. Usually it was always to some skin on my outsides. I couldn't eat or drink anything, at least not through my mouth. That really sucked.

Just a little bit after that new doctor left, Dr. de Pascual came into my room. "Hey, Lefty, what's happening?" I asked.

"Hello, Miguelito, how are you doing today? You look like you're in a good mood," the doctor said.

"Yeah, I think it's the buzz from the painkillers they're giving me. Am I going to have to sign up for Betty Ford after this?"

"I don't think they admit children, so you'll probably just have to find another place to dry out."

"OK, I'll start looking. Um, do you think I need to have surgery this time?"

"It's too early to tell. You've only been in here for two days and I have the feeling we're not going to know until you've been here for a whole week. But I'm optimistic."

"Duh, who isn't? But you know what? Sometimes I get real tired of being optimistic, and maybe I'd just like to forget all about it."

"Forget all about *what?* What do you mean?"

"I've been thinking about Jorge a lot lately. He told me something right before he died, that I need to do. Or else I'm going to get a lot worse."

"Well, what was that?"

"He said that I definitely have to get rid of all the fear we learned from...Mom. You see, Mom loves me a whole lot, and I love her too, but she doesn't let me do too much of anything 'cause she's afraid all the time."

"Afraid of what?"

"I don't know. Everything."

"But, Miguelito, you know your mother is so devoted to you. She's a major benefactor to the Children's Hospital, and she especially supports the E.B. gene therapy research done here. Without her money, I mean, her contributions, our progress would certainly be hindered. She's a saint."

"That's for the hospital though, I'm talking about me. Sometimes Mom gives her money away so people will like her more. I think that's the main reason she does it." The doctor's face looked completely shocked by what I was telling him, but I continued, "You know what? I think the reason I got sick this time is because of the man who's her new boyfriend. I don't know if he's so good. My gut tells me bad things about him. Part of me thinks that maybe I should move in with my Aunt Shirley right now. She always tells me good things about my future, and she said I'll only have one when I'm not afraid anymore. Maybe she's supposed to be kind of like my mom just for right now. Until I get better."

"Your Aunt Shirley?"

"Yes, don't you remember her? She always comes to see me when I'm here. She just moved to Berkeley."

"Of course I remember her. She's very...creative in the way she thinks. We've had many...interesting discussions. Do you think she has the means to support you, and care for you properly?"

"Aunt Shirley says that money will always be there when you really need it the most. You must *believe* it will be there. 'Act like you already have it,' she says." "Well, she certainly seems to have some unconventional notions. But for the moment you're going to remain with your mother, yes?"

"Yeah. I guess so."

"I'm not so sure you're giving your mother enough credit. She's a wonderful woman. To us here at Stanford, she's a hero. I can't imagine she would be so devoted to us here if she weren't doing it all for your sake. She does love you, Miguel."

Maybe I was wrong about Mom, and she probably was doing everything just for me. Sometimes I forgot about all the cool stuff she bought me.

Three days had gone by before she ever visited me once at the hospital though because Hunt needed her to be with him in L.A. He told her she had to be with him to meet with movie star people down there, so she couldn't be in two places at once. It's kind of like whatever he says goes. That's OK, because I knew Mom would come to see me some time when she could.

Aunt Shirley came to visit me a lot, and she had to come all the way from across the bay. All I could think about when I knew she was coming was to figure out new ways I could ask her about moving in. I thought if I could live with Aunt Shirley, even just for a little bit, I could make myself well. Or, maybe she could help me think of some way I can live someplace else where I won't be forced to be afraid. Then I thought, maybe I could live at a place where they do lots of E.B. research, like Stanford, and be their guinea pig. Then they could do as much tests on me as they wanted. I thought that maybe these kinds of places needed people like me.

Dr. de Pascual said that most of the tests being done were on animals though, and not humans. Plus, the kind of tests they were doing sounded kind of gross anyway. It's called skin grafts, and that's when they take off bad skin and put on good skin. I figured I already had enough going on with mine. I didn't need anyone ripping if off, and putting new skin back on again. Even if it was supposed to help me.

When I wasn't thinking of ways to move, I remembered all the things my Aunt Shirley taught me when she had visited. I looked forward to her visits all the time.

In the middle of my stay at the hospital Aunt Shirley came to see me for the third time, and taught me some new ideas.

"What's in that bag you put on the floor?" I asked her.

"Well, it's a gift for you, doll," Aunt Shirley answered, as she reached down and picked up a small box from inside the bag.

"Cool. Can I open it now?"

"Sure. Here, all you have to do is lift up the lid, so it's easy to open. If you need help, let me know."

Inside the box was a wristwatch, but it looked completely different. Not at all like a Timex or Casio.

"I'll put it on you," Aunt Shirley said.

"Thanks. I never saw a watch like this before. Is it supposed to light up or something?"

"No, it doesn't light up."

"Well, maybe it needs new batteries, right?"

"No, it doesn't use batteries."

Wow, I thought no one had a watch like this. It had a strap that was real soft, but I couldn't see any dials or numbers or anything. It had a glass piece that was dark, so I figured part of it was probably just broken. "Is it supposed to look like this?" I asked.

"Oh, yes. Absolutely," Aunt Shirley said.

"But, I'm not so sure how to tell time with it."

"It doesn't tell time."

"Oh, I get it now. So, it's *not* a watch then."

"Of course it's a watch. Every time you look at it, it will remind you that time doesn't really exist. Time is an invention of man. There is no beginning or end. It's something that goes on and on and on."

"I don't know if I get this. Does this mean that I don't have to wear it then, since it doesn't tell time?"

"It means you should wear it as often as you can. When you look at it, it will be a reminder to you that you'll live forever. You'll always be around, just like *I Love Lucy*."

"Just by looking at it?"

"Sure."

"How come other people don't have this watch?"

"You're the only person who owns one. I had it made specifically for you. Maybe what you can do is tell other people what you've learned from wearing it. You can tell them all that time never runs out, because it never existed in the first place."

"Like those people who're always in a hurry. *They* should be wearing this watch," I said.

"Bingo. Tell them that being in such a rush ain't all that. Now, tell me about your *To Do* list. How are you coming along with that while you're here?"

Before I was able to answer, Dr. de Pascual surprised Aunt Shirley and I by coming into my room. He said, "I'm sorry to interrupt, I just wanted to see how Miguel is feeling this afternoon."

"No, don't be sorry. Miguel loves it when you visit him anytime, I'm sure," Aunt Shirley said.

"And how about you, how have you been?" Dr. de Pascual asked her.

"Just great. Really fine. Before you came in I had asked Miguel how he was doing with his *To Do* list. It's very important for him to be jotting down ideas every chance he gets."

"I have been. Seriously. I think I must be up to about nine or ten pages just since I've been here," I said.

"That's fantastic, Miguel. Excellantro," Aunt Shirley said.

"I don't think I've ever seen this list. A list of things to do?" the doctor asked.

"A list of things I've *got* to do. It was Aunt Shirley's idea. You see, the more I have on my list of things I've got to get done, the longer I have to

27

stay here. Not here in the hospital, but you know, on earth."

"Earth? Were you planning on going to another planet after this one?" he asked.

"No, duh. You don't get it. This list helps to keep me alive because I've *got* to do what's on it, everything," I answered.

"Like Rocky, doctor. Tell him, doll."

"Yeah, that's a good one. Rocky's my hero. He had kind of a *To Do* list."

"I...don't recall that part in the movie," Dr. de Pascual said.

"*No!* I can tell you're thinking about the other one, Rocky, the guy in those shiny shorts who fights. I'm talking about Rocky Dennis from *Mask.* You know him, right? He's just like me, except he had lion-itis, or something like that. Remember how he always had that map of Europe on his wall 'cause he was going to go motorcycle riding acrosst it? And he'd put pins in all the countries he was going, I mean, had to go to. Do you get it now?"

"And the cards."

"Oh, yeah. Right. And he had to keep collecting the baseball cards of all the players on the Brooklyn team. Remember? He couldn't stop until he got them all. The map of Europe and his baseball cards were his *To Do* list. Now you get it, right?"

"That kept him alive. Kept him going," Aunt Shirley said.

"Well, I must admit they never taught us about instructing patients to formulate lists when I was in medical school. Perhaps they should have." The doctor sounded a little bit sarcastic when he said that, but my Aunt Shirley didn't seem to mind. Then he left with kind of a clueless look on his face, leaving Aunt Shirley and I by ourselves so we could be in private again. He probably knew we were going to talk about him after he was gone.

"He doesn't get it, does he?" I asked.

"Nope. He never will either."

"You said before 'cause he's a doctor, and doctors think like scientists."

"Well, that's part of it. This guy's pretty cool though. But most doctors need evidence to come up with answers. You and I don't. Who needs evidence? We can figure things out and know what's going to happen just by believing, making it happen by believing it will. Needing evidence to make sense of life is becoming a very old-fashioned way of thinking. Who needs it?"

"Like when you believed you'd buy your house when Mom said you couldn't?"

"Totally! I was the only one who knew it was going to happen because I had faith, absolute faith. I worked hard to make it happen, so why shouldn't it? If you question, even for a second, if something's *not* going to happen for you...it won't."

"Then I think I'm just going to keep on believing in what I want to happen. And I'll let the doctors believe what they want, too."

"You believe you're going to get well. Period. That's all that matters. So, maybe that's why it's more important than ever for you to realize that the very best doctor for you right now is you."

Aunt Shirley was right. I had to know that all my doctors were doing good things, but the only one who could really make me well was me. I made sure to add that one to my *To Do* list, becoming a doctor someday. Then I could teach my patients the ways to really make themselves well. I could teach the beginning doctors too, the ones who just practiced medicine before they did it for real.

It seemed like most of all the things on my *To Do* list came from Aunt Shirley. To a lot of people her ideas were way too different and kind of way "out there," but she always said that without new ideas and change, there's not much to learn. And, if there's nothing new to learn, then why was the world still going on? How come most everybody didn't die off a long time ago?

It's like when the Jehovah's Witnesses came to visit Aunt Shirley's house when I was over there. They said, "Wouldn't you love to be living in a place that's full of happiness *all* the time?" And she told them, "Hell no. What a bore. If everyone were happy *all* the time, then there'd be no obstacles to overcome, nothing to learn from. What's the point?"

After Aunt Shirley visited me my time at Stanford didn't last too much longer. I knew it wouldn't. Staying at the hospital made me think that being there was one of those "meant to be" kinds of things because I ended up getting exactly what I asked for. I got to spend time with my aunt, someone who helped me believe I'd have a future. Plus, in a weird way it got me some time away from my...fear. That's so amazing the way it all worked out.

As soon as I got back home, all I hoped for was another surprise. What was going to happen to me next? I guess only God knew the answer to that question.

CHAPTER FIVE

After dropping Hunt off at the airport the limo ride home was pretty routine until my mom said, "A letter from your father arrived yesterday."

"Are you serious? I mean, no kidding?" I asked.

"Yes. I knew how excited you'd be so I decided it would be better to tell you about it today."

"Thanks, Mom. But I probably could have handled it."

"Well, I just wanted to make sure you stay healthy. An ounce of prevention is—"

"Yeah, I know."

My mom didn't say anything for a while and while no one was saying anything we passed an accident on the side of 280, just after the vista point. Outside one of the cars was a Latino man with a boy my age. The man was holding onto the boy's shoulder, comforting him, as they both looked at their car all wrecked up. They both looked like they were OK though. Seeing the father and son together made me immediately think of my own dad.

"Miguel, it's best not to look at them. It'll make you sad, and we don't need that. Do we, dear?"

"But, Mom—"

"Just erase everything bad. That's what I do. Erase it completely, as if it never existed in the first place."

I guess Mom was right. Maybe that was the best thing. Not much was left to say after Mom said that, so we were both quiet all the way home. My mind just kept thinking about Dad's letter. Where was he? When was he coming home again?

As our limo drove past the garage's gate to get into our building I had a new feeling inside me. It felt like something totally different was about to happen to me. Just like Aunt Shirley always said, "Change is the most important thing in life." I wasn't so sure what was going to happen, but I

30

knew for sure that some sort of change was coming real soon. It was like I could tell it was supposed to.

When my mom and I got inside the elevator I pressed the button to our floor with my knuckle. Then she pointed to my left wrist, and asked, "Where did you get this?"

"Aunt Shirley gave it to me. Isn't it cool?"

"When did she give it to you? I didn't know she visited you at the hospital."

"Yeah. She was there lots of times. I like it when she comes to see me when I'm there."

"Well, you know I would have liked to visit you more often but Hunt really needed me to be with him. I couldn't really tell him no."

"How come?"

Mom didn't answer me. It was like she was trying to think of an answer but couldn't. Her face looked confused for a while, then out of nowhere she said, "You know, Danielle Steel will more than likely be coming to that fundraiser at Davies next week."

"Who? Is she that singer you're always talking about?"

"Singer? You mean Linda Ronstadt? No, she doesn't live here anymore. I heard she moved to Arizona. Danielle Steel is a famous author. She's fabulous. She lives in Pacific Heights on—"

For some reason I didn't really care about hearing Mom talk about some writer I didn't know. So, I interrupted her by saying, "I can't wait to get inside and read my letter from Dad."

"Before you do, make sure to do your deep-breathing and relaxation exercises I taught you. Remember, it never pays to become too excited about anything. It'll only raise your anxiety-level."

It's a good thing Mom told me that because my heart started pounding a lot when she handed me the letter. It was definitely from El Salvador. I could tell mainly because of the weird stamp of some man I didn't know that was on the envelope. I took the letter with me into my room so I could be alone. And, while in there I saved Dad's letter for last. I wanted to read all my e-mails first and get them out of the way.

One of them was from someone with the initials E.B. in their e-mail address. Just like Dad's letter I wanted to save that one for last, too. But when I finally got to it I couldn't believe it.

Hi Mikey,

I don't know how to spell your real first name, so they told me to just call you Mikey. You don't know me, but we both have recessive dystrophic E.B., so I'm just like you. My name is Henry, and I'm eleven. I live in Roseville. Do you know where that is? It's close to Sacramento and it's real hot in the summer. I hate it.

I got your e-mail address from Dr. de Pascual at Stanford. He said you like to write e-mails to people. He also said your brother's name was Jorge. That's my friend's name at school. Do you miss him a lot?

Maybe I can be your new friend. Maybe I will see you at Stanford someday. I don't get there too much because it's too far. And my Grandma can't drive me there because her eyes are too bad. She's the one who takes care of me now because both my parents are gone.

In the beginning, when I got too sick from E.B. my Mom and Dad left me for good. First it was my Dad and he blamed my Mom for making me have E.B. Then my Mom left, but she had always blamed my Dad. At first I thought they blamed me, but why would I decide to make myself have E.B.? That doesn't make sense.

What are your parents like? I just tell people I don't have parents because the story's too long to tell. I think Dr. de Pascual told me you don't really have a Dad either. Is that right? Is he dead? Or, do you just tell people that? Well, if you're ever in Roseville call me. I hope we get to see each other someday.

Bye,

Henry G.

That e-mail made me real mad. I *did* have a father, and he *wasn't* dead. How could somebody I didn't even know say something like that? Dr. de Pascual sure didn't do a very good job of telling this guy about Dad.

Not ever once did I think that my dad was dead. Maybe he ran out of money, so he just couldn't call me anymore. But I knew he was always going to stay my dad. And he always loved me. I was sure.

I picked up the letter from him that I had put on top of the table next to my bay window. I looked out it, but I knew that no matter what I really saw out there I pretended to see him. I believed he was right there somewhere in front of me and his letter was sent from a place not so far away. I thought he'd be coming back to see me very, very soon.

I opened the letter and began reading.

My dearest Miguelito,

    I know you will get this letter because I gave it to a friend to mail from Guatemala; not from El Salvador.

How are you? Are you still making yourself well when you need to? I think about you all day and night. You are the best thing that ever happened to me. And when I pray, I pray for you, and for goodness to follow you always.

It's taken me so long to write this letter to you because I was afraid of how you'd react to it. But, over and over I remember how smart you are, and how you tend to make sense of almost anything.

Anyway, I'm so very sorry for not being able to call you or see you. I want to so much. But right now I can't.

I'm still in San Salvador and I can't leave. I'm in prison. And I don't know when I'm getting out. Please realize that I was placed here unjustly. I've truly done nothing wrong. This country is unlike America or most other countries. They think I have done something wrong, but all I have done is be myself.

I can't tell you more than this right now, but you know me well enough to understand that I would never hurt anyone. All I want to do is see you again.

How's school? Is your Aunt Shirley still helping you? She is someone who is very wise. It's important that you listen carefully to everything she has to say. She will teach you all you ever need to know about life. More than anybody else, please listen to your Aunt Shirley. She is the one who will help you to become well more than anyone.

How's your mother? I imagine she's still able to give you everything you need. Always appreciate that, because that's her own way of showing you how much she loves you. And, always know that whatever she does is the best she can do, the best she knows how.

I want to see you so much, and I will do whatever it takes to make this happen. But, I'm sorry to tell you that they may never let me out. Trials are uncommon here, especially for American-Salvadorians. All I can do is pray.

Whenever you think of me, always see me coming to see you because someday this will happen. I can't tell you when or how, but if you keep imagining this inside your head, it will. Believe. You have the power. You are rare, and when you grow up, you will be able to teach many others, and they will be grateful to you for this.

The last thing I have to tell you is that I love you very much. And, just as important, I believe in you. I know you will become well, grow up, and be someone very important in life, because you already are.

If there is a time you think you're too alone, remember that God is with you every minute of the day. With God and myself continually loving you, and believing in you all the time, you can never be alone.

Please, please remember this.

I will certainly write to you again, as I always do, and I will do all I can to make sure my letters get to you. I'm sorry there is no place you can write back to me. Even if your letters were given to me by someone else, outside of prison, I would most likely be punished.

Until the next time I see you, stay positive, stay healthy, and keep believing in your head that YOU can make anything happen in life.

I love you always,

Dad

Right after reading that letter I didn't know what to think. I was really glad to hear from Dad, and at least I knew for sure that he wasn't dead. But why was he in jail? He didn't really explain that part.

I guess the most important thing is that he said he loved me, but what he told me about Aunt Shirley was the complete opposite of what Mom kept saying about her. Maybe what Aunt Shirley had to say was really good after all, and not way too weird or wrong.

But then I thought, what should I tell Mom about the letter? I knew it would make her real worried, so I decided not to tell her Dad's in jail. But she brought it up anyway.

"Miguel, I'm so sorry," my mom said.

"How do you...I mean, why do you say that?" I asked.

"I didn't need to read the letter. I know exactly what's going on. I was so terrified of how you'd react."

"But, Mom, he said he loves me, and all he thinks about is seeing me again. I'm really glad he wrote to me. I feel so much better."

"Glad he wrote to you? Well, then that's good. You're not...alarmed?"

"Yeah, I am. But, Mom, you know what? In the letter he said he didn't do anything bad, and I believe him."

"Oh, then that certainly is a relief. What else did he have to say?"

"He also said I should listen to Aunt Shirley because she's so smart. And the things she teaches me will definitely help me get well."

"Oh now, I think it's wonderful the way Shirley feels about...whatever it is she practices. But I don't think her philosophies apply to everyone. Everyone's circumstances are unique, dear."

"What about Dad then? You knew about this? Do you know why he's in there?"

Mom had a blank look in her eyes. But I could tell that when her eyes went blank always meant that she was just not telling me something. "My goodness no. I mean, I knew he was in there but I have no idea. I truly don't know why," my mom said, and paused a minute or so before saying, "but if your father didn't discuss it in his letter, he'll tell you the next time."

Staring at Mom's face was all I could do for a while. It made her uncomfortable, but I couldn't stop. Differences and secrets. All I could think of then was that it's so hard to believe that Mom and Aunt Shirley are related. One didn't like to tell things and the other believed that secrets were evil. One believed that holding things back and "playing it safe" were the best ways to live life. And the other sister had no secrets, told everything, and loved having obstacles in front of her. These differences were starting to become way more obvious to me.

What my mom and Aunt Shirley had in common though was that they both loved me a lot, and I was glad about that. I loved them a lot too. Sometimes I thought to myself, 'Which way was I going to turn out?' Like Mom? Or like Aunt Shirley? Was I going to turn out to be anything at all? Or was I going to die way before I ever had the chance?

With Mom still standing in front of me, she asked, "Did your father happen to mention when he might be here again?"

"No. He didn't say that part."

Next, Mom said something really strange, something that made me focus real hard on a thought I didn't want to believe in. "You know, Miguel, the culture in El Salvador is so entirely different. I know you may not want to believe this, but it's possible that your father may never be able to see you again. Don't let yourself become too optimistic."

"Oh, no way, Mom. No way."

"He will always love you just as much as I do. Even if he can never see you again I'm sure he'll always love you."

"Mom, why are you saying that?"

"For you, dear. Maybe it's best to prepare you now for the worst possible outcome. This way you won't be expecting too much. I'm only thinking of you, Miguel."

After Mom said that, I realized for sure that that was all Mom could do, prepare for the worst possible outcome. Why?

CHAPTER SIX

"On the seventeenth we'll be checking into the Crillon in Paris for five nights. Am I going to fast for you, dear? Would you like me to repeat any of it?" my mom asked Khadijah.

"No, Ma'am," she answered.

"Mom, why don't you just print out your schedule? Then give it to Khadijah. That way she won't have to write all this down," I said.

"Because it's excellent practice for her should she want to become a secretary someday. It's an opportune way to meet someone."

"Ma'am, I don't think I'll ever be a secretary. I'm a dancer, and hopefully I'll become part of a touring dance troupe at some point in my life."

"Oh, that's right. But the chances of meeting a male dancer who isn't...you know, aren't going to be that great."

"Oh, that's really not a priority for me right now, Ma'am," Khadijah answered, while looking kind of disgusted.

I could tell right then that Khadijah was maybe a little sick of Mom and her old-fashioned ideas. I was surprised Khadijah's lasted as long as she had. Every night I prayed she'd never leave me. But maybe with Mom going to be with Hunt in Europe for three weeks Khadijah could relax a little bit and enjoy our home. I was sure going to miss Mom, but I thought that maybe I'd finally get the chance to do some fun things I normally wasn't allowed to.

"After Paris we'll be staying at the Grosvenor House in London for another five nights," my mom said. "Oh, Khadijah. You're not writing this down."

"Oh, I'm sorry. But, you know, Miss Kirkland, I'm sure everything will be just fine here. I'll make sure your son is well-cared for," Khadijah said. She always said "your son" to my mom, because she told me she started to feel uncomfortable calling me Mikey, and she still couldn't say Miguelito just right.

"Mom, I've got it all memorized in my head," I said.

"Well then, that's perfect. I see there's much I have to catch up on. I'm nearly two hours behind on today's schedule. If you'll excuse me I've got a multitude of errands."

"Miss Kirkland, if you can think of anything else I should know before you leave, perhaps you can write it down."

"Oh, I think you already have a good understanding of Miguel's needs. You're doing a great job. I'm certain you'll be able to care for him when a crisis comes up. So, goodbye for now. I've got to run."

"Goodbye, Ma'am."

"Bye, Mom."

After my mom left the room Khadijah asked, "*When a crisis comes up?* What makes her assume there's going to be a crisis?"

"She's always expecting one. Sometimes they happen just because that's what she's always expecting. She *makes* them happen. That's what Aunt Shirley's says."

"Does your mother do this a lot? I mean, go off somewhere, and leave you here?"

"I guess she's doing it more now than she used to. Whenever she went to Europe before she called it 'husband shopping.' If she doesn't marry the guy she's with now she may find a better one over there."

"You're joking."

"No. I heard her on the phone tell one of her friends that. That's her goal in life, to find a man. And not just any man. It has to be just the right kind of man. She said that when she gets married our home will be normal again because there'll be a man in it."

"Well, what *kind* of man is your father? How did your mother end up with him in the first place? He's supposed to be more down to earth, isn't he?"

"That was way before she got to be like she is now, before she inherited most of my grandparent's money."

"Your mom wasn't always like this?"

"No way. If you can believe it, she used to be a lot more like Aunt Shirley."

"You've got to be kidding. That's so hard to believe. They seem like complete opposites to me."

"I know. My mom used to go to Berkeley when they were just...what's the word for people before they get those bigger degrees?"

"Undergrads?"

"Yeah. That's what they both were. But when my grandparents died and left Mom most of their money she didn't finish school. Mom changed right about then."

"I think money changes most people. What was your mom's major while she was there?"

"Central American Studies. She even went there, too, to Central America. That's how she met my dad. They were both at those big ruins in Guatemala, Tikal. Dad even arranged for Mom to visit El Salvador at the time when Americans weren't allowed to go there at all. And, while she was there she met some pretty important people," I said.

"Wow, it's hard to imagine any of this. I just don't see her as the type to visit Central America. She's so sophisticated."

It felt real good telling Khadijah about the way Mom used to be before she changed. Khadijah knew how much I liked staying with Aunt Shirley, so she asked, "Do you want to go over to Berkeley with me when I have one of my classes? That way you can see your aunt."

"Oh, yeah. Definitely. I like it a lot at her house. But don't tell Mom. She doesn't let me go there. She thinks Berkeley is way too dangerous."

"Yes, I remember what you told me."

As my mom was getting ready to walk out the door, I asked if I could go along to the airport. She said, "No. You might get sick on the way. The traffic might make you too anxious." But in the back of my head I could tell the real reason. She always knew I was kind of embarrassed by the way I look. Mom could tell I was ashamed, so she always made it so I wouldn't have to suffer any more than I had to.

The first few days with Mom away ended up being like a total present from God. The nervous feeling I usually had in my stomach was gone, and part of me felt sort of free. It was still summer vacation, so both Aunt Shirley and I had time off from our schools. I couldn't wait to go over to see her.

Aunt Shirley lived in a place that was like magic. She planted a garden with lots of different kinds of colored flowers and plants. Some looked like they had blue balloons hanging from them. No kidding. And by putting all her plants in the garden it made her feel like she was more planted, I mean, grounded.

The garden was shady for most of the time, so when I went out there I wouldn't get burned from the sun. And the front of her house was heck'a special. Out of her window I could see all the way across the bay to Mount Tam in Marin. I'd pretend to go hiking there. I could also see the

Golden Gate Bridge, all of it, the whole thing, not sideways like the way I'd see it from my house.

Khadijah ended up taking me over to Aunt Shirley's house to stay, not just to visit, on her way to summer school. As long as Mom didn't know, it was cool. When we got there the first thing Khadijah said was, "Wow! I thought your aunt didn't have any money."

"How come you said that?" I asked.

"Because this is such a nice house. I thought your aunt was more...simple."

"Aunt Shirley says that everybody is always able to have exactly what they want. Plus, she really, really wanted this house. And, she bought it with almost no money."

"Well, I'm going to have to ask her how she did it someday."

"Hi, dolls. How's my dumpling today?" Aunt Shirley asked, as she met us both in her front yard.

"I'm doing good. Aunt Shirley can I please show Khadijah your garden in the back?"

"Of course, doll. First, let's bring all this stuff inside. Then we'll go out back and relax for a bit."

"Thanks a lot, Shirley. I can only stay for a short while though. I've got to get over to the campus for a rehearsal. If I'm late Professor Hays is going to murder me. You know the way he is. Don't you?"

"Yeah, I sure do. But always remember, he's got a loud voice, yet he's a softy inside. Let's hit it!"

We carried all my junk into the house, and as Khadijah looked around she was totally shocked. "This is such a beautiful place. I can't get over it," she said.

"I'm so grateful to live here, it's my haven. Away from everything."

"This is probably one of the most comfortable place I've ever been in. It's so gorgeous too. And, you can see the entire bay," Khadijah said, while looking out. "My God."

Since she was standing right next to the window I showed her the special chair that's just for me. It's kind of mushy but real cozy. Sitting in that chair always made me feel great long after I sat in it. "Here is where I make my dreams," I said.

"Oh," Khadijah answered. I could tell she didn't really know what to say, so I just talked more anyway.

"Yeah. When I sit in this chair I just look out in the day or night and make up more things to put on my *To Do* list. This is also the place where I talk to God out loud. That way He can hear me for sure."

"Miguelito and God have a great relationship happening. They're becoming best buds," Aunt Shirley said.

"Yeah. Aunt Shirley always says that whatever you speak out loud is what's going to happen for you. And if you say negative things, then that's what you're going to have, too," I said.

"Well, if that's the case, I *positively* have to get to the dance studio so I can put in a great rehearsal."

The minute Khadijah left to go to school, the whole feeling in Aunt Shirley's house changed. It wasn't like it got better because Khadijah left. It was peaceful because I was there with Aunt Shirley, alone in her special house. Everything got so quiet and she became more serious as we both sat down in front of the window.

"I'm so glad you remembered what I told you about paying attention to what you say out loud. Maybe Khadijah will practice that more, now that you've told her about it," Aunt Shirley said.

"Yeah, it's a cool thing to know," I said.

"Have you been practicing this yourself?"

"Um, yeah. I guess so."

"This is such an important lesson for you to learn. And don't forget that if you say something as a joke about yourself, God won't know that. So, what you've said will actually happen to you. God doesn't know when you're joking. Whatever you've spoken out loud to someone is exactly what you've created for yourself."

"Like that lady you told me about in the city who always said she could never find a parking space in Union Square?"

"Yes, that's a perfect example. She said that over and over when I was in her car. She drove me nuts. So of course she never found a parking space in Union Square because she kept *saying* she'll never get one. I got so sick of hearing her say that."

"Well, how did she ever park her car?"

"You got me. I just asked her to let me out. For all I know she's still driving around Union Square in circles. You know what else she'd always say?"

"What?"

"'I'll never meet a man, I'll never meet a man, I'll never meet a man.' You know what happens by saying that, right?"

"That lady will never ever meet a man because that's what she made up for herself, her destiny."

"And, as far as I know she hasn't yet met any men. What she should've been saying all along is, 'I look forward to the time when I meet just the right man for me'."

"Maybe she should've just been thinking more positive thoughts, instead of negative ones."

"But, what's more important than positive thinking? What actually *makes* things happen?"

"Believing. Faith."

"Bingo, doll. Thinking positively is great. But, believing things to happen is like *extreme* positive thinking. Instead of wishing for your destiny, you create it. *You* make it happen because you've already believed it will. *You* create your destiny. Got it?"

"Yes, Ma'am."

"Since you don't happen to be driving in circles right now, what are some of the things you're creating for yourself?"

"Um, I want to go see Britney Spears the next time she comes here. I want to go on that paddlewheel boat at Lake Tahoe. You know, the one that has the glass bottom so you can see right through the water. And someday, I might want to meet more people in person who have E.B. so we can figure out how to make ourselves well all the time. And, I guess most of all, I want to get away from being afraid so much."

"But, doll-face, guess what?"

"Did I forget something big?"

"Yeah. All those things may never happen for you. Do you know why?"

"'Cause they're too many things to ask for?"

"No. Remember? You said, 'I want.' *Asking* for anything doesn't *make* it happen. *You're* going to make it happen. So, now say them all over again without saying the words 'I want'."

"Oh shit. Oops, sorry. Now I'm going to have to remember what I just told you."

"It doesn't matter. Make up new ones if you want. But tell me what you're going to create, not wish for."

"Um, let's see. I w—, I mean, I'm going to see Britney Spears the next time she's in the Bay Area. I'm going to go to Lake Tahoe to ride on the boat that has the glass bottom to see everything in the lake. I'm going to become a doctor, so I can cure all the kids like me who have E.B. And, most of all, I'm going to move out of my apartment on Nob Hill and live somewhere else, hopefully with Aunt Shirley."

"Wow. That's what you're going to make happen, huh? That's good. And I'm glad you want to live with me. But instead of saying my name, say 'in the perfect home for me'."

"Why can't I say your name?"

"Because there may be a more perfect place for you, a more perfect situation that you don't even know about yet."

"OK. And I'm going to move out of my home on Nob Hill and into the perfect home for me."

"Well then, start packing, doll. You're on your way."

CHAPTER SEVEN

"So, you're all packed up and ready to go?" Aunt Shirley asked.

"Yeah, I've been ready for a long time. I'm so excited," I answered.

"I'm not much of a picture-taker. How about you?"

"Well, I've gotten pretty good at using that camera Dad gave me for my birthday. It's digital. Can we stop off at my home to get it?"

"Sure, why not? We have to go through the city anyway. And when we're there, remind me to pick up more bandages for you," Aunt Shirley said.

"Yeah, I'll remember to tell you."

"Well then, that's it. Let's hit the road, doll."

I couldn't wait to get to Big Sur. I didn't even sleep too much the night before because I was so excited. Big Sur was a place I'd heard so much about. So many people told me that it's like a place they'd never been to before, like another planet.

Aunt Shirley and I went to my apartment for a while, but right before we left it to head down the coast, she asked, "Do you feel like listening to your messages since were here?"

"No, not really." I didn't tell Aunt Shirley the real reason I didn't want to play them though. One of them could have been from Mom, then I'd be busted for all the stuff she never would've allowed me to do.

"Maybe your mother called you? I bet she did," Aunt Shirley said.

"Well, that's OK. I'll call my machine from your house when we get back there later."

Driving with Aunt Shirley was so special for me. We talked about everything. And, she seemed to have a story for every town we drove through. "Do you know what the major industry is here in Half Moon Bay?" she asked.

"I guess some kind of farming 'cause there's cows and stuff like that here," I answered.

"Well, you're right, farming. Actually, horticulture. That's the main business in this town, growing flowers. Flowers are grown here and sent all over the world." I was glad she explained it to me because I never would have guessed what the word *horticulture* meant.

For miles and miles all I could see through my passenger window was the Pacific Ocean. It was massive and seemed like a whole other world to me because I couldn't see the end. For the longest time driving, there was no town after Half Moon Bay. I'd never experienced anything like that before, where every town was so spread apart. In San Francisco mostly everything is smashed together.

The next town we came to was Santa Cruz. Aunt Shirley said there were lots of car accidents in Santa Cruz because everybody there smokes pot all the time. Then we drove through Moss Landing, then through Monterey, and then we got to a real cool place called Point Lobos. We stopped there, and saw all the tourists taking pictures of the huge waves crashing, so I did too. I bet they were crashing higher than the TransAmerica Pyramid and all the other tall buildings in the financial district.

"Looking out at this very point, at these pounding waves, is what inspired Robert Louis Stevenson to write *Treasure Island*," my aunt said.

"Wow, no kidding?" I pretended to know that book, but I didn't. Maybe it was one I probably should have read in school.

After about an hour we left Point Lobos. And next, there was a really long part of the road that got pretty curvy, and we saw no towns at all. But, out of nowhere, there was a huge lighthouse on a kind of island. Aunt Shirley said that that island-thing looked a lot like Mount-something-something in France. Without even seeing the expression on my face Aunt Shirley said, "If there's anything you don't understand, or happen to be confused about, please ask. That's what I'm here for, to teach you. Sometimes people are too afraid to ask questions, but the absolute smartest people on earth are the ones who ask questions all the time."

After hearing that I asked questions nonstop. By the way, it's Mont-Saint-Michel. I found out later, because I asked.

"Now we're getting away from the ocean. So, I guess Big Sur isn't near the ocean after all, is it?" I asked.

"Just wait, you'll be surprised," Aunt Shirley answered.

We kept driving and driving. We drove through a town that was so country-like that it looked like it was straight out of *Dukes of Hazzard*. But, finally we got to a place and stopped, a restaurant called Nepenthe.

"Is this where we're going?" I asked.

"Yes, I've already called ahead, and they are fixing you up a great meal that'll suit you just fine." We got out of the car, and then walked up about a million stairs.

"You know, Mom has been to this place. She always tells people over and over how she sat right next to Jane Fonda and Ted Turner here. You know, before they got divorced. Mom always says how Jane Fonda was dressed up like a movie star, but Ted Turner just wore jeans and wasn't fancy at all. And Mom says Ted Turner wasn't too happy to see Jane Fonda eating some of his French fries. You know, 'cause she has stay perfect-looking all the time."

"I think your mom gets a bit star-struck sometimes. Maybe she secretly wants to be one herself."

When Aunt Shirley and I were seated our waiter asked, "My name is Rudy."

"Hey, Rudy. My name's Mikey," I said.

"You mean, your name is Miguelito. And I'm Shirley. Hi," she said very quickly.

I didn't know why Aunt Shirley had to say that. But when we looked out at the view I couldn't believe what I saw. It was like something that could only be made up in my imagination. The view was like a mixture of mountains and sky, but still all right on top of the ocean. There's no way I had ever seen anything like this before. It was from another planet, just like other people told me it would be. Big Sur was definitely the most special place I'd ever been in California that's quiet. It wasn't big like San Francisco, even though it's called *Big* Sur.

Catching me by surprise, Aunt Shirley said, "At some point you're going to be an adult, you know."

"You really think so?" I asked.

"Sure, you're going to grow up and have your own family someday."

"Babies, you mean? But what if the lady I have them with has the same genes as me? The genes that make E.B.? Then the babies we make will get it."

"Uh oh, what did I tell you about questions that begin with 'What if'? Every time you ask, 'What if?' you're moving yourself onto Plan *B* automatically. Then you'll never have the chance of pursuing Plan *A*. Don't even spend any time thinking about things that may never happen. You should think about all the good things coming your way...only the good things. How's that? Just as we agreed, right?"

"Yeah. I forgot." Then I changed the subject. "You know, how come *you* don't have any babies, Aunt Shirley?"

She didn't answer. I asked again, "Aunt Shirley, did you hear me? Why don't you have any?"

She still didn't answer. "Aunt Shirley, why are you crying?"

I guess she wanted to keep it a big secret, because she didn't say anything for a long time.

Then she finally said, "You know, I think this must be what heaven looks like. I'm sure this is the closest thing to it I can imagine."

"Sometimes I try to do that, think of what heaven looks like. But every time I see it I make sure to see Jorge there too, since I'm looking there anyway. Maybe Jorge's even looking down at earth right now."

"Do you think about Jorge a lot?"

"Yes, but I'm definitely not ready to visit him all the way in heaven yet. He would be so pissed at me if he saw me there already. He told me I definitely have to wait for a cure. So, I think I'd like to stay here on the ground for right now. It's funny though how some people live in heaven and some people live here. I wonder why all of us just don't live in the same place."

"Miguel, I don't know. I sincerely wish I knew the answer to that question, but right now I can only guess."

Out of nowhere, at the end of the deck where we were sitting a lot of people started to gather and look out into the ocean. "Hey, what are all those people looking at over there? Something's going on," I said to Aunt Shirley.

Aunt Shirley and I walked to the crowd of people and I didn't even need to ask what's happening. Far out into the Pacific there was one whale, all alone, jumping up and down in the water, making huge splashes. It was a baby whale, but there was no mother whale and no other kinds of whales around him. It seemed obvious that he was trying extra hard for us to see him out there.

"Hey, Aunt Shirley! Maybe that's really Jorge. Maybe this really is like heaven and Jorge turned himself into a whale just for today, just so we could see him. Let's wave. Hey, Jorge! Can you see us?"

The baby whale stayed around for a little while longer. I thought it had to be Jorge for sure because he was jumping up and down all the time in the same place, being kind of obnoxious. Then, a bigger whale finally came along and tried showing him which way to go, but the baby whale wasn't listening. Mom said Jorge never listened to anybody. She said he's the independent-type. Maybe he still is.

Eventually the whales swam away. Maybe I saw Jorge and maybe I didn't. In my head I pretended I did. And it would remain my own secret, well actually mine and the other people at Big Sur who heard me yelling out at him. I thought, maybe when I'd get to heaven I'd turn myself into a whale sometimes, too. That way I wouldn't have E.B., and no one would ever make fun of me, because I'm pretty sure whales never make fun of each other the way people do.

After seeing the whales at Nepenthe restaurant, Aunt Shirley and I drove a little bit more south, but we still stayed in Big Sur. The next place was called the Julia Pfeiffer Burns State Park beach. We parked off of the side of the highway instead of in the parking lot and paying the man, because Aunt Shirley said the state gets too much money already they don't know what to do with.

I had no idea beforehand that where we were off to next was going to be even better than where we'd just been. At the end of a short trail, all full of thick ferns and tall trees was a bench all by itself. Where we were was at some sort of old, torn-down mansion, but parts of it were still there. The view was awesome, and just like before, I felt like I could see the border that separated earth from heaven.

Aunt Shirley and I sat all alone on this bench with no other people around. "Isn't this incredible?" she asked me.

"I've never seen anything like this before. This is even better than at Nepenthe."

"You know the waterfall we just passed, the one that emptied into that pretty emerald-colored cove?"

"Yeah, it's beautiful."

"It's the only waterfall on the entire West Coast that empties directly into the Pacific Ocean."

"Wow. You sound like a tour guide, like the ones who you can hear talking through a loudspeaker outside of those fake cable cars in the city."

"*Fake* cable cars?"

"Yeah. Those ones that have rubber tires instead of the real cable cars that are hooked up to the covered tracks. The ones the tourists ride on who don't care that they aren't on the real cable cars because they just want to listen to someone on a microphone telling them about the city."

"If you had a Mr. Microphone, what would you tell God if He were a tourist and didn't know about this place we're at now?"

"Well, that's kind of dumb. No offense. Because after all, God made this place, and so He really should know all about it already. Unless He forgot."

"Yeah, I guess that's true. But what would you like Him to know about how you like being here?"

"I'd tell Him how great it is and that there should be more waterfalls around like the one we saw."

"The first thing *I* would say to Him, without a doubt, would be 'thank you.' I think I'm going to do that right now. I feel so blessed to be able to experience this vista He created. I'm going to be quiet for just a little bit. If you feel you may want to thank God for what you're experiencing right now, go right ahead. I bet He'd like that."

"Yeah, sure. What the hell. I mean, why not?"

Both of us got real quiet and started to thank God in our heads, not out loud, but sometimes I would look over at Aunt Shirley. The way she looked on her face was a strange mixture. She looked real, real happy, but it looked like she was maybe crying on the inside at the same time. And, she didn't have her eyes closed like when people are praying. Then I forgot to be quiet and I said, "Your eyes aren't closed."

"They shouldn't be. When we have such a beautiful place to see, when we have eyes that possess the ability to see, why should they ever be closed? I'm so very grateful to be able to see all this."

Well, I didn't interrupt her anymore. Maybe it's just Catholic people who are supposed to pray with their eyes closed. When it got real quiet again I looked around me, at the trees, at the ocean, at the waterfall, at the leaves on the ground, at the mountains that came into the sea, and at Aunt Shirley. I began to feel so lucky. I felt like this was a very special moment, like we were already in heaven, but not really.

I thought of Jorge and how lucky I was to have known him at all. At least I had a brother for part of my life, and I was thankful for this. Having had him in my life was a miracle, just like all the other good things I had. The more I looked around me, the more I wanted the quiet to last forever. I didn't want to leave.

Then, after a pretty long time Aunt Shirley looked over to me when she was finished. She must have known I was done too. "So, how're you doing?" she asked.

"Great. I thought about a lot of great things."

"Did you happen to thank God?"

"Well, I just started to feel lucky about all the good stuff in my life, and how lucky I am to be here right now."

"That's the same thing. By taking the time to recollect all the goodness in your life, you're thanking God and that's very, very important."

"Well, would God get mad if people didn't thank Him for all the good things they've got?"

"No, I don't imagine He'd be mad at all. But you know what He might think?" Aunt Shirley asked.

"That people who don't say 'thank you' aren't really good people anyway?"

"No. I bet He'd think, 'Well, why should I provide any more goodness to those people who aren't appreciative of the goodness they already have?' When you thank God, and recognize Him for creating such miracles around you, you're telling Him that you're ready for more. You'll appreciate the next one as much as the miracles you've already received."

"Hey, that makes sense. Well, right now, I just like being here at this cool place with you. I can't even think about the new miracle I want to happen next."

"Then when it does happen, it will come to you as a nice surprise."

CHAPTER EIGHT

More than ever I didn't want to wake up that morning. It meant that it was my last day to stay with Aunt Shirley. Soon I'd have to go back home. Somehow I just couldn't understand why I'd have to go back, considering Aunt Shirley and I got along so well. Maybe I could have been the kid she never had. Maybe she didn't want one in the first place. Maybe she was just acting like she liked being with me, but she really didn't.

On that day, my last morning with Aunt Shirley, the weather was very strange. It was like earthquake weather that usually only happened close to the fall. I sure wasn't in the mood for one of those, you know, an earthquake. I was hoping it would end up being so hot that I would have to stay indoors all day, and not go home. But it didn't turn out that way.

The first thing I saw when I got up was the light coming from Aunt Shirley's office. I walked in to say "good morning," but found her asleep while she was still sitting in front of her computer. She must have been there all night. When I saw her there I thought to myself that she must've done a lot of rearranging to let me stay with her all this time. She told me the most important commitment she had was to her thesis and how she had to finish it very soon. Maybe I had been in the way, and she never told me.

"Hey, doll. You're up," Aunt Shirley said in a half-asleep voice. I don't know how she even knew I was there because I didn't make a sound. Aunt Shirley always seemed to know everything early.

"Yeah. Have you been here all night? In front of your computer?" I asked.

"Oh, yes. This has to get done, and as usual I'm a bit behind. School's starting soon. But, I'll be finished when I'm supposed to be."

"Maybe I can help you get it put together. Or, maybe I can help you with your research. What do you think?"

"No. I can handle it all myself. Thanks though, doll. Hey, I want you to be enjoying life, not spending most of it hunkered over a computer like me."

"Well, how about if there's other stuff I can help you do, that doesn't have anything to do with computers?"

"I have this feeling you want something. Am I right?"

"Oh, no. There's nothing I want. Well, yeah, maybe to ask you something."

"I'm absolutely sure I know what the question is. So instead of me answering it now, let's have a talk first. Let's discuss why you want to live here with me, and let's discuss why I think that living with your mother in San Francisco would be better for you."

"How did you know I was going to ask that again?"

"I've known you long enough to know the way you think, and *that* combined with my instinct gives me all I need to be able to communicate with you without saying a word."

"But the bottom line is that you don't know what it's really like, living with Mom. No one does. No one except me and Jorge. Remember that letter I showed you, the one he wrote just before he died? The one I keep under my mattress?"

"Yes. Sure I do. A lot of what Jorge said is the truth. He was a smart boy. As I recall, he knew how important it was to have faith, not fear. That's fantastic. But, he was wrong about your mother. She may have nothing but fear inside her, but she'd never intentionally inflict those fears upon you. She wants you to survive and—"

"No. I don't know about that. Now she just cares about this new boyfriend. She just does whatever he tells her to. What's going on with me doesn't seem matter to her anymore."

"Oh my. I think we've had this conversation before, doll. Let's try to look at this from a different perspective. You can't argue that your mother is capable of giving you the best care you could ever have, right? I'm not so certain I'd be capable of providing that."

"Yeah, but just medical care. I need to be around someone who has faith. That's what's most important for me. Isn't that what you taught me?"

"But, you've got to remember that no one can give you faith. You must develop it and maintain it yourself, that's your lesson. It's impossible to rely on someone else to fulfill your own destiny. God created us all to have individual destinies, all unique and independent from those belonging to anyone else."

Aunt Shirley wasn't mad when she talked to me, but she sure didn't seem like she was going to think any differently. I thought the best thing to do was to wait until the afternoon, and maybe bring it up all over again. But first, I'd have to think of another way that would maybe make her change her mind. "I'm going to go back to bed. Maybe it was too early for me to get up after all," I said.

In bed I thought of a lot of stuff. I thought a lot about what Aunt Shirley had said to me. Maybe it was my destiny to be living with Mom for some reason, a reason I didn't really know about yet. Or maybe it was just that the time wasn't right. I guess I should have been thanking God for the time I had with my aunt, instead of just thinking about what more I wanted to get.

While Aunt Shirley was still at her computer I went to my chair, the one where I make up my dreams. It was a perfect time for me to go there because the morning sun was starting to light up the bay, and I usually never got to look at it this early before. All I wanted to do was think up other ways of living somewhere else.

I thought that if my mom did find a new husband, or marry Hunt in Europe, then maybe she would have to stay there with him, and leave me here to live with some other family. Or, maybe she'd let me live in the hospital all the time. Maybe the new husband wouldn't want me to be around. That would be good. Then I'd be forced to find another place to live for sure.

"Have you thought up some excellent dreams?" Aunt Shirley asked, while walking up to me.

"How did you know that's what I was doing?" I asked back.

"Because that's what you always do in this chair."

"Yeah, well I've been thinking up a few good ones."

"Like going back to school? You always liked that. You must be glad you're going back in a few days. Or that your mother is going to come back a changed person, full of optimism, hope, and faith. How about that?"

"Oh, that's a totally good one. But hey, let's get real. If she comes back home with just one of those three, I'll celebrate."

"Celebrate anyway. Pound it into your head that she loves you and she's showing you that the only way she knows how. This may be the last time you're able to learn lessons from her, so appreciate them, and appreciate her for giving them to you."

"Mom sure gives me tough lessons to learn, that's for sure."

"But, do you realize that you've gotten where you are now because of her? It's possible she may be coming back several more times, whereas you might have already moved on from her in your young life."

"Coming back to where?"

"Earth, life...here. She may have a long way to go, being unreceptive to change and the fears she has to overcome. Her soul may be destined to regenerate a few more times, until she learns a few things."

"And, you think I won't be coming back?"

"No, I didn't say that. It may be that you might not know your mother again, in your next lifetime. You've already learned so much. Certain souls reconnect with each other lifetime after lifetime, until lessons are learned. Then, once they are, they're free to move on and choose a different destiny, different lessons."

"So, does that mean I can decide what I am next? And if my mom will be my mom next time?"

"Maybe yes, maybe no. It depends on what you learn in this one, this life. And right now, I don't think you're supposed to know exactly what lessons are ahead of you. We'll just have to wait and see."

"Wow, I wonder what I'll be next time. What if I'm more like Ricky Martin next time? That would be way cool."

"Thinking about your next life while you're still in this one isn't so hot. You've got a lot in front of you, doll. It's fun to ponder. Perhaps in my next life, I'll be your mother. Perhaps you'll be mine. There are a million possibilities. All I can say is that you're doing a great job right now. You're one of the wisest young men I've ever met. I'm so extremely proud of you, Miguelito."

"Thanks. I guess I'm lucky to have you as my aunt right now. And, if next time you're still my aunt, then that's just a bonus prize."

"So, why don't we get ready to leave soon? How about if we fix up some sort of *Welcome Home* celebration at your place for your mother?"

"Yeah, OK. She'd like that. We already have some stuff at home. It's leftover decorations from when those charity people gave Mom a surprise birthday party."

"Perfect. She'll be thrilled, especially since you'll be right there welcoming her back. That will make her so happy."

"Good. I hope so. So, I should get ready to leave *now*?"

"Yes. That way we could get into the city before the commute traffic begins. That always gives me such a headache."

"OK. Thanks a lot, Aunt Shirley."

"Thanks? For what?"

"Well, just for letting me stay here this past week. It was like a vacation for me, especially when we went to Big Sur. I hope we can do that again. Or, maybe next time go to some new place."

"And I should be thanking you for your company. I feel privileged to know such a good person. I love you."

"I love you too, Aunt Shirley."

"Well, now that we both know how we feel about each other, how about some sort of breakfast, or lunch, or whatever it's time for?"

"That sounds good."

Aunt Shirley made me my favorite, a cheese sandwich with white bread. The white bread's good for me because it's so smooth going down. What a cool treat. I think one of the best rewards I got every time I stayed with Aunt Shirley though is that sometimes I forgot I had E.B. She always thought of me as Miguelito, the boy who happened to have E.B., rather than my mom, who always thought of me as the tragic kid with E.B., who's called Mikey. I liked Aunt Shirley's way a whole lot better.

After lunch Aunt Shirley and I both sat in the living room looking out the windows at the beautiful bay. The city looked so special with all the big buildings lit up by the sunny sky. There were boats all over the place, but the ones I paid attention to were the tourist ferries that went to Alcatraz. "Have you ever been to Alcatraz?" I asked Aunt Shirley.

"Yes, it's interesting. The entire island doesn't have any electricity, you know?"

"How can any place not have electricity?"

"I'm not really sure, but there are many places in this country that don't. Miguel, you're very lucky to be living here. The Bay Area is a fascinating place, full of innovators."

"What's *innovators*? What does *that* mean?"

"Innovators are people who think up new ideas, new ways of doing things. Innovators are people who welcome change. And, it just seems to me that I've never been anyplace where there are so many people who possess so many different ways of achieving their goals. It's great!"

"Is *innovation* from the word *innovators*?"

"Yep, it's certainly related. Right over there is a huge innovation, the Golden Gate Bridge. The only reason it was able to be built is because everything about its construction was innovative, new. Mostly all of the standard guidelines regarding bridge-building were tossed out because they would've never worked. So when everybody said the bridge could never be built there was one person who insisted it could. I forgot his name, but *he* was an innovator. And, he must have been right because it was built in 1932, it's still standing, and people continue using it decades later."

"That's really old. I wonder if there'll be a person who'll come along who says there'll be a cure for E.B., or maybe a cure for AIDS and cancer. Because, there's lots of people who think there won't ever be."

"Then those are the people to ignore. It's only the innovators you want to listen to. And someday they will be proven right. I'm sure of it."

"I guess I'm lucky to live here then, and besides all of it is so pretty to see, you know, scenic. And, since I live here anyway, maybe that's what I should be when I grow up, a professional innovator."

"I think you already are."

Wow, at first I never knew the word *innovator*, and suddenly I found out that I was one. Cool. "Can we take BART back to the city instead?" I asked Aunt Shirley.

"Sure, why not? You don't want me to drive? You don't like my driving, do you?"

"Well, you are kind of nutty when you drive. No offense. But, I think it would be cool for us to walk to BART, then take it to Powell St. Station. And after that take the cable car up to my house. We could act like tourists and point at everything."

"That's fine. But, what's so nutty about the way I drive, doll? I think I'm OK."

"Well, it's just that when you drive you're always in the fastest lane. How come you get so *speeded-up* when you drive? You know what I mean?"

"Oh my goodness, I never knew I was talking to Mr. Jeff Gordon."

"You know who Jeff Gordon is?"

"Absolutely, but my favorite race-car driver was Dale Earnhardt. I try to learn a little something about every subject, even if I am the nuttiest driver on earth."

"So, BART, right? Is that OK with you?"

"Oh, definitely. Let's walk up to the first car, and ask the driver if he can pop a wheelie while we're crossing the bay underwater. Wouldn't that be rad?"

"Aunt Shirley, nobody says 'rad' anymore."

After Aunt Shirley and I were done goofing off we carried all my stuff out the door and were ready to go. Then she had to go to the bathroom. She did this a lot right before she leaves to go somewhere. While she was in the bathroom the phone rang. Instead of letting the machine get it Aunt Shirley yelled out, "Miguel, could you please answer that? I'm expecting a call from a friend of mine. Thanks, hon."

Clint Adams

I grabbed the phone just in time and answered, "Hello." But on the other end it was totally quiet. I continued, "Hello...hello." I thought no one was there so I hung up. Then the phone rang again. "Hello," I repeated.

The frantic voice said, "Miguel? Oh, thank goodness. Are you all right? I've been so worried about you. I've been calling and calling. No one ever answered. What are you doing there? I've never been so scared in all my life. You can't imagine what went through my mind. I thought I was going to have a heart..."

CHAPTER NINE

"And when you drop off Miguel, please don't come up. Just leave his things in the lobby. The doorman will deliver them when he has a chance," my mom said to Aunt Shirley when all three of us were on a conference call.

"Yes, I understand. But Sharon, I hope you won't stay angry with me. I love Miguel so much. Taking Miguel on trips is so healthy for him," Aunt Shirley said.

"Miguel, I'll see you in a little bit," Mom told me, but didn't answer Aunt Shirley.

Aunt Shirley ended up driving me over to the city. The ride in the car was awful, but I wasn't going to let Mom's mood ruin the time I had just spent with Aunt Shirley. When we were going over the Bay Bridge Aunt Shirley had a look on her face like she didn't know what to do next. Part of her face was mad, and the other part looked like it just gave up.

She spoke almost no words. I could tell that a huge part of her felt real guilty because she went against what my mom had said about not letting me do fun stuff. Maybe I was the one who should have felt guilty because I wanted to stay with Aunt Shirley so much, and be in a place where I didn't have to be afraid. But, something was happening. I knew I was probably going to get into big trouble when I got home, but whatever. I didn't care.

The fog in the city was so think that day. It hid the tips of the tall buildings in the financial district. I guess it was meant to be that Berkeley had stayed so sunny and bright, but when I got home to San Francisco it turned really dark and gloomy.

When Aunt Shirley parked in front of my building in the loading zone she spoke her first word to me in a long time, "Miguelito, I promise you, your life will only get better from this point on. Please don't let what happened between your mother and I upset you. Today was meant to be, something quite good will come of it."

"I believe you, Aunt Shirley. I had that feeling already."

"You're a real champion. That's the word for what you are. And, I don't know what your mother is going to do when you see her, but I know that seeing me will make her very upset. I don't care about your mom getting upset with me, I just don't want her to take it out on you. I told her that I was the one completely responsible for the things you and I did while you were with me."

"But, that's not really true."

"Sure it is. I always want you to stay with me. But, I went against what you're mother wanted. I was wrong, and your mother has a right to be angry with me. You'll be fine though."

"When will I see you again?"

"I'm not so sure. But, keep remembering that I'm always with you. Keep sending me e-mails. And, another thing, please remember how much I love you. In just a little while we'll know why this happened today. The explanation of these *meant-to-beeees* always comes shortly after a confrontation like this. So, expect it."

"I will. I'm not afraid." After I said that Aunt Shirley hugged me, took all my suitcases out of her car and gave them to the morning doorman, John. She hugged me again and drove off. John was glad to see me and together we went up to my floor. My mom wasn't at the elevator door like I thought she would be. Then John dropped my stuff off in front of my apartment, and left.

I tried opening the door with my key, but the lock was dead-bolted. I rang the bell, and tried real hard not to be nervous. My mom opened the door and she didn't look mad at all.

"Hi, Mom," I said.

"Well, Hunt isn't quite sure if he'll choose the Ecole Chantemerle. You see, it happens to overlook Lake Geneva and Montreux. Or, should it be the Leysin American School? Or, perhaps the Gstaad International School near Bern. And, oh, there's the St. George School, but I think they only admit girls," my mom said.

"What are you talking about, Mom?"

"Oh, the boarding school you'll be attending. In Switzerland. Hunt thinks that that would be the best place for you right now."

"Switzerland? Are you serious?"

"Absolutely. He said it will give you culture. You're going to love it, I just know. Hunt spent his childhood in a Swiss boarding school, and he said you should do the same."

"I'm sorry I went to Big Sur with Aunt Shirley when you didn't want me to. But how come I have to go to a boarding school?"

"Hunt doesn't like you disobeying me. He really loves you but he says you need more discipline. He knows what's best."

"But what about you? I'm just a kid, and you're my mom. What do *you* think?"

"Miguel, I love you. But, I love Hunt too. We're going to be married someday soon, so I pretty much have to go along with whatever he wants. And, Hunt told me he doesn't think it's good for you to be around Shirley. He said her philosophies, her ideas, aren't good for you."

"I love Aunt Shirley and I always will. Her ideas keep me healthy. They keep me alive."

"Healthy? I'm not so sure about that. Her background is drama, not medicine."

"But what she's taught me is more important than medicine."

"We're getting off the subject. I'm so certain you're going to be pleased with this move. Just positive. You'll see." Then Mom changed the conversation by asking, "Don't you want to know who I met in Europe?"

"I'm sure you met a lot of cool people, Mom."

Talking about other people just then wasn't important to me at all. And, in a split-second everything sunk in. I wasn't going to put up a fuss about boarding school because being sent off somewhere is exactly what I wanted. I didn't know how it was going to happen, but somehow I got my wish in a total unexpected way. Thank You, God. Mom thought I would hate the idea, but it was like the total opposite. Anywhere in Switzerland suited me just fine. I wanted to act like I didn't like the idea though, just to be kind of a brat. But inside I became so totally excited. I couldn't wait.

I actually liked going to school, any kind of school. The next day I was supposed to return to my regular one, Notre Dame, that's kind of halfway in between Nob Hill and Chinatown on Pine Street. It's really called Ecole Notre Dame des Victoires, but nobody ever calls it all that. And they let me go there even though I wasn't French.

It would be my first day back after summer vacation. I knew that one of my favorite teachers, Mr. Ramirez, from my old elementary school was supposed to transfer over to Notre Dame, so I really hoped I would see him there. He's great.

I was only seven when I had first met him, but what he had said to me then will always be important to me. At seven I had realized that every day that I went to school I learned something good. I knew the reason I learned so much was because my teacher was Mr. Ramirez. He was real special to me and made me feel smart all the time. He was one of the main teachers at my old school, but one day I found out he wasn't going to be my teacher anymore because they were going to make him a principal. I ended up missing him a lot.

On the very first day of school he had taken me to the front of the class and said, "Everyone...Can I have everyone's attention please? This is Miguelito Estes, and he's a very courageous boy. He's a courageous boy because some boys like him don't go to a regular school. Miguel has E.B. Does anyone know what E.B. is?"

No one said anything. They just looked at me.

"E.B. stands for Epidermolysis Bullosa. It's a rare, skin disease, and Miguel was born with it. E.B. is not contagious, so that means nobody else can catch it from him. Do you understand that, boys and girls?" he had asked.

"Yes, Mr. Ramirez," they had answered.

"Good. Miguel is just like all of you, but he has to be extremely careful. It hurts him very much if you touch him. If you touch him he may get a sore, and then he may have to go to the hospital. You kids don't want to see Miguel go to the hospital, do you?"

"No, Mr. Ramirez."

"Fine. Boys and girls, do you have anything you want to say to Miguel?"

"Hi, Miguel," half of the kids in the class said at the same time. If Mr. Ramirez hadn't brought me up there, the kids never would have understood what I was like. And when the times came when I did get the sores, the kids knew what they were. They always asked extra questions though, and some of them still even made fun of me.

One boy in my class, Myron, called me a bad name. He had asked, "Are you a fag? Is that how you got it, fag?"

But when Mr. Ramirez heard that, Myron got in big trouble. Mr. Ramirez kept Myron after school and then called Myron's parents. Mr. Ramirez explained what E.B. is, but then he still kept Myron after school for two more weeks because he said, "using that kind of language is unacceptable." Then he told me, "Miguel, make sure to let me know anytime anyone says something like that to you."

I asked him, "Mr. Ramirez, why did Myron call me a fag?"

"Because he probably doesn't know any better, and maybe his parents don't either. That's why I explained it to all three of them. Now they know. When people don't know any better it's up to us to teach them, so they won't be ignorant. Do you know what *ignorant* means?"

"Ignorant? Yeah, I guess it means when a person isn't so smart."

"Yes. But sometimes ignorant people *are* smart and they just don't want to listen or learn anything new. They want to believe what they want, even though it may not be the truth. *Those people* are ignorant."

"Is *fag* really a bad word?"

"Absolutely! It's a very bad word. It's a bad word, especially for gay people, and it's used only by ignorant people."

"My mom said to me before that you're gay, and you're married to a man. Is that really true?"

Mr. Ramirez didn't answer real fast. "Yes, that's true. In the world some people are gay and some people are not. And when I was in school many kids made fun of me."

"Just like they make fun of me?"

"Exactly."

"Did your teacher make those kids stay after school?"

"No, they didn't. All my teachers did was ignore what the other kids called me."

"My brother Jorge said that when you ignore things they don't really go away, they get worse."

"Jorge's absolutely right. You must *do* something. When you tell the truth you are always the winner. When people don't know the truth, you must tell them."

"Like the people who don't know what E.B. is?"

"You're right once more. You can be their teacher. When you explain it to all the kids who don't really know what they're saying, they will no longer be ignorant."

"Is it that easy? Then they won't make fun of me anymore?"

"No, not quite. There's one more thing. You must always be proud of who you are. You are a very smart and good boy, Miguelito. You also happen to have E.B., and that makes you even more unique. If the kids don't know that, you must tell them. Tell them how proud you are."

When Mr. Ramirez had told me that, I thought he was the smartest man I ever knew. I was so proud that he was my teacher. And I became proud of myself.

I wished all my teachers were like him. As I got older the students got better too, I mean, smarter. In those days people were more dumb about AIDS. And, if those kids had only known better, they would have known that my sores didn't look anything like K.S., which is what mostly people with AIDS get.

I didn't understand much about boarding schools, and I didn't even know why they were called boarding schools. But it ended up sounding like something I might like. And, it didn't even matter because I was going to be free. Yippee!

For a few days I wondered how I was going to let Dad know that I was moving. He couldn't get letters, and I didn't know if Mom would tell him where I had gone. I thought, Aunt Shirley's so smart, I'm sure she'd figure out a way to let him know. So I called and asked her, "Couldn't I write directly to the El Salvador government? Wouldn't that work?"

"I don't think so. I'm not really sure that would do much good."

"Are you ever going down to Central America, Aunt Shirley?"

"Gee, doll. I really don't think so. Are you so sure you really want to go to Switzerland? I still feel so horrible since all this mess happened because of me. I'm going to speak to your mother again."

"Definitely not! Don't *even*! You don't get it...I got my wish, my biggest wish ever. I get to move away, to a place where I don't have to be afraid all the time. And, don't ever tell her I'm happy about leaving or else she might keep me here. I'm pretending like I'm mad because I have to go. So please, please don't tell her. That would ruin everything."

"I promise you I won't say a word. She may not even accept my calls these days anyway. But I must say that you do sound glad to be going. So in that case, I'm very happy for you. And, you know I'll be visiting you there as often as I can," Aunt Shirley said.

"Oh, for sure. We'll go hiking in the Alps, just like in *The Sound of Music*, even though that was really Austria. I guess they're kind of the same, right?"

"I'd imagine so. Or, I should say, 'Natürlich'."

"That sounds like a German word. I guess I should start studying right now or else the people there are going to think I'm a dumb ass."

"I wouldn't worry about it, doll. I think most of the people in Switzerland speak English."

Aunt Shirley and I still never did figure out a way to let Dad know where I was going. But, right after I got off the phone with Aunt Shirley I looked on the Internet to find out what all my favorite words were in German, not just the swear-ones. That was fun. Then Mom came right into my room and asked what I was doing. "I guess I should be practicing German words, you know, since I'll be leaving and everything," I said to her.

"You won't need to practice."

"How come?"

"Because you won't be going after all. I've heard back from almost every school I've queried. None are able to care for you. None of them have ever heard of E.B. before."

"Well...what about families over there? Or hospitals? Couldn't there be somebody I could live with who could take care of me?"

"No. I'm sorry. Hunt wants you here now."

"But Mom—"

"No. I promise you, Mickey. We're going to have a great new life in Los Angeles. You, me, and Hunt."

"Why did you call me Mickey?"

"Oh, ever since you told Hunt that Mickey Mouse in Spanish is 'El Raton Miguelito,' he insists I call you Mickey. Isn't that adorable?"

CHAPTER TEN

"Hi, I'm here to see Mr. Ramirez," I told the secretary at my school. My appointment with him wasn't really until 3:00, but since I was already out of class I thought he might be able to see me early.

"Oh, yes. You're Miguel, aren't you?" the secretary, Mrs. McCready asked.

"Yes, Ma'am. I'm a little early, so I can just wait out here, if that's OK."

"Certainly. Mr. Ramirez has told me a lot about you. You knew him when he was at St. Benedict's. You even had him as your teacher, before he became principal there. My goodness, that sure was a long time ago. And now, Mr. Ramirez is your principal here. What a small world."

"Yeah, I guess so. Mr. Ramirez is my friend. He told me I could talk to him any time I wanted. He's real smart. You probably like it that he's your boss, right?"

"Oh, of course. Such a nice man, very fair. And by the way, how is your mother?"

"You know my mother?"

"My goodness no. But I see her name all the time in the society pages of *The Chronicle*. She's involved with so many charities, isn't she? What an angel. If only there were more people like her."

"Yeah. Um, maybe Mr. Ramirez can see me now? You think?"

"Well, no. I'm sorry. At the moment there's someone in his office. It's not quite 3:00 yet."

"I'll just wait then."

Mrs. McCready began working on her computer, but I could tell she was going to say something else to me again. I heard she was kind of a nosy person, so I was half-way expecting her to ask me questions that were really none of her business. "You know, a few years ago, before Mr. Ramirez was here, I used to spend time talking to your brother, Jorge," she said.

"My brother? Jorge?"

64

"Oh my, yes. There were days when I would even take my lunch the same time as his, just so we'd be able to talk in the cafeteria together. Jorge used to inspire me so."

"Wow. I had no idea you knew him. He didn't really talk to that many people."

"I recall that. I remember Jorge being alone most of the time. He sure talked about you though. Oh, and how he liked the time he spent with your father. I met him, you know."

"You knew my father too? I can't believe this."

"Yes. His name was...Wallace, no...it was Joaquin. Isn't it? I remember him being such a handsome man. He looked so much like that movie actor, Antonio Bandero. How is he doing?"

"Antonio Bandero? I don't know him. But Dad's, well, he's been out of town for a long time. And I'm really not sure when he's coming back."

"Well, when you see him again, please tell him Margaret McCready from Notre Dame says 'hello'."

"Yeah, I will."

"And, before you go in to see Mr. Ramirez, I want to tell you once more how highly your brother spoke of you. Sometimes when Jorge talked about you I felt as if he was your guardian or protector. He loved you very much. I just want you to know that."

"Gosh, thanks, Mrs. McCready. I'm glad you told me."

What she said to me was kind of shocking. I had no idea Jorge ever talked about personal things with anybody. He was alone a lot, and seemed to talk to almost no one. Hearing Mrs. McCready talk about Jorge and Dad made me feel somehow closer to this woman I had never even met before. I was happy I got to talk to her. Sometimes God put people in front of me to meet, out of nowhere, that ended up making me feel real good. It was always a surprise, and this time really loosened me up before I went in to talk to Mr. Ramirez.

Just like before, it got to be real quiet again, then Mr. Ramirez's office door opened. Nellie Fong, a real bitchy eighth-grader, stepped out of the office, but when she looked at me she didn't say "hi." I never liked her anyway. She was totally mean and was always, as Mom would say, "insensitive to my needs." But when Mr. Ramirez saw me he said, "Hey there, Miguel, how are you? Wow, it's so great to see you."

I went over to Mr. Ramirez and hugged him first. He was like a best friend I hadn't seen in a long time who happened to be a grownup. "Oh my God, you still look the same," I said.

"Well, come on in. I'm sorry I didn't have much of a chance to speak with you on the phone the other day. That's why I thought it would be better if we talk here. We'll have more time, and hopefully at this time of day we won't be interrupted."

"That's OK."

"I'm not keeping you from a class, am I?"

"No, my classes are over." I said.

"So, how have things been going? Do you like your teachers? Tell me what's happening."

"Yeah, I like my teachers a lot. You know, I still won't really be here full time. I take home a lot of assignments, you know, 'cause I've got to be so careful. But, that's going fine. And, I'm never usually behind. Actually, I'm ahead most of the time. Math is kind of hard though."

"So, is that what you want to discuss with me today? Math? Who's your teacher?"

"Um, I just wanted to talk to you. It's not really about my classes though, not about school."

"OK. You said on the phone that it was important to speak with me. And, I want to hear whatever you want to tell me. So, whatever is said is between us. I hope you know you can trust me."

I totally trusted Mr. Ramirez, but I was getting kind of nervous because I never talked about real personal stuff with anybody else except Aunt Shirley. But, most of me felt real right about it. And it seemed like I had to tell someone I trusted or things in my life were going to get a lot worse. "You know my mom?" I asked.

"Yes. I met her a couple of years ago, when I was at St. Benedict's School. What about her?"

"Um, well, she—"

"Just a second. I can tell this is important and it may be difficult for you. So, please do me a favor. Relax before you go on. Just begin when you're ready," Mr. Ramirez whispered to me after he got up out of his chair to sit next to me.

That really helped. I'm glad he stopped me. I just sat still for a little bit but then blurted out, "I don't think I'm going to live much longer if things don't change."

Mr. Ramirez looked totally shocked. And it even took him a few seconds before he could say, "Miguel, tell me all about it. Explain what you just said."

"Well, first they were going to send me to a boarding school in

Sweden. I mean, Switzerland. But the schools wouldn't be able to take care of me right, so they all said 'no'."

"Who's *they*, Miguel?"

"Mom and this guy she's going to marry. It's mainly just this guy, because Mom does whatever he tells her. And what happens to me isn't so important anymore."

"Are you sure? Wow. Miguel, I'm positive this has to be some kind of colossal misunderstanding or miscommunication...or something."

"And, at some point they're going to make me live in Los Angeles."

"In L.A.? But your treatment is up here. Your school is here. And over the phone you told me that your aunt now lives here. Miguel, it doesn't make any sense to me that you'd move right now."

"I know. I want to be closer to Aunt Shirley now more than ever. She told me that if I don't get rid of fear I won't get any better. It's fear that I need to be away from."

"Fear?"

"Mom's afraid all the time. Sometimes Mom thinks it's best to prepare for the worst, you know, like me dying. She thinks it's not a good idea for me to get my hopes up, about living into the future."

"Miguel, this is an awful lot to digest. I know that that isn't true about your mother though. She really loves you."

"Well, maybe she does. But she actually believes that I'm not going to live much longer. She told me that it's healthier for her to believe that. She said that it will be easier for me to just know that I'll eventually die, and that there won't ever be a cure for E.B. She also doesn't want me to see my Aunt Shirley too much, who thinks the total opposite. My Aunt Shirley knows for sure that I'll be alive as long as I want to be."

"Your Aunt Shirley. Is she your father's sister or your mother's?"

"She's my mom's sister."

"Would your mother for some reason be jealous of your aunt?"

"No. Definitely not. It's not really Mom that doesn't want me to see her. It's Hunt, the fiancé guy."

"What can you tell me that's positive about the way your mother feels about you? Does she make sure you have all the medical attention you need?"

"Yes. She always makes sure I have a nurse who takes care of my blisters every day. My nurse is nice, I like her. Her name's Khadijah."

"My God. Let me think a minute. Where's your father?"

"He's...not around for a while."

"When is he coming back? Your mother has legal custody of you, doesn't she?"

"Yes, for some reason the judge made sure I could only be with her. And, I don't think Dad's ever coming back. My mom told me I should just prepare myself that he'll never be back to see me again. Maybe he just might stay in El Salvador forever."

"He's from there, right?"

"Yes. But he's supposed to be here too because he has duo citizenship."

"Miguel, all of this definitely concerns me. I've got to talk to your mother. Where does—"

"But you can't say that we talked, or else I'll really get into trouble."

"Oh. No, I won't. I have to speak with her though. I want you to be safe. Where does she work? Where can I reach her?"

"She doesn't really work at a place. I guess you can call her at my apartment. She has an office number, and her office is inside our apartment, too."

"Either way. Is there anything else you'd like to tell me right now?"

"Yeah. Just before Jorge died, he said the same thing I'm telling you now. Except he told it to me in a letter. It's all about Mom and her fears. He said that that's what really killed him. And, I think all her fears have gotten a lot worse since Jorge died. It's like I should have died too, when he did, so now she's just expecting that for me. I think she's like guilty for making us have E.B. You know, because of her genes."

"Miguel, it's so hard for me to imagine that your mother doesn't truly care for you, completely. But, I am taking this all very seriously, very seriously."

"Good. I don't know who else I can really tell. Aunt Shirley, you know, leans Mom's way 'cause that's her sister. Nobody really knows the truth except me."

"Do you still have this letter that Jorge wrote?"

"Yes, I do. It's always hidden under the mattress in my bedroom. Mom never looks there. It's always cleaning ladies who change my sheets. Why?"

"I'd like to see it."

"Well, that's not such a good idea. If Mom ever saw it, she'd be really, really hurt. And, she'd be totally embarrassed that I ever let anyone read it."

"What I want to do more than anything is help you. And, reading that letter should enable me to help you all the better. Why don't you think about this, and decide later. How's that?"

"Sure, that's cool."

"Good. In the meantime I'll talk to your mother, and it will be very positive. I'm sure she's a bright person. I'm not going to confront her, I just want to talk. I don't think she'd be adverse to that."

Meeting with Mr. Ramirez was good, but I still didn't tell him everything. And, I wasn't real sure that he totally got it. But I knew I could count on him. It felt so good telling someone what was going on. And that way I didn't feel like I was all alone, too. Mr. Ramirez wasn't biased the way Aunt Shirley was either. I guess if I had a sister I'd kind of stick up for her too, no matter what.

I was hoping Mr. Ramirez was going to call my mom on a day when I was in school, but he called her right away. I heard his voice talking on Mom's answering machine when I got home, but Mom wasn't there to pick up or listen. I thought that it was going to be soon that they would talk though. But I was wrong.

Two days went by. Three days went by. Mom still acted the same way she always did, so I just figured they never talked, because if they had she would've questioned me. It was on the fourth day, in the morning before I went to school, when Khadijah was there and asked, "What's going on with your principal at school? Your mother wanted me to ask you."

"I wonder why my mom asked *you* about him," I answered.

"She didn't really ask me about him. She just said he's been calling here a lot, and wants to talk to her."

"And she hasn't called him back yet?" All of the sudden I felt very afraid. I trusted Khadijah a lot, but I thought maybe she would tell that I talked to Mr. Ramirez about Mom. And, I never lied about anything. I didn't know what to do. So I ended up saying, "I talked to Mr. Ramirez in his office about four days ago."

"So, you *do* know what it's about?"

"Maybe, I guess so. But—"

"Miguel, that's OK. You don't need to tell me. I'll think of something to tell your mother. And, this has nothing to do with her, but...you're OK, aren't you?"

"Oh, definitely." I guess the real truth was that I wasn't. But I didn't want to worry Khadijah. She already had enough to think about with mid-terms, or finals, or whatever they were, coming up at Berkeley.

When I went to school later that morning one of those meant to be things happened when I ran into Mrs. McCready in the parking lot, just as I was getting off the bus. "Well, hello, Miguel, how are you?" she asked.

"I'm fine. And you?"

"Oh, I'm doing well today. You know Mr. Ramirez has been trying desperately to reach your mother, but she hasn't returned any of his calls. Has she been out of town?"

"No, she's home. I guess she's just kind of busy right now."

"Well, why don't you come with me for a moment. Mr. Ramirez is probably in his office, and he's been wanting to talk to you again."

"Now? But I'm going to be late for my first class."

"Oh, don't worry. I'll write you a note. It should only take a few minutes." Mrs. McCready and I walked into the office where Mr. Ramirez was. I thought I was maybe in some kind of trouble, but he was real glad to see me. "Miguel, my favorite person. What a nice surprise," he said.

"Hi, Mr. Ramirez," I said, just as Mrs. McCready walked out of his office and shut the door.

"You know, I've phoned your mother many times, but she doesn't answer. And, she's never called me back after I've left several messages."

"Yeah, I know. She doesn't ever answer the phone unless the call's coming from someone she knows real well. Calls from people she doesn't know too good scare her."

"I see. But, remember what I said before? I want to help you. What I'm going to do next is to write your mother a letter. I'm sure she'd have a moment to respond to that. And, by the way, I still would like to read over that letter you told me about, the one Jorge wrote to you. Can you please bring it to school the next time you're here?"

Most of that night I panicked. I was hoping I wouldn't make myself sick, but I looked under the mattress over and over again, and all around my room. Jorge's letter wasn't there.

CHAPTER ELEVEN

Lots of times I dreamt at night. In my dreams I would go to all the best locations, and most of the time Jorge was with me. Together we went to places where the sun was warm but never burned our skin. Something like this could only have happened in my dreams.

When I was awake so many great ideas came to me while I was sitting in front of the bay window in my room. The whole world was out there. But whatever I couldn't really see out the window I'd learn about on the Internet. Like Playa del Carmen in Mexico. It's on the Yucatan Peninsula in the state of Quintana Roo. That's where I was one night, in my dreams. Jorge was there too.

"How many do you want?" Jorge had asked me.

"Just bring all of them down. I'll eat every one," I answered. Jorge had just picked a bunch of bananas off of the highest part of the trees, just for me. He didn't really like them too much for himself. I usually made milkshakes out of most of mine. Mom wasn't there, so we could do whatever we wanted.

After Jorge came down from the tree we we're going to go fishing, but we ended up looking through a pile of stuff in the sand instead. "Hey, this one's from Trinidad. Do we have anything from Trinidad yet?" he asked.

"No, not Trinidad. We still need to get one from Barbados, too. And, from that other place...Bermuda," I said.

"Duh. Bermuda's not in the Caribbean, it's in the Atlantic."

"Whatever."

"Hey, is this a beer bottle? Or some other kind of drink?"

"It looks like beer to me." Since Playa del Carmen was on the edge of the Caribbean, all the garbage collected there. Not in a messy way. The beach was still pretty, but there were lots of things that ended up on the shore. Like bottles, plastic jars, plastic bags, lots of things. What Jorge and I had to do was find at least one piece of garbage from every one of the islands in the Caribbean. Since we never did go fishing, this took up lots of our time. We could tell which county everything came from because most of it still had its original label stuck on.

"Miguel, let's walk over to that point. There's some people over there. Maybe one of them will buy us a beer," Jorge said.

Oh my God, when we got to where the people were they didn't have any clothes on. I never saw naked people in person before, just in the movies. I couldn't believe it. "Act like you're not surprised," Jorge whispered.

"Does this mean we have to take our clothes off too?" I asked.

"No, I don't think so." We stared at the people for a while since they were there anyway. But then we moved on. We didn't get a beer because we really stood out, and everyone could probably tell that we were way under twenty-one.

"Jorge, look at this bottle of liquid soap. It's from Venezuela. Venezuela isn't a Caribbean island, what's this doing here?" I asked.

"It's still on the Caribbean coast in South America."

"Is it near El Salvador?"

"Yes. I think it is kind of close. I'm not really sure."

"I want to sit down now. How about under those trees, where it's shady?"

Jorge and I sat under the palm trees and looked out at the blue-green Caribbean Sea. It was beautiful. And so peaceful. It's kind of what I thought the colors in heaven would look like. Then I asked, "You know what? This reminds me of the place I went with Aunt Shirley, Big Sur. She said that Big Sur must be like heaven."

"I've never been to Big Sur. I miss Aunt Shirley, but I never understood all that *believing* stuff she talked about when I knew her. But I found out later she was right. All that stuff was true. I wonder why she was the only one who seemed to know those things."

"She's pretty smart. So, what's heaven like? Do you like it up there?"

"Well, that's a made up thing. It's not really *up* anywhere, and I've never thought of it as *heaven*. It's just somewhere I got to go to before I come back here again."

"Oh. Well, I'm glad you're here for right now. I guess I'll learn about it when I get there."

"But, you're not supposed to be there for a while. You've got more to do here."

"How do you know?"

"I just know."

"So, you mean I'm going to be OK? And there's going to be a cure for E.B.? And I'll get to be alive for a long time?"

"I can't tell you. That's for you to discover."

"I wonder if anyone will ever discover heaven. You know, somebody like Christopher Columbus. So people can go there to visit without having to be, you know, dead."

"Never."

For some reason we stopped talking about heaven and started walking down the beach again. I was restless. We were getting real close to finding garbage from all the countries. "Here's a shampoo bottle from Antigua," Jorge said.

"Wow, all this stuff is way different from the stuff we have at home, but I bet the ingredients are identical."

"How are things at home? Did the Giants ever win the World Series?"

"No, not yet. You know, they don't play at Candlestick anymore?"

"I know. They call it 3com Park."

"No, it's a new place altogether, SBC Park," I said.

"Wow. So, how's the rest of the city? How's Mom and Dad?"

"The city's the same. And Mom's just the same, too. But Dad is in some kind of jail in El Salvador."

"He's *what*?"

"He's in jail. I don't know what for. He wrote me a letter but couldn't say why he's there. I know he didn't do anything wrong though."

"Miguel, you have to write back to him. But don't put your name on the envelope in the return address part."

"What? What are you talking about? I wouldn't even know where to send it. Plus, he told me he might get into trouble if I write to him."

"There's a way to get an address. Aunt Shirley will help you. She can find out anything. Just *make sure* you write to him. This is real important."

Jorge seemed to be so positive about this. He kept telling me over and over, "Write to Dad."

I thought I should. Maybe it was a good thing. But then I thought of Mom. Maybe Jorge knew something about her, something I didn't know. So I asked him, "What about Mom? Is she ever going to change?"

"You don't need to ask me because you already know the answer. That's why you're here in the first place. She's your biggest lesson here."

"So, she's not going to change? Is she going to get more afraid of things?"

"I don't need to say anything...you already know. If I tell you these answers, then what do you have left to learn? You would have no purpose here if I gave you all the answers."

"You're starting to sound like Aunt Shirley."

"That's another thing, you should appreciate Aunt Shirley every day. It's probably the last time she'll be around. There's probably very, very few lessons left for her. She may have no reason to come back."

"Am I going to come back?"

"Maybe. I'm not sure. It depends on what you do in this lifetime."

"What about Mom?"

"Stop asking about her. You're only responsible for yourself. But as far as she goes, her soul's pretty young. She's got a lot ahead of her. Mom may come back lots of times. Lots of lessons."

"You know what? That letter you gave me, the one where you talked about Mom?"

"Yeah. I wrote it just before I died. It was probably the most important letter I've ever written."

"Well, I know it was important. So, I kept it hidden under the mattress, tucked in a torn part near the top. But I looked all over for it a couple of days ago and it was gone. I'm real sorry. It made me sad because whenever I read it I think of you. But, I'll keep looking for it."

"You won't ever find it. It was meant to be found by someone else."

"Someone else? Like the cleaning lady? So you're not mad?"

"Definitely not."

"Oh, that's good. Should we get back to looking for more garbage?" I asked.

"Of course. I think we still need to find a few more countries. I see something. Look, it's toothpaste. And, it's from Puerto Rico."

"That's where Ricky Martin's from."

"Cool."

"And, here's something. It's a shaving cream can from...St. Lucia. Ooh, gross. It has barnacles on the bottom of it."

"Oh, is *that* what barnacles are?" Jorge asked, after making a weird look with his eyes. Then he said, "You know, pretty soon I'll have to leave again. But, I'll definitely see you another time. And remember, you will be here for a while. It's not time for you to go yet."

"Yeah, I know that. But let's keep looking. What's that over there?" I asked as I pointed to some garbage underneath some dried seaweed."

"I don't want to go over there. Look at all those flies hanging over it."

"Let's go see."

"It looks like some sort of dead fish. A shark, I guess. But what's that thing over by its mouth?" Jorge asked.

"Some kind of cardboard-thing. A cover from a book, maybe. I never knew sharks could read."

"Does it say anything?"

"I can't see. I'll have to touch it to find out. Way gross," I said. Touching it was such a strange, magical feeling. It wasn't that it was mushy, or because it was right next to a dead shark's mouth. It was like a book I should read if I could find one just like it that wasn't all disintegrated. All I could read were four words on it.

"Well, what does it say?" Jorge asked.

"*Joaquin Must Find Out.* It's probably one of those mystery books," I answered.

Then out of nowhere my dream was over. I didn't get to say "goodbye" to Jorge, and we never did get to find all the garbage from every country. But, it was so strange that the title on the book cover had Dad's name on it. What did that mean?

Later in the day I thought a lot about the dream again. I tried remembering what Jorge told me exactly, but I could mostly just remember the names of the countries where the garbage came from. Then, the letter I should write to Dad is what I remembered next. Jorge said this is something I had to do for sure.

Since my mom was out of the house I turned my computer on and began.

Dear Dad,

Lots and lots of times I've thought of writing to you, but I wasn't sure if I should. Now I'm sure. How are you? Are you doing OK there? When are you getting out? There are way too many things to tell you about what's going on in my life.

And, I still don't know if you're even going to get this letter because I don't really know where to send it, but I'll find a way. Maybe you were wondering if I still love you since you don't know what I'm thinking. The answer is yes. I'll always love you, and I know I'll see you again sometime. Even though you're not here I still watch Nick-at-Nite, but I watch it by myself. You'd be glad because they just had a *Munsters* marathon, but it was on TV Land, not Nick-at-Nite. And, they don't show *Maude* too much anymore. Do you get to watch TV where you are?

What do you get to do? Is it like the jails here? Aunt Shirley told me Alcatraz doesn't have any electricity. Does your jail have some? I hope so. Maybe you get to watch Nick-at-Nite in Spanish, that would be cool.

Well, you know what? There's another main reason why I'm writing to you now, and that's Mom. She's taking real good care of me. But I have the feeling that if I don't move somewhere else real soon I'm not going to be around much longer. I really need to get away.

But I'm all out of ideas. I told my school principal about what's going on. Do you remember him? He's new at Notre Dame, but he used to be my old teacher at St. Benedict's. His name is Mr. Ramirez.

I keep telling Aunt Shirley about what's going on, but because Mom's her sister she probably won't ever get it. She says it's part of my destiny and it will all play out, whatever that means. She tells me that Mom protects me so much because she loves me. I don't know about that one. And I know that love isn't what keeps a person alive. If I'm around fear much longer it might kill me.

Instead of just waiting to find out what's next I'm trying to make this change happen. Aunt Shirley said that this is important too, that if you at least try to make things happen, then God will see that you're trying, and probably give you a break. But, if you just wait, nothing will happen, because God doesn't think you really want it bad enough.

The best thing I can think of is for you to get out of there and then I can live with you somewhere. Are you trying to get out of jail? Because if you're not trying then you won't get out. Or else you'll just have to wait until after whatever time they said you have to stay in there. Are you ever going to tell me why you're there in the first place? I don't really care because I know for sure you're a good person, and you didn't really do anything wrong.

Don't forget, I still have those passes to the Monterey Bay Aquarium and they have to be used up by the end of this year. Plus, you told me you'd take me there. So maybe that's another reason for you to try to get out of El Salvador. By the way, I hope this letter doesn't get you into trouble. It shouldn't, because I don't think I said anything bad, and I didn't use any swear-words.

I miss you a lot, Dad, and I want you to come home. I know that El Salvador's your old home, but you belong here now. Maybe it's your destiny or something that you're there now, but pretty soon you need to come back to your new home, San Francisco, and live with me. Jorge would probably think that that's right too, since he told me how important it was for me to write this letter to you.

Well, Dad, I love you a lot. So what you have to do now is try real hard to get out of there, then God will give you a break. That's the way it works. Do this. Maybe you already are and I just don't know it. Anyway, I can't wait to see you again sometime. I know this will happen no matter what.

Love,
Miguel

CHAPTER TWELVE

'Biopsy: The removal and analysis of a sample of tissue from a living body for diagnostic purposes' is what the dictionary says. I got to be so sick of hearing this word, but I had to look it up to see if maybe it meant something worthwhile, just in case. The more times I had to go to the hospital, the more confused I got. The more time I spent in the hospital, the more I was reminded that I was probably going to die.

If God gave us life to live why did so many people on earth have diseases? Diseases like E.B.? We should either live or die. But what was the point in preparing us to die by being ill all the time? Diseases just make people sick so they can't even live life totally while they're alive anyway. So why shouldn't they just be dead in the first place? I didn't get it.

I was at Stanford for probably the zillionth time, and I was sick of it. Either I was supposed to live, or I was supposed to die. But, I got to be really tired of all this in-between stuff. This time I wouldn't have to stay overnight, so that was cool. But I had to spend most of the day in a hospital room. As usual I saw a lot of different people I had never seen before. The first person who came into my room was a nurse who asked, "And how are you feeling today?"

I didn't answer immediately because I could tell that's what she was going to ask. That's always what new nurses and doctors ask when they don't know you. Maybe they're trained to say that. "Fine," I said. *Fine* was my trained answer. I wasn't in the mood to say much more than that. The nurse said and did a few more things, but I pretended I wasn't even there.

Then Dr. de Pascual walked in. "Hi, Miguel. How's it going?" he asked.

"I'm OK. But, what is this new test for again?"

"Right now were going to test your blood for a T-Cell count. Then were going to take a small skin sample from the bottom of your left foot."

"A biopsy, right?"

"Yes, a biopsy."

"Then I can leave after that?"

"Well, no. You'll be here for most of the day. We'll conduct a few other tests after that."

When Dr. de Pascual said that I shook my head sideways, but I thought he didn't see me do it. I just wanted to go away. Not even home, because home was just getting to be worse. I didn't really know where I wanted to go, but I knew I didn't want to be at the hospital anymore. "What's wrong, Miguel?" the doctor asked.

"Um, I don't know. I guess I'm kind of tired of coming here all the time. No offense. I like you, you know. And, you do a good job, but—"

"I don't blame you. I wouldn't want to come here all the time either if I were you. Do you know why I come here every day?"

"Duh, because it's your job."

"No, because I like helping people to get well. I want to make them better. I want to help you, Miguel. You're a great kid and I like you."

"Well, thanks. But, why am I alive? I don't really get that part."

"What? You're alive because you're a fighter."

"No, I mean, why should people be sick while they're alive? People should either be alive or dead. Having a disease while I'm alive doesn't make sense. Why should I be alive in the first place if I'm alive with a disease?"

I liked Dr. de Pascual a lot, but I could tell he'd probably not be the one who'd have answers to the kinds of questions I was asking. The best person to answer my questions was Aunt Shirley. She would have known what to say right away. She never really felt that having a disease was a bad thing. "It is your destiny," she would say every time. Aunt Shirley said that I chose to have E.B. before I was ever born. But how can that happen?

I guess I needed to stop being mad for a while, or else I was going to make everything worse. After the nurse took my blood, and after the doctor asked me a ton of medical questions I asked him one, "You still want me to stay here for the rest of the day, right?"

"Yes, some of the results aren't going to be ready until about two o'clock. You're here with Khadijah, aren't you?"

"Yeah. She's in the waiting area."

"Why don't the two of you go get some food at the cafeteria? Or, how about taking a short walk through campus?"

I liked his idea of walking around, but not close to Stanford. "So, you don't need me to be here for like two or three hours?" I asked.

"Yes, about that."

I couldn't wait to get the hell out of there so I could find a place to be less mad about life. In the waiting area Khadijah was kind of in the same mood, sort of bitchy. "Do you know Palo Alto very well?" I asked her.

"A little bit, but not so well," she answered.

"Well, I don't have to be back here for another three hours. Maybe we can find a place to just relax, a special place."

Khadijah thought for a real long time. She always understood me on the inside and already kind of knew the things I liked and the things I didn't. "Well, let's go," she said.

"Where're we going?" I asked.

"You'll find out. But, there's one thing. If you don't recognize what's unique about this place I'm taking you to, we're heading back. I'm taking you there because you in particular should find it very interesting."

"OK. God, I hope I get it right then."

"You should."

Somehow she drove us out of Palo Alto altogether and we got right back on the freeway. We headed north. "We're not going all the way back up to the city, are we?" I asked.

"No, not at all. We're almost there," Khadijah answered.

We got off at some country-looking place, and then got onto some road that just had trees and no buildings. The town we were in was called Woodside. Then I saw a hanging sign that said *Filoli Center.* We parked and then walked up to this really huge house. "Oh my God, this is the *Dynasty* mansion," I said.

"You got it right off the bat. Good job!"

"But, how come it's here. *Dynasty* was in Colorado. What's it doing here?"

"Who knows? That's the way Hollywood is, I guess."

I couldn't believe it. Khadijah knew that one of my most favorite things is TV shows that aren't on anymore. I mean, old shows. So, seeing the *Dynasty* house was extra special for me.

"Some days it's open, some days it's not. It's part of a historical preservation something-or-other. But, what I really want to show you is behind the house," Khadijah said.

We paid some money to a person, then I saw one of the most beautiful places I had ever seen. The gardens there had every kind of plant and flower there probably was. "Oh my God. Look. That's the pond where Alexis and Krystle had a huge fight. Did you see that one? Where they both pulled out each other's hair? I can't believe this."

Khadijah looked real happy because I was. This place was so pretty. And it's the *Dynasty* mansion. Wow.

"You know, I wanted you to see this not only because I knew you'd like that parts of *Dynasty* were filmed here, but I wanted you to spend some time in this magnificent garden. Let's sit down for a while. We have lots of time before we have to head back."

"Look at that bench over there. Let's sit there." After I said that we both didn't say too much. It was just real quiet, like I was all by myself but not really. Looking out at beautiful things when it's real quiet was good. I wasn't too mad anymore. In the trees behind the gardens the birds were chirping. It was like being in a National Park, except it was the *Dynasty* house. When it was time to talk again I started and asked Khadijah, "Do you get mad at life sometimes?"

"Oh, all the time," she answered.

"What do you get mad about?"

"Injustice. I don't like people to get away with things that are wrong. It's not fair. But the older I get I realize that that's them, not me. When I was your age I thought it wasn't fair that I was born black. I was mad about that all the time."

"You wanted to be born white?"

"Well, I didn't have a say in it. I just realized early on that it seemed it would have been a lot easier being white."

"Aunt Shirley would tell you that you could've chosen what color you wanted to be. She says that we decide everything before we're born, and the reason we live life is to learn to accept ourselves whichever way we turn out."

"I tell you, the more I listen to you and Shirley, the more I think you both may be right."

"What do you mean?"

"Well, because now as an adult, I wouldn't be anything but what I am, African-American. I wouldn't have it any other way."

"I wish I could say that about having E.B. There are lots of times I hate it."

"But if your aunt is right, then there will come a time when you'll accept it, and appreciate that you've tackled it, or overcome it. If that's what you choose to do. I guess the only way we can be happy is to not be mad at what we have already chosen for ourselves."

"So when you were my age, was being black like having a disease for you?"

"Yep. It was. That's an interesting observation, that's how I saw it. But, I got to the point to where I didn't need...a cure. I thought I was fine just the way I am. I realized I wasn't sick at all. I'm black, and that's just fine, that's just great. Have you ever thought about developing friendships with other kids who have E.B.?"

"Yeah, other people asked me about that too. I've tried to do that a couple of times, but then I get real tired of them talking about E.B. all the time. Sometimes I don't like to think about it too much, and talking to them just reminds me."

"So getting to know other kids with E.B. hasn't helped you?"

"Um, no. I kind of like hanging out with adults more. Jorge was pretty much the only friend I had who was a kid."

Having just adult friends always seemed normal to me, and every time other people told me I should have kid friends I couldn't seem to understand why it never happened. Maybe because I didn't go to school as much as the other kids, only on some days of the week instead of five.

Oh well, I guess I thought that by hanging out with mostly adults I'd turn into one quicker than if I hung out with just kids. That's OK.

Khadijah and I didn't talk too much more, so we just looked into the garden and at the pretty pond with the lily flowers on top of it. I wondered if any of Alexis's hair was still left in there after Krystle pulled it out. Pieces of her hair or scalp would have made such totally awesome souvenirs.

Well, seeing those gardens sure was cool. Khadijah and I never did go inside the mansion to see all the fancy things there because we wanted to be in the garden more.

We headed back to the hospital a little bit before I was supposed to be there. And after Khadijah parked we walked from the car to the Medical Center, and I thought about what Khadijah said about being mad and choosing to get over it. I thought about all the time I spent being mad, but I never told anybody. I was mad at so many things. But being mad sure takes up a lot of energy, and it probably made me sick lots of times.

I decided that whenever I might get mad in the future, I'd first try to stop and think if being mad would even make a difference or not. Being mad at something I couldn't change was a total waste of time. Duh, why bother? And, I had to really watch it all the time, because getting mad was so easy for me to do.

Back in my hospital room I waited for Dr. de Pascual, and after he came in we talked about important stuff. "Do you think that being mad makes a person sick?" I asked.

"I think so, yes. Psychologists say that people who hold onto their anger are more prone to develop disorders, which are like diseases."

"Well, I'm going to try not to be so mad sometimes. That's what I'm going to do to make myself well this time."

"Great. I think if you accomplish that, you'll be giving yourself some very positive therapy. The trick is to practice that during the most trying of situations. But, I bet if there's anyone who can do it successfully, you will."

"Thanks for the confidence, Lefty. I'll definitely do my part. But I'm still counting on you to discover the cure for E.B."

"We're working on it. You'll see the day when we do."

Wow. What a cool thing to hear. Dr. de Pascual seemed so sure when he said that. I sure was hoping he was right. On the drive back to the city I told Khadijah, "Dr. de Pascual said that I'll be alive when there's a cure for E.B."

"Miguel, that's great. Wow, that should make you happy," she said.

"Well, I don't know if he was serious, or if he's just thinking positive because he knows that that's the way *I* think."

"I bet your aunt would tell you to keep that one in your head. Isn't that what she calls it?"

"Aunt Shirley would say to believe that one for sure, and expect it. What we believe in our heads is what we create for ourselves, is what she says. What do you believe for yourself?" I asked.

"What do I believe for myself? Well, I believe I'm going to be a part of a professional dance company and tour all over the world."

"Ooh, that's a good one. Then I will believe this for you, too. But, I don't know if I'm going to be so enthusiastic though."

"Why in the world not?"

"Because when you go off to be a dancer, that means you won't be my nurse anymore. And I'll be all alone."

"Oh, I see. Hmm. How about if I believe that I'm going to be a part of a professional dance company, tour all over the world, *and* you'll have someone new to take care of you? And you're going to like that new person a whole lot. By believing this, am I covering all the bases?"

"Sure, I'll go for that. That's the one I'll keep inside my head, too."

CHAPTER THIRTEEN

"Who'd have believed it? I'm giving up a life with a babe on each arm to be with this *Leona Helmsley-wanna-be*," my mom's newest fiancé said. Hunt was Mom's third in a row, but I knew for sure she'd end up marrying this one. Even though he was a few years older than Mom, I always felt like Hunt wasn't a real grownup, he was just trying to act like one. He seemed to think the way a baby does, only about itself. And by the way, who's Leona Hemsley?

Seeing Mom happy was good. Thinking that this guy was going to be around more wasn't. Aunt Shirley met him only once, and she said that that was plenty. She said he pity-mizes L.A. because he's plastic, fake, and full of himself. "I say let's have our wedding at the Hotel Bel-Air. Lots of talk if we have it there. The publicity won't hurt us a bit," he said.

"Oh, but darling. We'd be so far from my circle of friends. Everyone I'd invite would have to commute," my mom said.

"But *my* friends wouldn't. What do you think, champ? Who in their right mind would prefer attending a wedding in San Francisco over Los Angeles? All those important people. Couldn't you just groove to being around them?" the fiancé asked me.

"I still don't know if I like L.A. too much. No offense, sir," I said.

"What's this *sir* bullshit? Call me Hunt. I don't get it. Why don't you like L.A., pal? It's everyone's dream."

"Mickey really doesn't know Southern California so well. We've been up here for so long now. We'll have to bring him down more often, so he'll learn to appreciate it. I'm sure he'll celebrate wherever we end up marrying," my mom told her fiancé.

Actually my mom probably figured their match was perfect. So I tried my best to just be happy for her that she found a man. What I couldn't figure out was how I was going to fit into this new picture. Maybe they really didn't want me with them at all. Maybe I really would have to go somewhere else to live. Could I finally get the chance to live with Aunt Shirley? Would they be sending me off somewhere else far, far away?

"You know, you don't look that sick today. I mean, not as much as your mother keeps telling me. I keep forgetting, what's the name of this thing you've got? Epidemiolosis Billosos?" the fiancé asked me.

"Epidermolysis Bullosa," I answered.

"Well, you don't look too bad to me, except for those rashes. Now, it's not catchy? Is it? – Just kidding."

"No. It's not catchy, it's not a virus. It's an inherited disease."

"Inherited?"

Mom got a totally terrified look on her face when I told her fiancé that my E.B. was inherited. It's like I let the cat out of the bag. Letting this guy know that she has the E.B. gene made Mom's image look less than perfect, the way she didn't want it to. "Mickey, I think you may be confusing Hunt. E.B. is a rare, genetic disease Mig—, I mean, Mickey acquired from his father. I don't have it, and I never will," my mom said.

Mom wasn't exactly telling the truth. I did get the disease from both my mother and father. Both have the recessive gene in them, and when those genes were added together they made E.B. That's the way it goes. This guy Hunt never knew what's up. Sucker. I prayed to God that soon I'd really get to go far, far away.

"Mick, I know you're going to love the room we've picked out for you in my Malibu place. By the way, Malibu's the perfect spot for you to work on your tan. You do know that to live in L.A. you've got to have the perfect tan, right?" the fiancé asked me.

"I can't get very much sun. Sunburns make me real sick," I answered.

I decided right then that there was no way in hell I was going to live with them in HELL.A. That's what San Francisco people call it. "Well, Mom, are you sure that boarding school thing couldn't work out after all?" I asked.

"No. It's highly unlikely. Why? Is that what you'd like to do? Go to a boarding school?"

"Well, you know. Maybe it's not so bad. Maybe there are other ones that would take me."

"Why wouldn't they take him?" the fiancé asked.

"Mickey needs frequent and specialized medical attention. The schools I'd interviewed just aren't equipped to care for him properly," my mom said.

"*How much* medical attention?"

"I definitely have to have my own nurse. I have to be bandaged every day. I have to wear masks on my face sometimes too. I can only eat very specific things. And, most important, I need to be real close to Stanford. It's really the only place where I can have the best treatment and the best doctors. The only other place there is, is at the University of North Carolina in Chapel Hill. Sometimes I need to have surgeries on my hands and feet. See, look at my hands," I said. I could tell Mom didn't tell him any of this.

"Yeah. I noticed those before. I never did ask, but what's, I mean, how did that happen? Were you in a fire or something?" he said.

"No. All the skin's grown all over my fingers. So it's like I don't have them anymore. So much for the digital age, huh?" I asked.

"What?"

"Don't you get it? No more digits. I don't have digits anymore," I said.

"Hunt, Mickey is making it all sound much more severe than it really is. He receives excellent care from his nurse, Khadijah. She does everything for him. She's the greatest. I don't have to lift a finger."

"Well then, we'll just bring her with us. Done," the fiancé said.

"But she goes to Berkeley. She's in their dance department, and she's going to be a professional dancer," I said.

"Just give her more money. Pay her what she wants. I mean, a lot more than she's getting now. No problem. She ought-a go for it," he said.

"She'll never do that. Being a dancer is her dream. And taking care of me here fits right into her schedule perfectly. Money won't make her change her mind."

"Listen, champ. You've got a few lessons to learn about money. It has the power to change everybody's mind."

"And, what about Aunt Shirley?" I asked Mom.

"What about her?"

"Well, I know you guys don't want me to hang around her too much, but I don't want to be that far from her."

"Shirley? Oh, brother. Mick, let me tell you something. I think this aunt of yours is a bit of a nut case. Isn't she a little...Isn't Berkeley full of a bunch of leftover hippies? Sharon, am I right?" he asked.

"Well, it certainly is an unusual place to say the least. Mickey, dear, why don't you go to your room now. Rest for a bit, so you'll stay well," Mom told me, so I wouldn't say anything mean back to the guy 'cause of what he just said about Aunt Shirley.

This whole thing was the biggest joke I had ever heard. There was totally no way I was going to let my life get any worse. Having to be anywhere near this guy, in L.A., was like never going to happen. I hated him. I went into my room and immediately called Aunt Shirley but she wasn't home. Instead of leaving a message, I wrote her an e-mail with my Point & Speak.

Dear Aunt Shirley,
Help! I just spent more time with Mom's new fiancé. It's the same guy you met before, the same guy Mom was in Europe with. He's a total jerk. He's so L.A. He's got that phony kind of personality people have down there.
I forgot what he does exactly, but he's some sort of movie consultant, which is sad because that means when he talks people are forced to listen to him. Bummer. I know that what he is doesn't affect me at all, but where am I going to live? What am I going to do? There's no way I can live with them in L.A. That's where they want to take me, to Malibu.
Why would anyone ever want to live in Los Angeles? Unless they're in the entertainment business, and they absolutely had to.
Would you reconsider about me living with you? The guy even thinks that Khadijah will come down there too if Mom pays more money for her. Aunt Shirley, I want to stay here. Or, at least go to a place where he's not. You know what I mean? Do you have any ideas? Let me know, OK?
I'll write to you again, soon.
Love,
Miguelito

About an hour later Mom's fiancé must have left because Mom came in to talk to me. "Mickey, tomorrow morning we have a meeting with my attorney and we'd like you to come too. OK?" she said.

"Who's *we*?" I asked.

"You, me, and Hunt. You're not going to school tomorrow, are you?"

"No. I'm not. What's up with the attorney?"

"Oh, well, you'll just have to talk with him for a bit. We need you to come with us when we sign a few papers."

"Papers about what? Is that guy making you sign them?"

"That guy's name is Hunt. You do like him, don't you? He adores *you*. Please call him Hunt from now on, dear."

"Yes, Ma'am. But, what are these papers?"

"They're for protection, that's all. It's something I've neglected for far too long. Regarding the trust money you'll be getting from Grandmother and

Grandfather. Remember the money they left you when they died? You recall how it can only be awarded to you once you've reached your eighteenth birthday, right? Well, silly me, what I've always forgotten to do is protect myself. You know, just in case, heaven forbid, you..."

"What happens when I sign these papers?"

"It'll make everything so much simpler. It means that should you, you know...depart before you receive the trust when you're eighteen, the money won't be lost, or tied up in court. It'll come directly to me."

"Well, what if you die before I do?"

"Then you'll get all the money I'm leaving you too. Mickey, dear, it's simply best to get all this done now."

"Tell me something, Mom. Is this guy, I mean, is Hunt, *making* you do this?"

"He just *reminded* me. He's so good at that. He has such a keen legal sense. This is something I should have done long ago. As I said, it's for protection, that's the only reason. Mickey, I want you to be here forever, but Hunt keeps reminding me that we have to be realistic."

"Yes, I know that. But will Hunt get any of this money?"

"Hunt? I'm not sure yet. Well, you know what community property is, don't you? Whatever married people acquire after they're married becomes theirs. And, don't forget, the same applies to me. Half of what he acquires becomes mine, ours, yours and mine. And trust me, he's more than comfortable. Either way, we'll be living well for the rest of our lives. Isn't that fabulous? It's perfect."

"But I don't care about what he has, all of his money. What's going to happen to me?"

"Miguel, dear, I'm doing all this for you. Should you live a long life, you'll have everything you've ever dreamed of."

I guess what my mom didn't know was that all I've ever dreamed of recently was to get away. Having lots and lots of money was something I've never thought about. It wasn't important. Any mother who really loves her son should have been saying things like, 'You'll always be alive,' 'Of course we'll stay close to Stanford so you'll get all the care you need,' 'You'll always be near Aunt Shirley because she loves you so much,' and more than anything else, she should have said, 'I *believe* in you. I have faith in you. You Go!' How come Mom never told me these things?

Dreaming that my mom would ever think like this was wwwwaaaayyyy too much to ask for. So, why bother. All I could hope for was that somehow Aunt Shirley was going to write back to me or call with some great news. I went to bed thinking that I'd be woken up by the phone, so I didn't fall asleep right away.

But when I did, I started to dream. Jorge wasn't in it, which was kind of strange. Instead, that man, Hunt, was in it. We were driving to a grocery store in Malibu and he'd given me a list of things I had to buy. When we got there it was a mega-fancy grocery store, like just for movie stars. Hunt didn't come in though. He dropped me off and said, "I'll come back at 4:00 sharp. I'll meet you right here in front of the store, got it?"

"Yeah. But I don't know the kind of brands you like. I hope I get it right," I said.

"Just use your best judgment," the fiancé said, then he drove away.

The inside of the store was just as fancy as the outside. The ceilings were totally high, like skyscrapers. And, all the stuff on the aisles was stacked just right. It all looked perfect, like the store just had plastic surgery.

I started finding all the things on the list and put them into my cart. But then I came to something on the list I'd heard of before but didn't really know. It was hearts of palm. What's that? Was it the insides of a palm tree? Was it some weird kind of meat? I had no idea.

So, guess who I asked? Roseanne from TV. She was shopping in the store without too much make up on and she was buying bologna, the really thick kind with the peel still on. "Excuse me, do you know where this is?" I asked her, while pointing to the hearts of palm on my list.

"Sure, honey. I'll show you," she said.

She walked over to where the canned vegetable section was and showed me these cans of hearts of palm. I still didn't really know what they were but as long as I found them that was the important thing. Roseanne looked at my list and asked me, "You're buying *all this* by yourself? Isn't anyone with you?"

"No, Ma'am. My mom's fiancé dropped me off and I've got to get all this stuff. He's picking me up at...Oh my God, I forgot what time he said he's going to pick me up. He's going to be so mad if I'm not out there right when he is."

"Is your mom's fiancé a nice guy?"

"Well, I actually think he's kind of a jerk?"

"What about your mom? What's she all about? Where's she?"

"Um, I don't know where she is. She probably doesn't have time. I guess she's busy planning her wedding, or putting together a fundraiser. I'm not really sure."

"Hmm. Can I be honest with you? They both sound like a couple of assholes to me. Some people just don't know a good thing when they got it."

"I know what you mean."

"Well, you seem like a nice kid. I tell you what, why don't you come live with me."

"With you? At your house? Are you for real?"

"Sure, why not? You wanna think it over first? I need some coffee. I'm going to go over and get some while you think about it. I'll be back in a minute or so. I got a real cool place, you'll love it."

I couldn't believe it, Roseanne asked me if I wanted to live with her, in her own house. I didn't really need much time to think about it though. I mean duh, who wouldn't want to live with Roseanne? I never lived with a movie star before. Wow, this was going to be way cool. Maybe she could teach me how to become a movie star too.

But, before she came back to the canned vegetable aisle where I was, my dream was over. I couldn't remember anything else. That dream sure put me in a good mood though. I didn't have to think about Mom's fiancé. I didn't have to think about moving into a place I didn't like. Plus I got to hang out with Roseanne.

I wondered what was coming next. Maybe if I was real lucky in my next dream I'd meet Val Ewing, I mean, Joan Van Ark from *Knots Landing* in that same grocery store. I thought Val probably shopped there for sure, you know, considering how close Knots Landing must be to Malibu. And then maybe she'd ask me to live with her, just like Roseanne did. That would be so totally cool. I couldn't wait.

CHAPTER FOURTEEN

"So, what do you really think about Mom and this dude?" I asked Aunt Shirley.

"I think it's great for your mother. But in relation to you, the idea of you living in Los Angeles makes no sense at all," she said.

"I totally agree. I'm so glad you're on my side."

"I'm not on anybody's side. And, I'm not going to give it any thought either. It's absolute nonsense."

"But, what should I do to stay up here? Do you have any ideas?"

"Wait it out. Keep going. Keep changing, growing, and *believing.* I'm positive you won't ever have to live there, but the rest needs to be played out. Just know that everything'll be fine."

"If you say so. You mean I should just ignore what they're talking about?"

"Just wait it out. Speak your mind, but know that everything will be fine. Hey, why don't we get ready to enjoy a wonderful day. We're almost there."

It was Saturday so neither one of us had school. Mom was in L.A. for the weekend. And since Khadijah couldn't stay with me, Mom agreed for me to stay with Aunt Shirley. She was taking me to the Japanese Tea Garden in Golden Gate Park. I'd never been there before.

The park was packed full of people on the weekends, and all the ones I could see looked like they were having a great time. Golden Gate Park was so huge. It took us a long time to look for a parking place, but that gave Aunt Shirley and I more time to see different parts of the park as we drove around looking. We saw the de Young Museum, the Asian Art Museum, the Steinhart Aquarium, the Planetarium, and a bunch of other cool stuff. I think people mostly go there for the trees, the meadows, the paths, and the roller-blading though. "Wow, what's that thing?" I asked when I noticed some real weird-looking place.

"The building?"

"Yeah. What's it for? Conventions or something?"

"No, it's the Hall of Flowers. The whole building's made of white-painted glass, and it contains some of the rarest flowers in the world."

"That's so awesome. It's like that movie where the glass falls down and cuts up that lady. And then kills her. *The Hand that Rocks the Cradle.*"

"I never saw that one. She was in a greenhouse?"

"Yeah. That's what it's called, a greenhouse. Hey, there's a space. Are we kind of close to the Tea Garden?"

"Oh, let's grab it. This is close enough."

We parked in front of the Arboretum and I wasn't so sure what that meant, but I didn't care. I just wanted to get to the Tea Garden. "You know, for the longest time it used to be free to get in. I actually came here when I was a little girl," Aunt Shirley said.

"It's been around that long?"

"Hey, I'm not that old. Watch it, doll. The Tea Garden has been in this park since the late-eighteen hundreds."

"Sorry about that. Hey, guess where I went a few days ago? The Filoli Center."

"Oh, that's a beautiful place. It's on the Peninsula. Who did you go there with?"

"Khadijah. She took me there because it was so close to Stanford. She thought it would be the perfect thing for us to do while we were waiting, and she was right. That's where the *Dynasty* house is."

"Yes, I know. They also used it for the movies *Heaven Can Wait* and *The Joy Luck Club.*"

"Damn, you know everything."

"What made Khadijah think to take you there?"

"She knew, well actually both of us were in bad moods so she wanted us to spend some time in the gardens there. It was beautiful, so peaceful."

"That's rare. You? In a bad mood? What was wrong?"

"I guess I was just mad at life, you know, for having to go to Stanford all the time. I was mad just seeing Dr. de Pascual. But I was mostly mad about having E.B."

"You have a right to be mad, so get it out. I'll tell you something, having anger and not expressing it, or not getting beyond it, is lethal. It's almost as bad as fear."

"I know that. I could tell that that's maybe why Khadijah and I were meant to go to Woodside and just hang in the gardens at the Filoli Center."

"I believe that held-in, or sustained anger causes more diseases than anything else. I don't think most people realize how dangerous it is."

"You don't seem to get angry too much. Is that because you know how really bad it is?" I asked Aunt Shirley.

"Well, I've learned from the lessons I've been given. Too many times I realized that the anger I was creating, came right back in my face every time. I couldn't get away from it. It just kept coming right back to me like a boomerang. Just like all things, whatever you put out, is exactly what you'll get back."

"Kharma is what you're thinking of, that's what you told me before."

"I think it's more like instant kharma. I remember the time when a very, very long article I'd written was rejected. That made me so mad. I mean really mad. I was working at the *Oakland Tribune*, and began a new piece on my computer, but out of nowhere some scribbly lines started to appear all over my monitor, and my computer crashed for no reason. Then, an hour or so after that I drove home, turned on my computer there to check my e-mail, saw the very same scribbly lines, and my computer crashed. And all that time I'd been furious."

"So, just because you were mad you had to get new computers."

"No, I didn't have to get new ones. They were both repaired. The point is that anger, more than any other emotion, is horribly negative if it's not dispelled. It's so dangerous. It ruins lives. I think a lot of mental illnesses are misdiagnosed. Some of them aren't caused by chemical imbalances at all, they're a result of held-in anger."

"Well, I'm for sure not going to get pissed the next time TV Land shows a *Gomer Pyle* marathon when I'd really like to see *All in the Family* instead."

"That's a good idea."

Aunt Shirley always had lots of good ideas. We were at the Japanese Tea Garden for most of the afternoon. We sat under an enormous pagoda and drank green tea. Mine was cold. Together we watched the maple leaves blow by. Aunt Shirley and I were there so long in the same spot that we were able to recognize every little difference between all the goldfishes in the pond below us. They're really called koi and carp, but they still looked like the same goldfish that's in Woolworth's basement.

Aunt Shirley and I walked through the paths and even went over some arch bridges that we had to kind of climb up. There were so many beautiful little waterfalls, and lots of lily flowers in the ponds. Aunt Shirley and I found a spot where not too many people were, so we sat down on a bench in front of a huge golden Buddha statue.

"What is Buddhism all about, Aunt Shirley?" I asked.

"I just know a few things about it. I'm not that much of an expert on any organized religions, but I'm sure there are a few good elements in just about all of them. I do know that Buddhists believe that *you* must be in charge of your own life, no one else can be responsible for you. Not God. Not anybody," Aunt Shirley said.

"That's like what you told me before about taking responsibility for yourself."

"Yeah, I guess it's similar to that. It means that if someone else is paying your bills, paying for your survival when you're supposed to be responsible for your own life, then your destiny is not yours. You are living out the life, the destiny, of the person who is paying for you. Your life is not your own if you are dependent upon anyone else."

"But since I'm a kid, my Mom pays the bills because I don't have a job yet."

"Sure, oh definitely. But, you're sort of living out your mother's drama until you are free from her. Independent."

"Oh my God, her life *is* a drama, for sure."

"That's OK. But that's her life, not yours. Change is coming to you. Buddhists believe that it is your responsibility to create change, to re-claim your own destiny. In your case you're going to have to wait a bit, but eventually the decision will be yours. It'll be up to you to change your life. *You* will have that choice...for every aspect of your life. And you do want to hang around, right?" Aunt Shirley always used the words *hang around* instead of saying "staying alive."

"Yeah. I really want to hang around. I've got too much left to do, you know, pretty important stuff."

"Did you know that most people are destined to have what they really, really want? Because when their desire becomes so strong *they'll* inevitably *make* it happen. But expecting to get something, just because you've wished for it, or prayed for it, doesn't cut it. You know what I mean? So, once again, do you really, really want to hang around?"

"Yes. That's what I just said. Duh."

"Great. Well then, as you and Archie Bunker say, 'Case closed'."

That was totally like a non-question for Aunt Shirley to ask. I mean, who wouldn't want to be alive?

After the Buddha, we walked some more. Around us all the time were tourists from all over the place. Maybe we were the only people from the Bay Area there. "You know what, Aunt Shirley? I guess I really don't want to leave here...San Francisco," I said.

"Do you really, really not want to leave here?" she asked.

"Oh my God. This is like a re-run. No, I really, really don't want to leave here."

"Then you won't. You'll be here as long as you want. *You'll* make that happen. It'll be like an ongoing dream inside your head."

"Hey, guess what? I even had a dream about Mom's fiancé. But instead of having to live with him and Mom in L.A., I got the chance to live with Roseanne at her house, but then I woke up."

"Roseanne who?"

"Roseanne from TV. You know, Roseanne Conner from Lanford, Illinois."

"Oh, *that* Roseanne. Well, having dreamt of her certainly convinces me that you really, really don't want to live with Hunt in his house. Dreams are very telling, you know."

"Yeah. I always have lots of wacky ones. I mean, some of them are totally, totally way off."

"It's interesting. Dreams can be interpreted psychically or psychologically. Either way, they're significant and can provide fascinating insights and answers."

Some of the dreams I've had in the past I was afraid to tell Aunt Shirley about because they were just too weird. Most of them I always had were kind of scary. Instead of telling her directly about some of the ones I've had, I just asked her, "What do scary dreams mean?"

"Oh, that's an easy one. Every one of those has to do with the *f*-word," she said.

"Really?"

"Yep. Fear. Scary dreams seem to emanate from some sort of existing fear we may have about something. Usually not having anything to do with what we're seemingly afraid of in the dream. Whatever seems to scare us in the dream is not what we're really afraid of. What scares you in your dreams?"

"Um, well. I always end up alone. The people I want to be with are taken away, and at the end I'm all by myself."

"Those are the dreams you have about Jorge?"

"Yeah, and some other ones too."

"But, you know what? The clearest thoughts I ever have come to me when I'm alone. I love that. So many people today feel the need to be around somebody else all the time. And there's others who really have little choice in the matter and always seem to be surrounded by people."

"I like being around other people. But there's times when I like being by myself."

"That's very healthy, Miguel. For some people, constantly being around others means that they're so much less in touch with what's going on in their own lives, their life-lessons. Experiencing solitude allows us to deeper explore our own lives, our own life-lessons. Being alone sometimes makes people realize why they're alive in the first place."

What Aunt Shirley said seemed real right to me. The times that I spent by myself I'd think about things that really mattered to my own life. But, I still didn't really know the reason why I was alive. I figured, I'd just find out when I was supposed to.

Just as Aunt Shirley and I were about to leave the Tea Garden, I said, "I wonder if some people here on earth ever have the same exact lessons to learn as other people, like copies of lessons."

"I doubt it. Every individual is so damn complicated. All lessons are different. But, there is one thing that most people need to learn, the elimination of all fear. That's huge. That's got to be the biggest lesson of them all. And, for you to know this so early on is going to make your life so much easier to handle."

"Jorge said that too. He thought that having more faith would have saved his life. Maybe it would have, maybe it wouldn't," I said.

"Well, I know he had faith, even though he never admitted it, because he and I talked about it so much. And since he had faith rather than fear, he wasn't afraid of dying. He was so dear. I loved him so much. But, it was hard for him to learn. His mind wasn't as open an yours. I'm so proud of you for growing into such a wise, young man."

"Thanks. Well, what about you? What lessons do you have left, Aunt Shirley?"

"Oh my. I'm sure I've got plenty. Perhaps I'd like to have a relationship someday."

"That's something you don't ever talk about. It's like Mom is so desperate to have a new husband, but you're not. Is it because you're the independent-type, like Jorge? How come?"

"Good questions. You must have your instinct turned on because you've just nailed my biggest lesson. I need to learn to trust. Only when you can completely trust someone are you able to have a healthy relationship. And it seems like it's nearly impossible for me to trust anybody."

"Well, that's kind of weird. What's up with that? What about all the guys you must meet at school?"

"I don't really meet that many men on campus. They're mostly so much younger, the undergraduates. And a lot of the faculty I know are either married, gay, or conceited married men who think that it's OK to fool around."

"You should put an ad in one of those papers. There's lots of other people looking for somebody."

"Maybe it's just not my time yet."

"But, is it something you really, really want?"

"Maybe. I don't know."

"I think it would be really cool if you started to have a boyfriend." I said.

Aunt Shirley didn't say anymore after that. She actually started to look pretty sad. Then I remembered her looking that way before. I wasn't totally sure if it was none of my business so I asked anyway, "What about that time when you started to cry at Big Sur? When I asked why you didn't have any babies? Why were you crying then?"

CHAPTER FIFTEEN

Fall kept getting closer and closer and I could hardly wait.
That's when Mom and I usually take our vacations because that's when Mom said European people take theirs. Nothing really special was planned, but it seemed like we usually always went to a new place. Most of the time it was to a country somewhere in Europe, like last time when I got to go to Denmark and Norway. That was way different for me.

My mind was on fun stuff because Mom still didn't pick out a date for her wedding. And that meant I didn't need to think too much about moving or not moving. Cool.

When I began thinking about where we'd go for our Indian summer vacation I asked, "Mom, is there a good place we haven't been to yet that we can go to this time? A place you won't be afraid of?"

"Afraid? I'm not afraid. I'm just concerned. There's so much going on in the world right now, dear."

"How about if we go to Israel? We could see where Jesus was born. What about there?"

"Oh, Mickey. And be shot down by some terrorist lunatic? No. Hunt told me that going there on any vacation would be like a suicide mission. It's much too dangerous to even pass through. No, I don't think so."

"Well, here's the deal. You name the place. You tell me where we're going to go. Take a stand. *You* make the decision."

"Oh, dear. The whole world is so scary these days. Hunt keeps telling me that you never know where the next terrorist threat is gong to come from. And that's true. You know, I'm not even sure when we'll have time to squeeze in a vacation anyway. These wedding plans certainly are occupying so much of my time. I don't really see my schedule freeing up in the near future."

"Maybe I could go on a trip with someone else? What about that?"
"Who?"
"Well, what about Khadijah? She's having a three-day weekend soon.

And that would be good because she could also take care of me when we travel. That way I'll stay real healthy and probably not get sick."

"That reminds me. Hunt has been wanting to know more about Khadijah. How long has she been your nurse now? I don't quite recall."

"I guess about four months or so, something like that."

"He's been wondering...on the days when Khadijah isn't here, you manage to do well enough, don't you? You're doing all right?"

"Um, yeah I guess I do OK. Why?" I could tell Mom was thinking about something, something not so good. Three or four months are the most my past nurses have lasted with us, but there's no way Mom was going fire Khadijah. I mean no way. "Mom, why did you ask me that?"

"Oh, we just want to know, well, Hunt wants to know how you're doing, how you might manage on your own," my mom answered.

"You mean on a vacation?"

"No. All the time."

"What are you talking about, Mom? That's totally impossible. Are you talking about me having no nurse at all? Never?"

"Well, Hunt just feels that since you're twelve now...you'll be thirteen next month. He thinks it would be good for you to become a bit more self-sufficient at some point in the near future. He'd like to see how you'd do on your own."

"But Khadijah and all the other nurses I've had are trained. They know about medicines and ointments and bandages. Sometimes it's hard for me to reach the blisters on my back and on the backs of my legs. If I don't fix them and wrap them up right they'll get infected. Then I'll get really sick."

"Oh, you're so resourceful, Mickey. You'll be fine. Hunt has total faith in your abilities. Khadijah will be here tomorrow, won't she? While she's here, perhaps the both of you can create some sort of list of needs and directions in which you'll be able to follow. I'll help you jot them down."

"Maybe you can think about this a little bit more tonight, before telling her tomorrow morning. Maybe that's a good idea. And you know what, Mom, why do you always have to do everything Hu—"

"Oh, my. You know what? As it turns out I won't even be here tomorrow morning. I have an early breakfast engagement with Hunt at his hotel. He's at the St. Francis, in the very same suite Queen Elizabeth stayed in while she was here in '84. Isn't that something?"

"Yeah. So, then you're not going to tell her tomorrow?"

"I'm not quite sure when I'll have time. But, I'll speak with her shortly. Maybe this is what she wants, too. It'll all work out. You'll see."

I couldn't believe this was going on. I had to think real quick. What was the way to stop this from happening? I knew Mom did whatever Hunt wanted no matter what, so I didn't ask again why she felt she had to do what he said. But I figured, maybe out of nowhere, this really wouldn't turn out the way she wanted after all. And I knew that just hoping for this not to happen wouldn't be enough though, so I thought of some kind of specific plan.

Maybe Khadijah could adopt me. First I would have to get emancipated from my mom, or whatever it's called. And that way I could get away and stay healthy. I definitely didn't have anything to lose by asking Khadijah when she got here. If she said "no," then I'd just have to think of another idea, then another one, then another one.

Somehow the next morning Khadijah got to my house extra early. She did that sometimes. But my mom was still home too. Oh my God. When I found out that Khadijah was there I wanted to run right out of bed and get to her before Mom said anything. "Hi, Khadijah. What's up?" I asked, while sprinting up to her at the coffee maker.

"Aren't you going to greet your own mother this morning? Hi, sweetie," my mom said.

"Oh, yeah. Sure. Hi, Mom," I answered, without being able to see her.

"Good morning, dear. Khadijah, how long are going to be here today?" Mom asked.

"Well, the same as usual, Miss Kirkland. Your son has school today. So I'll just be here now for a few hours, then pick him up at three to bring him back home."

"Fine. I'd like to speak with you once you've brought him here. I've got to run out the door this very moment, so I'll see you sometime between three and four."

"Yes, Ma'am. I'll see you then," Khadijah said.

"Goodbye, darling," my mom said, as she aimed her face to mine. Most of the time Mom didn't like to kiss me when her lipstick was real fresh, so she just gave me a make believe one.

Mom walked out the door, and then Khadijah and I talked. "Do you know what she wants to speak to me about, Mikey?"

"Yeah, I do," I answered, but said nothing more.

"Do you want to tell me what she wants to speak to me about?"

"Um, well, yeah. But first, can I talk about something important to me?"

"Of course, sure. Yikes, something weird is going on. I can tell."

Khadijah started to get this worried look on her face. So, instead of making it a long story, I just asked her, "Have you ever thought about adopting a kid?"

"Adopting a kid? Well, no. Which kid? You?"

"Yeah. Maybe it would be good for you to adopt me. I could probably work it out so that it would still be your job, and you'd still get paid from Mom or maybe Hunt. Maybe even more than you're getting now. Did you ever see that movie from the eighties, *Irreconcilable Differences*?"

"No."

"Well, it's with Drew Barrymore when she was a kid. Not like she is now. It was way before *Charlie's Angels*, and way, way before she showed off her boobs on *David Letterman*. Anyway, what she did was divorce her parents. So maybe there *is* a way I can get away from here."

"What made you start thinking about all this? I don't get it. Why do you want to get away from here?"

"Don't get pissed, but Mom said I don't really need any more nurses. I think this afternoon she's going to let go of you."

"You mean, let me go?"

"Yeah, that's it."

"No more nurses? She wouldn't be hiring a replacement? You've got to be kidding. Mikey, you *definitely* need a nurse. What's she thinking? Did I do something wrong? Is she unhappy with the way I take care of you?"

"You know what? It has nothing to do with you. She does whatever Hunt tells her, and I know for sure that he just sees me like a total nuisance in their life. And, now that they're getting married soon, I'm positive Hunt isn't going to want to have anything to do with me. He's a massive jerk."

"But keeping you away from the medical attention you need is ridiculous. I think your mother may just want to get rid of *me*. She must be unhappy with something I've done. I'm sure if she did let me go she'd certainly hire someone else, another nurse for you."

"No, I don't think so. I'll try really hard to help you find your next job. OK? Sorry about all this."

"Wow. This is so hard to believe. Let's talk more about this while we get you ready for school," Khadijah said. She took her job real serious. As usual she got out the scissors to cut off my bandages from the day before. Doing this required extra careful attention. I was thinking that there was no way I was going to be able to do all this on my own, especially with my hands being the way they are.

Next, she cleaned out my mouth so it wouldn't become infected. I can't use toothpaste or a toothbrush like most people because the skin in my mouth is way too sensitive. Most of the time I can never open my mouth up too much because I don't have too much healthy skin to do that, it might tear.

After that, I'd have to take special baths with some sorts of chemicals in them. These special baths not only clean me but are real good for all of the skin lesions on my body that *weep* all the time. Even drying me after I get out of my bath is a tricky thing. I always have to have extra special care for almost everything I do.

When I get dry I have to have all different kinds of ointments put on me, the ones that keep my skin's layers from separating. The ointments are real moist but aren't supposed to stick to the bandages that kind of hold my skin on. Those are called Surg-O-Flex® flexible tubular bandages for large extremities. That's what really takes up the most time, putting them on just the right way.

Well, anyway, Khadijah knew all this particular stuff. And she was real good at it. All the time she was getting me ready she didn't talk too much. It's like she felt that when she was cleaning me, and putting my bandages on, she needed to just be talking about only positive and good things. Or, maybe she just didn't feel like talking at all.

I thought that Khadijah was more than a nurse to me. She was my buddy, and I didn't have too many of those. But maybe I really didn't matter so much to *her*, since she probably had so many other people who were her friends at Berkeley. I wasn't sure.

"Am I your friend, Khadijah?" I asked.

"Of course you are," she answered.

"Are you sure? Or are you just nice to me 'cause it's your job?"

"Mikey, I'm nice to you because I like you. I think anybody would be lucky to have you as their friend. You are so very special." Khadijah was going to say more, but then she began to get a little emotional. At first, I didn't know why. "Sometimes I can't believe you're only twelve. When I was your age I'm not so sure I could have handled any of what you've had to deal with in life. I know your family has a lot of money, but for you to have stayed as sweet as you are truly amazes me," she said.

"Wow, thanks," I said.

"No. There's no way your mother is going to do this to you. I won't allow it. No, no way. It's never going to happen. I can't wait to talk to her now."

Uh, oh. Damn. I could tell something was going to hit the fan at right about three-thirty or four o'clock. But, just like Aunt Shirley said, "You've got to get rid of your anger, or it's going to cause a disease." I was glad Khadijah was going to get pissed off for lots of reasons.

It was a great day at school when I found out I got an *A* on my Math assignment I turned in. That was so cool and totally unexpected. Usually when I even got a *B* on any Math homework I was real glad, because I always thought that Math really sucks big time.

At lunchtime I even got a table all to myself. There was no one there to bother me. Things in the day were definitely getting better. As the day got longer, the more I wanted to see Khadijah at three o'clock, so we could go home and I could watch her let loose.

It was two forty-five and my last period teacher, Mrs. DesJardins, let us out. Getting out early was like icing on the cake, heck'a cool. I went to the parking garage, and it was two-fifty, then two-fifty-five. Hooray, it had turned three o'clock. Then it turned three-ten, then three-fifteen. What was going on?

Finally, I could see Khadijah drive up at almost three-twenty. Her face looked like she was just in a car accident, kind of in shock, not knowing what to do next. She didn't even say "hi" when I opened the passenger door. "Khadijah, what's up?" I asked.

"Um, I went back to your house before I came here. And I talked with your mom then. The truth is, I didn't want you to be around when I spoke to her."

"That's OK. I don't think I would have been surprised by what you were going to tell her anyway. So, how did it go?"

"It went fine. Completely under control. I was wrong about...well, actually we were both wrong about assuming what your mom's going to do next. She *does* have someone else to take care of you. That means I am out of the picture. And, it's not because your mom is displeased with me. She knows you can't take care of yourself. It all has to do with moving to L.A. All about her fiancé, so you'll both be able to live with him there."

"No kidding. Wow. I had no idea that that's what this is about. But then, this means you're still leaving?"

"Yes. I'm sure going to miss you. Your mom asked me if I could go to L.A. to take care of you there. But I just started my fall classes. And I've got to finish them in order to graduate on time. It would've even been difficult for me to continue commuting to the city. These days I not only have to spend afternoons there but now mornings on campus, too."

"I'm definitely going to miss you, Khadijah, a lot. I'm real glad you'll be getting closer to graduating, but what's going to happen to me?"

"Well, that's what your mom and I talked about more than anything else. I asked her a million questions about you. Apparently the new nurse she's hired is excellent. He used to work full-time at the UCLA Med. Center in their Dermatology Department. And he already lives in L.A. It sounded like your mom still isn't quite sure exactly when you two'll be moving, but at least you'll be receiving great care no matter when you go."

"I can't believe you're leaving."

"Well, we'll certainly stay in touch. There's no way I'm going to let you forget about me. I want to hear more of these stories your aunt tells you. It seems like those help you the most."

"Yeah, they do. But without you here, I'm going to get pretty lonely."

"There's no reason for you to ever be lonely because you and I are going to be friends for a very long time."

I didn't like hearing that too much because that's exactly what my last nurse, Stephanie, had said to me on her very last day. I've never talked to her since.

A couple of days went by, and then it was almost a week. I hadn't heard from Khadijah at all, and I kept expecting to meet my new newest nurse.

After a whole week passed, I asked my mom, "What day is my new nurse going to start again?"

"A new nurse? I never hired a new one," Mom said.

CHAPTER SIXTEEN

One morning I took a cab to school. Mrs. McCready noticed this when she saw me get there and asked, "Is it your nurse's day off?"

"No. Khadijah's not my nurse anymore," I said.

"Oh my goodness, that's a shame. So then, how are you doing, Miguel? You're doing all right?"

"Yeah, I guess so," I answered, but I wasn't telling the truth. Mrs. McCready knew it too, but she made things worse by asking about my mother. I didn't feel like saying anything, but then I told her, "My mom's fine. She's marrying some guy from Los Angeles."

"Yes. I know all about it. I read about the two of them in *The Chronicle* again. Hunt Manly is such an important man. A big movie business executive in Hollywood."

"I'm really not too sure what he does. All I know is I might have to move to L.A. because that's where Mom's going."

"I certainly hope you'll be able to finish out this term. Mr. Ramirez will surely miss seeing you. You know, he never was able to reach your mother and he tried so many times."

"Yeah, I know."

"He'd still very much like to speak with her. And, I think he even wrote your mother a letter. No response there either."

"Yeah, well, I don't really care too much about the whole thing anymore. I was supposed to bring him a letter too, but I never found it. Whatever."

"I know Mr. Ramirez is supposed to have a pretty lengthy meeting with the counselors this morning, but what if you could come in to see him right before lunch? Could you do that? I'm sure he'd be willing to talk to you again."

"Um, I really don't want to, if that's OK. Today I just feel like going to my classes, and then going home."

"All right then. And you're sure about that?"

"Yeah, I don't really care anymore."

I definitely didn't care anymore. Not about what my mother had to do because of Hunt, and not about the lessons in my life I was supposed to be learning. And, I didn't care anymore if I was going to die. Since my own mom didn't care, why should I?

At this point in my life, maintaining it, was just too much trouble. Since I started taking care of myself I realized even more what all the nurses had to do. And, they never had to live with all the pain that goes along with it. It's like a double dose. What a total nuisance. I was absolutely going to puke if I ever had to look at one of my lesions in the mirror again. I sure didn't see anything changing in my life, and I figured I'd tried real hard to come up with lots of ideas to make it get better. And it just never did. I thought I'd tell Mom that I was too sick to go back to school anymore. I didn't even care that I was doing better in some of my classes. Who cares? I always knew I'd never grow up to be an adult anyway, so what did I need an education for?

Towards the end of the day, when I was headed to my English class, I ran into Mr. Ramirez. I guess I should have known that that was going to happen. There's no getting around it. That's the way things were meant to be. I wasn't in the best mood, but I talked to him anyway. "Hi, Mr. Ramirez," I said to him.

"Hi, Miguel. Are you headed to a class right now?" he asked.

"Yes, I am. I'm going to English, and I've got to be on time."

"Oh, I won't keep you. But, Margaret...Mrs. McCready, told me you took a cab to school this morning. I'm leaving a little early today, so I'd be glad to give you a ride to your house. How would that be?"

"That's OK, but you don't really need to."

"No, I *want* to. And, you never know when a cab's going to show up in this part of town anyway. I can never seem to get one when I need one. I'll pick you up in front of the parking garage on Stockton Street at three. OK?"

"Yeah, I guess so. Thanks."

"Great, I'll see you then."

I thought Mr. Ramirez was being a little pushy, but he was generous at the same time. Maybe he couldn't tell that I wasn't in a good mood and I didn't really want a ride. That was strange though, that he was getting off so early from school. He usually worked way after all the kids left. Somehow it seemed like it was a meant to be thing though, so I knew I shouldn't question it.

Then English happened, then Math, then I was done. Hooray. And way before I got to the parking garage I could see Mr. Ramirez waiting there, and it wasn't even three yet. He looked real impatient, like he couldn't wait to get going. "Is that your car?" I asked him, while he was almost sitting on top of a lime-green Jaguar.

"No. I like spending my free time leaning on other peoples' cars. Duh," he said.

"That's what I usually say. Duh."

"So, how was school today?"

"It was OK. I guess maybe I'm going to miss it a little, especially since it may be the last time I'm able to come here."

"Are you definitely moving?"

"It looks that way, and I hate it."

"Let's get in. You're at the top of Nob Hill, aren't you?"

"Yeah. I live right across from Grace Cathedral. But I'm actually closer to the Fairmont."

"Oh, that's a great neighborhood. And, the Fairmont is such a beautiful hotel."

"That's where the second TV team did the show *Hotel*, you know. But on TV they didn't call it the Fairmont. They called it the St. Gregory," I told him.

"Oh, good old Holly-weird. A town where image is more important than substance."

I didn't really know what he meant by that because I was talking about the hotel here in San Francisco, not Hollywood. Whatever.

"The man your mom's marrying is in the film business, isn't he?" Mr. Ramirez asked.

"Yeah, I guess so. I'm not totally sure what he does. That's what Mrs. McCready asked me this morning. I don't really care. He's some producer consultant."

Mr. Ramirez definitely took the long way to get to my house. He drove all the way through the Cannery and Fisherman's Wharf, two places that were always packed full of tourists. Then he drove through North Beach, Washington Square, Chinatown, and finally up to Nob Hill. Driving over the cable car tracks on Powell Street was fun. I liked hearing the chains underneath the tracks rattle as they turn around in circles. Mom never drove on the streets with cable car tracks underneath because she thought the tires might get stuck in them.

"I have an idea. How about if I park in the garage at California and Mason? It's hard to stop and let you off without being able to park on the street. And up here it's impossible to find a space."

"Well, isn't that parking just for the Masonic Auditorium?"

"No. It's public parking. I'll pull in there."

Again, Mr. Ramirez was kind of pushy. He definitely could have stopped in front of my building without having to park, no big deal. I didn't get it.

"You don't mind, do you?" he asked. Then he drove in, paid the guy, and parked his car.

"No. I can definitely walk from here. No problem," I said.

"I'll walk with you."

"Oh. No. You don't have to. I'll just walk by myself."

"Well, I'd *really* like to see your building. Would you mind if I came up for a minute? I bet some of the views from up there are awesome. Are you on an upper floor?"

"Yeah, but—"

"Miguel, let me be honest with you. I wasn't quite sure you'd want me to, but I must speak with your mother, in person. She's probably home right now, isn't she?"

Oh my God. I should have figured that that's why he wanted to give me a ride home. And he knew that Mom, never in a million years, would go for him just showing up. I didn't know what to do.

"Um. I don't even know. I'm not sure. You know, she usually likes to know beforehand if someone is coming to see her. She's kind of proper."

"Well then, I don't have to talk to her. That's fine. Maybe she's not home. She sounds like a busy person. Perhaps she's out on an appointment."

Mr. Ramirez still walked with me to my building, but when we got there I thought, what the hell. "Do you want to see it?" I asked Mr. Ramirez.

"Absolutely," he answered. Al, the afternoon doorman, greeted us both, then pressed for the elevator. Mr. Ramirez and I got inside, and I pressed *Thirty*.

"Wow, you're on the thirtieth floor. How do you like high-rise life?"

"I guess it's OK." Mr. Ramirez was acting kind of weird, not the way I was used to seeing him. We got off on my floor, and then stepped out. I opened the door to my apartment, let him in, and took him right over to see the view of the bay. I still didn't know if Mom was home, but then she came into the living room almost right after Mr. Ramirez and I got there. Mom was totally shocked to see him. "Mickey, you didn't tell me Mr. Ramirez would be visiting us today," my mom said in a scared voice.

"I didn't know he was going to either. He just gave me a ride home from school," I said to her.

Mr. Ramirez didn't waste any time and said, "Mrs. Kirkland, it's nice to see you. But for some reason you haven't responded to any of my calls or letters. So, why don't we have a chat now?"

"Oh, my goodness. I'm so sorry. I'd very much like to speak with you, but...you see, I'm just about to step out once again. It's been such a hectic day. There's so much left for me to do."

"It'll only take a minute. May we speak in private?" he asked her.

"Mickey can stay here."

"No, that's OK. I can go to my room," I said.

"No, dear. Stay here with us, please," my mom said to me.

Holy shit. I massively didn't want to be in that room with them. I thought that if he told her any of the things I told him in secret, I was definitely going to get killed. Maybe I could just be off to the side, so I asked, "Can I go into the kitchen? I really need a sandwich, you know 'cause of my anemia." The kitchen was close enough so I could get something to eat *and* listen to what they were saying at the same time. Perfect.

"Yes, indeed, hon. Go make your sandwich. And then come right back," Mom said.

The same second I walked into the kitchen Mr. Ramirez asked, "So, who's Miguel's new nurse?"

"New nurse?"

"Yes, I understand that Miguel took a cab to school today. And I know that Khadijah usually drives him. Will he continue to take cabs? Or will Khadijah resume giving him rides in the morning?"

"Maybe Khadijah was just too busy. I'd think that in San Francisco many children take cabs to school. I've never thought of that as being so unusual."

"So then, Khadijah is still Miguel's nurse? Or does he have a new one? He does need a nurse, correct?"

"Well, yes, Mr. Ramirez. I'm in the process of hiring someone new. And I do appreciate your concern, but it certainly does take time to screen all the applicants."

"Mrs. Kirkland, from what I can tell, Miguel has become extremely despondent ever since Khadijah left. He needs medical attention *now*. I know it's not my place, but when he's in my school he becomes my responsibility. And while he's there I won't have his needs neglected merely because the most suitable applicant hasn't yet been found."

"Actually, you see, my fiancé Hunt believes that it would be better if

Mickey learns to become more self-reliant. And in terms of hiring a new—"

"Mrs. Kirkland, as principal of Notre Dame, it's my duty to report situations which I feel may be endangering the lives of my students. I've known Miguel for quite some time now, and I'm well aware of his condition. I know he needs regular medical care in order to survive. Should I ever feel his life is in danger, without hesitation I *will* file a report with the children's protective services for the City and County of San Francisco."

The living room then either got totally silent, or I just couldn't hear anything they were saying anymore. It was the first time I thought that maybe I could come out carrying the sandwich I just made, peanut butter and mashed bananas. I acted totally dumb by asking, "So, how do you like the apartment, Mr. Ramirez? Isn't it cool?"

"Mickey, come over here. You know I love you very much. Don't you, dear?" Mom asked.

I didn't know what she was getting at so I said, "Yeah, sure Mom."

"For some reason Mr. Ramirez thinks I'm not going to hire a replacement for Khadijah. Now hon, you know for certain that I'll find you only the best care, the best care money can buy. Where on earth did he get the idea that we weren't hiring a new nurse? Someone perfectly qualified?" my mom asked me.

"I figured it out on my own, Mrs. Kirkland. I observe what goes on very closely, especially with regard to the lives of my students, and even more so when that student is Miguel. I look forward to meeting his new nurse someday. Someday soon," Mr. Ramirez said.

"Be assured that she, or he, will be introduced to you at school. Definitely. And, I'm so sorry for the misunderstanding, Mr. Ramirez. I don't know how you could have been so misinformed. I guess those things happen sometimes." Mom reached to shake hands with Mr. Ramirez and said, "Mickey, please show Mr. Ramirez to the door."

"Yes. Being misinformed seems to be the cause of so many problems. And, Mrs. Kirkland, if I may, why do you call Miguel Mickey?"

Mom looked at Mr. Ramirez real confused, like she wasn't sure how to answer, but then she said, "It's my fiancé's pet name for him. I've just gotten so used to hearing him called that, I decided to call him that myself."

"Oh, I see."

"Well then, Mr. Ramirez, I'll make sure you know of Mickey's new nurse," Mom said.

"Very soon I hope," he said.

"Quite soon."

Mom then nodded to Mr. Ramirez, went into her room, closed the door, but looked too afraid to ever turn around to say "goodbye" to him. I walked Mr. Ramirez to the front door, and even though he did say "goodbye" to us both, his wink to me from the elevator was like a victory speech. It felt so good having somebody else on my side.

Mom and I never discussed what went on with Mr. Ramirez and his surprise visit. Instead she called Hunt right after. She always talked to him instead of me about things that really mattered. But what happened when she hung up with him wasn't a surprise. Through her bedroom door I could hear Mom crying again. I could tell that Hunt had yelled at her about something. Why was she still with him? What made her put up with his orders? How could a person love someone who could be so mean? How could Mom do things he told her to do if it ended up hurting me?

I had wondered this many times before, but when I'd talk to Mom about it the subject always got changed. Knowing that no one would probably give me the answer I was looking for, I forced myself to remember a word Aunt Shirley used to keep telling me about Mom. "The c-word," she used to say. "Try to have compassion for your mom. You have no idea what she's been through."

CHAPTER SEVENTEEN

"Aunt Shirley, can you hold on a minute? There's another call," I said, while I was on the phone with her.

"Sure, no problem," she said.

"Hello."

"Yes. This is Robert from the mailroom downstairs. There's a small package here. Just arrived, that needs a signature," the man said.

"My mom isn't home right now."

"This package is for a Mick-ul-eetoo Estes."

"That's me."

"Well, can you come down and sign for it, please?"

"Yeah. OK. But, I'm not really expecting anything. Can you please tell me where's it from?"

"Let's see...it looks to me like it's a 10 X 13 envelope. And it's from Amnesty International USA, 322 Eighth Avenue, New York."

"Wow. I don't have any idea what that is. But yeah, I'll come down and sign for it right away. Thanks," I said to the man in the mailroom.

I clicked back to Aunt Shirley and told her, "That was the mailman, or whoever the guy is who's in charge of our mailroom. I've got to go downstairs and sign for a package addressed to me. It's probably just junk mail. It's from some place called Amisty International."

"Oh my God. Do me a huge favor, Miguel, and call me right back as soon as you're upstairs again," Aunt Shirley insisted.

"Then you know what it is?"

"I'm not sure. But, go sign for it. Then call me right back, OK?"

"Yeah, Aunt Shirley. I'll call you after."

I was kind of reluctant to say "goodbye" to Aunt Shirley because it sounded like she knew something about this package that she wasn't telling me right off. Oh well, whatever. I decided I'd go downstairs and find out for myself. As soon as I got off the elevator Al stepped away from his desk in the lobby and came up to me and said, "Sounds like you got something important. I would have brought it up to you, but we're not supposed to handle the mail. Federal offense if I did."

"That's OK," I said. I could tell he wanted to know more, but since I didn't even know myself I just went ahead to where the mail was. Al walked right in back of me. There was an open door to a room that was behind where the mailboxes were, so I said to the man sitting in there, "Hi. You called me? There's something I have to sign for?"

"Yes. You're Michal-ee-noe Estes? In 30-01?" He totally didn't pronounce Miguelito right for the second time in a row. But who cares?

"Yeah."

"Can I see some identification, please." he demanded.

"Oh, this is definitely Miguel," Al explained.

"OK, sign right here," the mail person said. He handed me a clipboard full of signatures, and then realized that I don't have any fingers to hold onto it with. So he put it down on the counter. "Are you able to sign this?" he asked.

"Oh, sure. Watch," I said as I showed him how I signed things by holding the pen in the middle of both my hands while they're pressed together. That's the only way I can write. It usually goes kind of slow, but I always get the job done.

This was way cool. I thought for sure it was something I bought off the Internet but forgot all about. Maybe it was the new 50 Cent CD. I couldn't remember if I ordered that one or not. The insides of the package felt too mushy to be a CD though.

I tried opening it right when I got inside the elevator, but it was closed up pretty good, so I thought I'd open it when I got back upstairs. When I was opening the door to my apartment the phone was ringing. I answered it and it was Aunt Shirley. She asked, "Did you open your package yet?"

"Not yet. I need to get scissors, or a knife, or something to get it open," I said.

"Well, can you wait just a minute before you do that? I want to tell you something first."

"Yeah, OK. I think it's just a magazine or some free gift I got from signing up for something on the Internet."

"No. I don't think it is. Do you remember when you gave me that letter you wrote to your father? And you asked me to find a place to send it, so he'd receive it?"

"Yeah."

"Well, I found someone at the Amnesty International office right here in San Francisco who was able to help me. They—"

"Wait a minute. What's Amnesty International again?"

"Amnesty International is an organization dedicated to freeing political prisoners. They help them get fair trials in foreign countries. Your father is now considered to be a political prisoner."

"Dad? Is he going to be freed?"

"Oh, Miguel. I certainly hope so...at some point."

"But, what are they mailing to me? Do you know?"

"They may have sent your letter back to you, because I gave them your address. I should have told you all this before. I just wanted to get things moving."

"OK. Well, let me open it up and see." I took the phone with me as I went into the kitchen to find something I could use to cut the thick envelope. "Wow, this thing is wrapped pretty tight," I told Aunt Shirley.

"Don't cut yourself," she said.

I started to get it open and then I saw a lot of different, littler envelopes inside. And, wrapped around them was a letter from the place that sent me this package, Amnesty International. I didn't even look at the letter from them because I wanted to look closer at those other envelopes instead.

"Miguel, what's inside? Did you open it yet?" Aunt Shirley asked.

"Yeah. It's a bunch of envelopes that are kind of stinky. The writing's all blurry and smudged on all of them. It looks like someone drove over them with their jeep."

"Were they ever mailed? Is there a postmark on any of the them?"

"No. There's not."

"Open one up. Maybe you can read what's inside."

"I already opened one." And as I tried reading another, I said, "And this one is the same. It's like they're all moldy." But, a miracle happened when my eyes saw the writing on the next envelope. "Except here. Here's one that isn't. It looks...oh my God, it *is* from Dad," I told Aunt Shirley.

I kind of didn't know what to say to Aunt Shirley next because I couldn't believe it. I wasn't so sure I'd ever get a letter from him ever again. I think Aunt Shirley didn't know what to say next too. Before I read this letter Dad had written I looked through the rest of the stack of about a dozen just to see if I could read any more of them. I couldn't. This one letter, the one I was holding in my hands, was the only letter I would be able to read.

"What's going on, Miguel?" Aunt Shirley asked.

"Out of all the stuff here, there's just one letter I can read that's not totally smudged. The rest of them are too ruined," I said.

"You want some privacy as you read them? Or would you like me to stay on the phone?"

"What?"

"Why don't you open your letter, read it, and if you'd like to talk about what's inside, call me. How does that sound?"

"Fine." Aunt Shirley absolutely read my mind. I definitely felt like I had to hang up, because I was only able to concentrate on the letter I was holding in my hands. Then I read it.

My dearest Miguelito,

It seems like I always have something unique to tell you in every letter I write to you. But this one in particular is very difficult. It's difficult because I'm not so sure you will understand what I have to tell you.

So before I begin I will tell you again what I say in all my letters to you – I love you so much. I'm so very proud to be your father. I'm proud of your courage, your tenacity, your intelligence, the respect you have for others, and your mighty perseverance and optimism. You are the epitome of all that is good in this world. ¿Entiende? I know you do.

I hope you're keeping up with your Spanish; it's a great language. When you practice your Spanish, I feel that you are remembering me. Do you think of me once in a while? I sure hope so. I think about you all the time. Most of the time I feel completely alone here. I'm still in prison and more than anything I miss not hearing from you at all. I used to love getting your e-mails. They still don't let me receive mail, so don't bother writing me back. I haven't talked to you in so long. I hate this. I feel I have let you down tremendously.

All I can do is hope that you are receiving excellent care from those who love you up there. How's your Aunt Shirley? Are the two of you still great amigos? I imagine she's still teaching you some very valuable lessons. And your mom? I'm sure she's still buying you everything you could ever want.

I wish I could send you lots of gifts, but I know they'd never reach you. I no longer censor my letters to you because I have found that only the truth is worth telling. The consequences no longer matter to me. I'm sure you already know the value of truth. So, under no circumstances be afraid to tell it. Speak only the truth, and you can do no wrong.

What I have to tell you next is the most difficult part of this letter

I write. You deserve to know the truth, so I will tell it now. I am in prison now for living the truth and being honest with myself, the only way I know how. What you have never known about me is that I'm gay. And, I always have been. When I was married to your mother I wasn't living the truth, and I deeply regretted this for such a long time. But now I don't.

Since I know you realize that everything in our lives happens for a reason, I hope you will believe what I tell you next. When I look back, I know the reason I was with your mother was so we both could create you and Jorge, the most perfect children I could ever imagine. I feel privileged to be your father. I no longer question why I married your mother because the answer is now so clear to me. But, if I am to be an example to my dear son, then I must be totally honest with him. And, I hope you will try very hard to understand what I've just now told you.

Please know that I have committed no crime. I have merely begun to live a life that is truthful, yet found myself being punished for it. Since I am now a U.S. citizen, I am persecuted even more. The government, as well as the culture here in El Salvador is extremely antiquated and primitive, and seems unlikely to change in the near future.

I still don't understand exactly why I'm here in prison. I might as well tell you what I know. The government claims I was soliciting a young boy for sex, but this is completely untrue. I have never had a trial, and I have no one to defend me here. Being gay in El Salvador today is illegal. And there continue to be death threats against human rights advocates here. Somehow I believe I was set up. I've thought about it constantly, but I still can't imagine who would want me sent to prison.

All these things are my concern, not yours. The reason I am writing all this is my attempt to explain to you why I'm not with you now. I have no idea how you're going to react. All I can do is hope for the best and trust that providing you with the truth that you deserve will somehow make things a bit better.

Another reason I'm writing this to you is because I truly don't know what will happen to me next. I've thought about this day and night, but I guess now I have to tell you that it's quite possible that I may never see you again. Of course I will remain optimistic; something I learned from you. But they don't like keeping prisoners in their jails here for long periods of time. Hoping that they will let me go is only a remote possibility, and thinking that I can get out of this country to come back to America is perhaps even more remote.

Does this make sense to you? I hope at some point in time you will be able to forgive me for not being there in your life. I want to be with you more than anything. I hope you know this too. I hope that someday you will receive these letters I write to you, and you will keep them. I hope when you see them, you will remember me, and know that there was someone who loved you very much.

I'm not quite sure what else I can say in this letter; I guess that gives me more to tell you in the next. Stay well and be happy. You're an extraordinary young man with a wonderful future ahead of you.

My love and prayers are with you always. And remember forever that you are the creator of your own destiny.

I love you always,
Dad

Not being able to read any of the other letters was now OK, because reading just this one was enough for me. All I could do was sit in my chair at my bay window, looking out for answers. I was so confused, and felt like I never knew my dad in the first place. The phone in my room kept ringing, but I didn't bother to answer it. I knew it was Aunt Shirley, and since I never lied, I'd have to tell her what the letter was all about. And I wasn't so sure I could.

Then I thought that maybe I just didn't understand what I read. Maybe the government down there just accused Dad of being gay, but that's not what he really is. Then that would help everything to make sense. The best thing to do, I thought, was to re-read his letter. But first I needed to look up *solicited* because I didn't know what that meant. It was good for me to do anyway, especially since I never knew what the sign *No Solicitors* meant, and that way I'd never become one.

The way dictionaries talk I'm not really sure if I got an answer. And after re-reading Dad's letter, I was more confused than ever. What I read the first time ended up being the truth after all, even though I wasn't sure I wanted to believe it.

That's just not the way it goes. If a man is gay, they're not supposed to be married to a woman, and then have kids. Why did Dad do this? Maybe he had amnesia or something. Maybe since Dad did this when he wasn't supposed to meant that I didn't count. Maybe I wasn't ever supposed to be born. I wished someone could tell me the answers.

Unfortunately though, I was beginning to realize that the number of people who usually gave me those answers was starting to shrink. Who was left? And who was going to be gone next?

CHAPTER EIGHTEEN

Maybe Mom had some answers. She walked through the front door at the same time that my phone was still ringing. Then she came into my room and asked, "Dear, why aren't you answering your phone?"

"I'm not in the mood. It's probably just a solicitor," I said.

"A solicitor. Oh, well then...I see what you mean," she said as she walked back out of my room.

"Mom, wait! Can I talk to you for a minute?"

"Of course, hon. But I only have a minute. Not too long?"

"No. Not too long. I wanted to ask you something about Dad."

"Your father. OK. What do you want to know about him?"

"I got a bunch of letters from him today, altogether in one package. They were sent in a cluster, but I could only read one. The rest were ruined. But, this one letter was in totally perfect condition, like I was meant to read it."

"Oh good heavens. I feel like I'm talking to Shirley, where everything is *meant-to-be*. Letters from your father? Are you sure they're from him? I didn't know he'd be able to send mail out from...where he is."

"No. He didn't mail the letters. None of them were even postmarked. They were sent to me from a place called Amnesty International in New York. They even wrote me a letter—"

"What did you just say? They were sent by whom?"

"Amnesty International. It's a long story, but one night I had a dream. Jorge was in it, and he told me I definitely had to write a letter to Dad. So I did. But I had no idea where to send it. So I gave it to Aunt Shirley and then she must have given it to somebody at Amnesty International. So I guess maybe that had something to do with me getting this package from them. But in Dad's letter to me, he didn't know I had written to him. Get it?"

"Yes. I think so. But I've got to say I can't believe it. Why did you feel you had to write him a letter? Why didn't you tell me about all this? And if you didn't know the address, why didn't you ask me?"

"I don't know. I just figured you wouldn't know about, you know, prison stuff. Now they're calling Dad a political prisoner, and that's exactly the kind of people Amnesty International helps."

"A political prisoner? Amnesty International? I don't understand this – it doesn't make any sense. I thought Amnesty International gets involved with criminals, people who most likely deserve to be in jail. Oh, Mickey. I'm so sorry. You must be so ashamed of your father."

"No. You don't get it, Mom. They help—"

"That's OK. I want to know what your father had to say to you."

"In the letter...Dad told me he's gay. Is that true?"

I could tell that in my mom's head she was trying to decide whether to tell me the truth or not. If you looked real closely at her face you could tell. "Yes, he is...what you said," Mom answered.

"So then you knew this all the time?"

"Well, not at first. Not in the beginning. Mickey, I'd rather not talk about any of this."

"So, he wasn't gay in the beginning? Is that why you married him?"

"I married him because I thought we were in love with each other. I had no idea he was a...you know. Once I found out, we decided to divorce."

Again, I could tell by looking at her that Mom was either hiding something from me, or she was getting ready to make up something totally different to tell.

"What I don't get most is that I don't know why I was born," I told her.

"What? What are you saying?" Mom asked.

"Well, does it mean that I don't matter because the people who made me were never supposed to be together in the first place?"

Mom had an extra confused look on her face, and said, "I still don't understand what you're trying to ask me."

"What's supposed to happen is that straight people are supposed to be with straight people, and gay people with gay people. If you were with a gay man and had a baby with him, then that wasn't what's supposed to happen, right? Don't gay people just adopt kids if they want to have a family? Isn't that the way it's supposed to be?"

"Sometimes I have no idea what anything is supposed to be anymore. All I can say is that I was embarrassed beyond belief that I'd made such a mistake. Can you imagine how that made me look? How that made us all look?"

"But I count, don't I?"

"Do you count? Of course you do, dear. You're alive aren't you? I'm the one who's being punished. I'm the one who suffers the most. You and Jorge being born the way you were. I must have done something terribly wrong. It's God's way of punishing me." It wasn't so often that I ever heard Mom say Jorge's name, so it shocked me a little. The only time she ever did was when she'd talk about being punished.

I stopped listening right away because I knew God didn't do those things. Aunt Shirley told me that having a disease was never a punishment. God doesn't punish anybody. It was part of my destiny, part of who I am. All of the sudden I regretted that I was talking to Mom in the first place. The way she talked never made me feel better. I thought she could have given me some answers, but instead I felt sorry for her.

More and more I felt like I was changing, but Mom wasn't. I was maturing, but Mom was still a child inside. How come she never took the time to learn from the lessons God gave her? What made her not want to change herself by growing and "getting on with it," as Aunt Shirley would say. Who knows? I just knew I had more work to do.

One of the things I was really good at was getting answers to kind of weird questions. I eventually got over being embarrassed about asking about Dad. So, once I was alone in my room, I called Aunt Shirley but she didn't answer. Then I thought of someone who may have better answers than anyone I knew, Mr. Ramirez. I waited until the next day when I was at school to think any more about it.

As soon as I got there I went into the main office. Mrs. McCready wasn't there so I walked right into Mr. Ramirez's office. He always got there extra early. "Hi, Mr. Ramirez," I said.

"Hey there, Miguel. How are you? Do you have a new nurse yet?"

"Yeah, I do. My mom just hired her. She starts tomorrow. I think she's like a fill-in though. You know, not full-time. But that's OK. Her name is Mrs. Stern...hobben, or something like that. She's from Germany or somewhere."

"Perfect. Well, you make sure to tell me how she's working out for you. And, I'd like to meet her here at school sometime. Maybe you could arrange that."

"Yeah, sure. But you know what? Can we talk about something, something else?"

"Of course. Only, you have a class soon, don't you?"

"I don't mean right now, but maybe later today."

"Absolutely. How about during lunch? That would give us plenty of time to discuss anything you like."

"Yeah, that's cool." I said.

"Great. I see you brought your lunch with you. So did I. Why don't you bring it along with you and meet me here at noon."

"You don't want to have lunch with me in the cafeteria?"

"No. Let's meet here."

Out of nowhere I started to think that Mr. Ramirez was maybe ashamed to be seen with me because he didn't want to eat in the cafeteria, where everyone else ate. Sometimes my imagination kind of works overtime. But when I saw him at noon I asked him about it anyway, "How come you didn't want to eat in the cafeteria?"

"What?" he asked.

"You're not ashamed of me? Are you?"

"Oh, Miguel, you're not serious. You're thinking that I didn't want to eat in the cafeteria with you because I was ashamed of you? Oh, no. That's nonsense. There's no way I could ever be ashamed of you. I think you're great. Being the school principal I probably shouldn't tell you this, but you deserve to know. You're my favorite student here. And I know it's unfair to all the other kids, most of whom I like very much, if they should ever know this. Everyone should be made to feel like they're the favorite sometimes. I'd appreciate it if you wouldn't tell anyone this. But I wanted *you* to know the truth."

"OK. Wow, you just said kind of what my dad said about deserving to know the truth."

"You're dad's back in town?"

"No, he's not. But that's kind of why I wanted to talk to you today. I got a letter from him, actually lots of letters. He's in El Salvador, in a jail."

"In jail. Why? Why is he there? For how long?"

"Well, that's the thing. In the letter he told me he's in jail because...he's gay. Or, for something they thought he did that gay people do."

"Wow. Oh, Miguel. I'm so sorry. I'm assuming you're confused about all this. Confused and concerned, right? That would be completely natural."

"Yeah, I guess both. But what I don't get is if he's gay, then why did he marry my mom, a woman, in the first place? And why did they have me and Jorge? That's not right. And if they weren't supposed to have us, does that mean that we don't count?"

"You don't count? I see, you wanted to talk to me about this because you know I'm gay."

"Yeah, probably."

"Well, first of all, thank you for trusting me. And, I'll tell you something. This is really amazing. But if you can believe it I had the very same experience you just now had, and I was *extremely* confused. Maybe it would help if I told you about it."

"As long as it's not a St. Olaf story. You know, the ones Rose Nyland tells on *The Golden Girls*."

"I promise, it's not one of those. By the way, I love that show. Anyway, when I was twenty-one I was very new to San Francisco. And I met someone who was very nice, a man named John. We got to know each other and I knew he was like me, gay. We started to spend more and more time with each other. And one time, when I was over at his house, I saw some framed photos on top of his piano. They were pictures of two, cute little girls. When I asked who the two girls belonged to, he said 'me.' Then I said, 'Oh, you adopted two girls?' And he answered, 'No, they're mine. I was married.' I was utterly baffled. How could that be? I bet the explanation he gave me was similar to one your father could probably tell you."

"What *was* the explanation?"

"First let me point out that he loved his girls, his daughters, very much. That photo reminded him of them every day. He missed them so much because they still lived in Dallas with their mother. And he had to be far away from them since he took a better-paying job in San Francisco. But, as it turns out, he married his wife because that's what he thought he was *supposed* to do. He thought *that* was normal. Now that I've been around for some forty years I can say with some certainty that that's how the majority of gay people in America still live their lives. They live their lives the way they feel they're supposed to be lived. Times haven't changed that much, and in my lifetime, I'll never see it the other way around."

"There's more gay people who are pretending than there are gay people who...are honest about being gay?"

"Yes, I think that's right. All because they believe that's what they're *supposed* to be doing. So, I'm imagining your father did what most gay people feel is expected of them."

"Did you ever marry a woman?" I asked.

"No, I never did. Somehow I always felt comfortable about who I was. I never had that kind of pressure to pretend I was something I'm wasn't. I knew all along I was *supposed* to be gay. God made me this way. You know, Miguel, may I ask you what else your dad talked about in his letter?"

"He told me it was important for him to tell the truth about everything. He said he loved me. He always says that. He said I should keep listening to my Aunt Shirley. And he didn't really say it, but he made it sound like he

123

won't ever be able to come back. Because if he even tried, eventually something bad might happen to him."

"Are you sure about that?"

"Yeah, I think so."

"But, you know what? At some point you're really going to appreciate that your dad told you the truth."

"Oh, he did say one more thing. He said something like the reward for being married to Mom is that they made me and Jorge. That was heck'a cool."

"Maybe that was the whole point he was trying to make, the bottom line. I'd be flattered. So how does that make you feel?"

"Well I guess I'm glad about that part. You know, like after all, it means that I *do* matter. I *do* count. And since Mom couldn't explain it to me, at least now you made me understand that I at least matter to Dad."

"*And* to your mother. To your Aunt Shirley, to your friends, to your nurses, to your doctors, to your teachers, to your e-mail buddies, to your doorman, to me, and I imagine to everyone else who's ever had the opportunity of knowing you. To me, it sounds as if your father loves you more than any father could ever love his son. It was very brave of him to be so honest with you, not knowing how you were going to respond. That tells me he loves you no matter what. Even if, for whatever reason, you stopped loving him."

"Oh, but I do."

"Would you miss him if you never saw him again?"

"Oh, totally. I definitely would."

"Well, I bet you can see him again if you want to badly enough. Didn't you tell me your aunt tells you something like that?"

"She always says that if you really, really want something you'll get it. Expecting it doesn't make it happen. And, what else is important is you have to believe in your head that something is going to happen, to have total faith...in yourself. Absolutely no fear, zero percent. Then what you want will end up happening because you made it happen by believing it already would."

"Then, if I look at this as your aunt does, you'll probably see your dad again if you really, really want to him to come back."

"OK, yeah. You're right. I might as well start doing that then, even stronger. I'll keep that one in my head for sure."

"So now you feel like you understand a bit more of what your dad was trying to tell you? You feel better about all this?"

"I definitely understand some more. Like I already said, the thing I didn't get the most was if I mattered or not. You know, because they really weren't supposed to be married in the first place."

"But, Miguel, they were supposed to be married. They were supposed to create you and Jorge. And, you've got to know this one thing, you definitely *do* matter."

"Yeah. OK, thanks."

"So, you're all right?"

"Yes, Mr. Ramirez."

"Good, I'm glad. How about if I ask you one more question that may be a bit off the subject?"

I nodded yes, and he asked, "Didn't your mother mention before that it was likely you'd never see your father again? Are you sure she doesn't know the real reason why he's in prison?"

CHAPTER NINETEEN

"Jesus Christ taught people that whatsoever a man soweth that shall he also reap," Aunt Shirley said to me.

"But I don't know how to sew. It would be kind of hard anyway with my hands the way they are," I said.

"No, it has nothing to do with sewing. Jesus was saying that what you give, what you put out there, is exactly what you're going to get back. If you feel hate towards certain people, then that's how they're going to feel about you."

"So, it's best not to hate anyone?"

"Well, yes. But, what I'm trying to tell you is that the way in which you give, is the same way you'll get. Got it? And, the same goes for preparing for what you want to make happen."

"That's like when you moved into here."

"Exactly. I started preparing to move in by packing up all my things months before I ever knew I'd be able to buy this house. I started filling out those change of address cards, picked out my new phone number, called the movers, and so on, at a time when I never had any proof at all I was qualified to buy it. I gave out the belief that this house would be mine, and that's what I got back. The real estate agents and mortgage brokers said it would never happen, and even though they know their business very well, their way of thinking is still far behind the times. So that just shows you, because I prepared for it, and believed it would happen, it did. *I* made it happen."

"Maybe I should start packing. Maybe I should pick out exactly where I want to move next."

"If that's what you want, then that's exactly what you should be doing. And don't forget to tell people what you're going to do. Then that will definitely make it happen. Saying it out loud turns it into a reality."

"I remember. You've told me that a lot."

"And, how about your mother? If you genuinely feel glad about your mom marrying Hunt, then they'll probably feel glad for you. Give them both love, not...whatever, and see what happens."

"Well I'm definitely glad she let me stay here with you while they're in France right now getting married. That's a real good thing."

"Perfect. Love your mother for letting you do this. Be grateful. And see what happens when she returns. Maybe it's all somehow connected to one of your desires, you moving out of your apartment. After you've done this."

"But, you know what I really mean by *wanting to move*, right? I want to be free. I don't want to be near Mom when she's around Hunt. I kind of want them to go away."

"How about if you give them love? You may find that things work out just the way you want, and they may never go anywhere, but *you* might. You have no influence on their destiny, but you can certainly affect your own. It's all about giving and receiving."

"OK, I'll go for that."

"Great. You're going to be quite surprised at how well this works."

Sometimes I felt like the times I got to spend with Aunt Shirley would eventually come to an end. So I decided to enjoy them while I had them. The weather was getting to be so much nicer, and Aunt Shirley and I spent more time in her garden in the back. All the flowers were blooming. It was like being inside heaven.

"Isn't spring great? I just love everything about it. For almost all cultures it's a time to celebrate new beginnings. And you should be doing more celebrating than anyone. Something big is about to happen for you. I can feel it," Aunt Shirley said.

"Wow. I hope so. That would be great. But the only thing that's new right now is my new nurse, Mrs. Sternhoffer."

"How's she working out?"

"She's totally different from Khadijah, she's—"

"Oh. You know, Miguel, I'm sorry to interrupt, but I ran into Khadijah on campus two or three days ago, and I told her you'd be staying with me now. She says 'hi'."

"Yeah. I miss her a lot. I only get e-mails from her once in a while now. Oh, well."

"She looked pretty frazzled. She's got finals coming up quite soon, and then she has to turn right around and prepare for the beginning of summer session."

"Anyway, the woman who's the new nurse is way different from Khadijah. She's really only at our house part-time. She has her own family. They all live in Redwood City, so she only comes in for a few hours at a time, and then she drives all the way back."

"I'm assuming she treats you well though."

"Yeah, she takes care of me pretty good, like she's supposed to. But we don't talk about anything, nothing. One time I tried telling her about the two reasons, and she totally didn't get it. She said it's not proper to talk about religion."

"The two reasons? The reasons why we're here?"

"Yeah. I tell everyone that a lot. Number One, to learn from the experiences we've been presented. Number Two, to help others when given the opportunity."

"Perfect. Good job. Wow, I'm glad you remembered that."

"But it didn't do much good. Mrs. Sternhoffer doesn't care. She doesn't even try to say Miguel right. And that sucks. She just says Mikey. So, anybody now who's around me a lot and still can't get my name right isn't so cool."

"Have you ever asked her anything about her life? How about if you do that, ask her about herself? So many people tend to be so self-absorbed in today's world. The only way they begin to open up is if you ask them something about themselves. Then, hopefully, they will notice you."

"No. I've already given up. And, she says she won't drive me to Stanford the next time I need to go there. So Mom said I have to take a taxi."

"A taxi to the hospital? From San Francisco to Palo Alto? That's crazy, doll. I still don't understand why your mother doesn't take you."

"She's always got those social events, those charity things. She pretty much just always does stuff for Hunt."

"Miguel, these days I seem to be understanding your mother less and less. Her life is so much more complicated than I thought. Much to learn. I guess her mind is mostly on Hunt for the moment, getting married again."

"And they still haven't decided what's going to happen to me. It's like I'm invisible."

"It'll work out, I'm sure. Your mother will make sure you're comfortable with the decision, whatever it is."

Just at the time when I thought Aunt Shirley definitely got it, she went back to thinking that my being with Mom and Hunt was going to turn out OK. I gave up. "Can we do something fun today?" I asked.

"Like what?"

"Let's go up the inside of the Campanile. That would be cool. I've never done that, and you said someday we would."

"Oh, gosh. I'm not so sure I'm up for that. Today's my one day off from school, and I'm not really in the mood to go back over to campus again."

The Campanile's a tower that always looked so awesome, and I always wanted to ride up it. Somebody told me once that you could see all the way to San Jose from the top. It's only like ten stories or something like that, but it's way old. Since Aunt Shirley wasn't in the mood, I thought I could go with somebody else. "Maybe Khadijah and I could go together. Maybe that would work out," I told Aunt Shirley.

"Oh. I have the feeling she's extremely busy right now."

"But, don't forget about what you tell me about *expressing your want*. How would I ever know if Khadijah does or doesn't want to go with me unless I ask? Right?"

"Yep. You got me there."

"I still have her cell number. I'll call her right now."

It was so meant to be that I couldn't believe it. Right when I called her she happened to be studying and said she'd been craving a break for days, something that would take her mind off all the tests that were coming up. She decided to pick me up at Aunt Shirley's house and in just a few minutes she arrived. Khadijah was so excited to see me. But I was even more excited to see her. "So, are you a professional dancer yet?" I asked her.

"I'm getting there. In no time at all I'll begin to see some sort of reward for all this hard training I've put in."

"God will give you a break for sure. That's the way it goes. Right, Aunt Shirley?"

"What? I missed what you just said. God will give you what?" Aunt Shirley asked.

"Miguel said that God will give me a break. I hope so. I could use one," Khadijah said. Since Khadijah didn't work for Mom anymore she started calling me Miguel instead of Mikey or Mickey. I liked that she did that.

"Yes, absolutely. It's a matter of you taking the first step...then you'll get your break. And in your case you've taken, what, about a million at this point? Steps, that is. Buh-dum-bum," Aunt Shirley said, while trying to be funny at the same time.

"The first step I plan to take after graduating is to live in Paris, just for a while anyway. I've never been there before. I can't wait. If I can't afford to do that, then I'll just find some job in the financial district here. Perhaps I'll end up moving over to the city. Who knows?"

"Uh oh. Plan *B*. Khadijah, can I tell you something, doll? Once you've got a Plan *B* you can kiss Plan *A* goodbye. It'll never happen. Only have a

Plan *A* and no other. You've got to *believe* it will happen. *You're* going to Paris!"

Khadijah shook her head yes, then said, "Yes, Ma'am. Plan *A* it is."

"Mom's close to there right now. In some town near Paris, getting married," I said.

It seemed like the same second I said the word *Mom* Khadijah made her face look like she was going to barf. I knew she didn't like Mom too much, but I could tell she knew something else. "Why did you make your face look like that?" I asked.

"Oh, nothing. It was nothing."

"You're not telling the truth, I can tell. What's up with that face?" I asked.

"Well, I know how big you are on honesty, Miguel. But, can I also be honest with you, Shirley?"

"Yeah, sure. Feel free to say whatever you want. It's impossible to offend me, or shock me. I think I've heard just about everything at this point in my life," Aunt Shirley said.

"It's just that Miss Kirkland and that fiancé of hers, I don't know what's up with him. Well, they really tried to persuade me to move down to Los Angeles to take care of Miguel. The fiancé, I forgot his name, was—"

"Hunt Manly," I said.

"Yes. Hunt, that's it. And by the way, what is with that name? It sounds to me like he should be on *General Hospital*. But anyway, he offered me a lot of money. I mean a lot, if I would keep Miguel," and then she quietly mouthed toward Aunt Shirley, "out of their hair." Then Khadijah continued, "Miguel, I'm so sorry. But I want both of you to know what this man is really like." And she looked away while she said, "He told me they 'have better things to do than...' Again, this is my opinion, but I don't think Miguel should have to live with this man under any circumstances. I don't trust him at all."

"Holy Shit. I never cared for his personality much, but I never knew he was this bad. Why on earth does my sister think he's such a catch?" Aunt Shirley said.

"It's not just him. Now, I'm sorry to tell you this, but I've got to. Your sister is, well...like Silly Putty. She does whatever he tells her, she can be molded any which way. And sometimes it's as if she's more concerned with her image than with her own son. I hope you can forgive me for saying this about your own sister. I'm telling you this for Miguel's welfare, to protect him."

Aunt Shirley then looked a little surprised at how honest Khadijah was being. "My goodness. That sure is a strong opinion. Has she ever done anything to you specifically? Something that upset you?" Aunt Shirley asked.

"Well, not to me directly. But I can't get over how much of her identity revolves around this guy, Hunt. While I was there I could see her becoming more and more like him. And it's as if he gets off on trying to make her feel more afraid, more fearful than she already is. Has she ever...been to therapy? I think she may be a bit troubled."

"Mom told me she's afraid of therapy because they might tell her she's nuts," I said.

"And, Shirley, most of all I'm afraid for Miguel."

"Khadijah, wow. I should tell you that on behalf of my sister, I apologize. I wish she hadn't let you go. I know you did a super job. Miguel told me so. He adores you."

"Yeah. I do. But, let's not get mushy," I said.

"The feeling's mutual, to say the least," Khadijah said to the both of us.

"When Sharon gets back we're going to have a long talk. Thanks a lot for sharing your thoughts with me. I appreciate it," Aunt Shirley said.

"Remember, my main purpose in telling you all this is not for my sake. I told you because of Miguel. I mean it, Hunt or Miss Kirkland, or both, for some reason, seem to be neglecting Miguel's needs purposely," Khadijah said.

"Well, then something definitely has to be done. I thought this new nurse was taking care of everything."

"No. I'm talking about his emotional needs as well, support that a parent should be able to provide for their child. A parent who believes in them."

"But, I already know not to expect that from Mom now. She's never been like that. She thinks it's a good thing for me not to believe in my future," I said.

"See, I did this for a reason, speaking to you this candidly, especially in front of Miguel. Shirley, I was hoping it would help you to see the truth. I realize you and Miss Kirkland are sisters, but Miguel has told me over and over how much the truth means to you, to you both. So I'm hoping that what I've said, what we've both said will sink in."

I felt so good after Khadijah came over and told Aunt Shirley what was really going on. It was totally meant to be that I called her up to go over to

131

the Campanile, and that she went to Aunt Shirley's house first. This was definitely an example of where I had to take the first step, and then God gave me a break. If I hadn't called, even when Aunt Shirley warned me that Khadijah was probably too busy to go, this whole conversation never would have happened. That's so cool the way things work out.

When we were both in her car headed for campus I told Khadijah, "That was so perfect, what you did."

"And, you know what? It felt real good saying it. Maybe this is what your aunt was talking about a long time ago, when she and I first met. She knew there was some reason for the coincidences we shared. She said either I had to tell her something, or she had to tell me. Your aunt was meant to know this information, and I was the one who was meant to tell her," Khadijah told me.

"Isn't that heck'a cool? The way it all goes? And like Aunt Shirley said, I'm sorry too, for the way Hunt and Mom let go of you."

"And, frankly Miguel, I'm real sorry you have to move. It's a tough situation you're in. The best way I can see you getting out of all this is through some sort of legal action, like we talked about before. And that's a horror for anybody to deal with. For your sake, I sure hope there's an easier way."

"Yeah, me too."

"You know, another thing I never picked up on when I worked for your mother was other family. Do you have any other family members in the Bay Area? Besides Shirley?"

"Well, yeah I do. But to me, they're kind of not really my family at all. I mean, they're probably nice people, but the reason I don't do too much with them is that they all don't know the truth. They all see me the way Mom does. They feel sorry for me because they think I'm going to die soon. Now, I guess they don't like me. They probably think I'm anti-social 'cause I don't go over to their houses. Maybe they're always going to think that about me."

"Do you think your Aunt Shirley's going to change her attitude? Now that she knows the truth about Hunt and your mother?"

"But, that's just it, I think she's always known the truth. She never liked Hunt, and she told me before that she feels sorry for Mom for some reason. I'm not sure exactly why. They're sisters, and Aunt Shirley is the kind of person who thinks we should love everybody."

"Do you think she really is going to talk with your mother?"

"Maybe not. I don't know. But if she does, I know one thing for sure,

Mom's going to have a shit attack when she finds out we've all been talking about her."

CHAPTER TWENTY

I started to get a little bit afraid because I didn't know what was going to happen next. It was great staying with Aunt Shirley just like it always was, but it's kind of like I just betrayed her sister. And, the only thing that happened was that the truth was told. I knew Mom would always love me though, so I talked myself into not worrying about what's next.

While I was sitting in my chair where I make my dreams at Aunt Shirley's house, Aunt Shirley came up to me, and out of nowhere she said, "You never told me what was in the letter your father wrote you. You said you were going to tell me when you got here."

"Oh, he said lots of good things."

"But, he's still in prison there? In El Salvador?"

"Yes, he is. It kind of sounded like he didn't know when they're letting him out. I think he maybe wrote the letter to kind of say 'goodbye' to me, because he didn't say 'I'll see you soon,' or 'I'll see you when I get out'."

"Did he discuss why he's there?"

"He said that they, the government or somebody, set him up. They said he was a solicitor."

"A solicitor?"

"Yeah. They said he was a solicitor for a boy. And he told me he...was gay."

Aunt Shirley didn't look shocked like I thought she would. She just nodded her head, like she didn't want to have to say anything. "You knew this, didn't you?" I asked.

"Yes, Miguel. I did. I mean, I knew he was gay. I don't know if I believe the other part. I knew at some point you'd be told. I always felt your mother would tell you. Once you were old enough to understand it, once you were able to understand that some people are gay."

"Duh. Relying on her to tell me anything that's kind of shocking is like never going to happen. And, duh again. Mr. Ramirez, my principal, is gay, and we're like best friends. I definitely understand about gay people. What I never knew is that they could have kids that weren't adopted."

"I'm sorry I never told you."

"Well, that's OK. But you know what? I think *you* need to take more first steps, and not be so afraid of what's going to happen next if you speak up to Mom. Just like you told me, God will always give you a break. And, the other thing you always told me, 'Do the thing you're most afraid of, because when you finally face what you're afraid of, it's usually disappeared by then.' Like that time when you learned to drive. You were so afraid of freeway traffic more than anything. Remember? You told me you were scared you-know-whatless. But then when you decided to get out there, there was almost nobody on the freeway anyway."

"I guess it's time I learn a few lessons from you now. You're right."

"Good. And getting back to Dad, I'm more cool about it. Maybe he married Mom 'cause he couldn't find a man or something. Whatever, I don't care anymore. I just hope I get to see him again someday."

"My feeling is that you should write him another letter. Why don't you do that."

"But I'm not really sure he'd be able to get it. In the letter he wrote to me he never talked about the one I wrote to him."

"Do it anyway. You'd be expressing your want. Even if he never gets it, you're letting it be known how much you want to see him again. Yes, do this. And tell him everything that's going on in your life. Tell him all that you and Khadijah told me yesterday."

"Yeah, OK. I'll do it. But I'll have to wait until I get home because you don't have Point & Speak or a voice-activated word processor on your computer, do you?"

"No, I don't. I forgot that that's how you write your letters at home."

"Yeah. That's the only way I can."

"Well, why don't you dictate to me what you want to say, and I'll write it for you. I'll send it off, exactly as I did last time. Are you all right with that?"

"I think I'll just wait until I get home. That's OK."

"Miguel, I'm positive you should write it now. Somehow this seems urgent to me."

I shook my head to show that that's OK, and Aunt Shirley went into her office to get some paper and a pen. She seemed real serious to do this. When she came back I had to tell her something before we started. I said, "Aunt Shirley, the thing is, I'm always *way* honest when I write to my dad. That's the only way I know how to be. So, you know, don't be too shocked about what I say."

I could tell that that was all right with her, so I began.

Dear Dad,

Well, the first thing to tell you is that I got your letters, a bunch of them. Did you ever get mine? I guess yours weren't ever mailed from the prison. They were all sent in a bunch from Amnesty International. Do you know them? Are you OK down there? I hope so.

The next thing is that almost all of the letters I couldn't read. They were all messed up, like they were in the garbage for a while. But there was one that wasn't messed up at all, and I could read every word of it perfectly. It was the one when you told me why you're there in the first place. And in the beginning I got real confused, but then I figured out that it's OK to have a dad that's gay. But someday I hope you'll tell me why you married Mom at all. I don't really get that part.

She's getting married again. Actually she's probably married right now, to a new guy in France. The guy's American, but I think they got married in Europe so none of their friends would have to see me. I think most of the time the guy's embarrassed by me and the way look. And because he thinks this way, I'm positive Mom now thinks this way too.

Right now Aunt Shirley's staring at me because she's hearing things that are the truth about her sister and this guy. Things she might not have known about for sure. I'm at her house right now, and she's helping me write this letter to you. And, yes, I'm listening to her all the time, just like you told me to.

But, telling you the truth about what's going on right now is pretty much the real reason why I'm writing to you. I want you to know the truth so you'll want to come home, here, even more, to help me. Plus, I just want to see you again, and I want to have a real dad again, not this new, loser guy who's marrying Mom.

Anyway, getting back to her. Did you know she always tells me that it's a whole lot better for me to think that there's never going to be a cure for E.B.? Do you know she tells people she doesn't have the gene that makes E.B.?

I remember one time at Stanford when my doctor said, "He's so healthy and strong, he's going to live forever," and Mom actually looked kind of disappointed that he had told me that. And, another thing, they made me sign papers that make her and Hunt get all the money Grandma and Grandpa left for me if I die before I turn eighteen.

Aunt Shirley is looking at me right now, totally shocked. Well, at least I told her I was going to be completely honest before I even started. And, one of the worst things, for a while there, I had no nurse at all. And, I can't really do all the things by myself to keep myself well, it's really hard. So now, Mom hired a new nurse who talks to me like a robot. Remember the one from the show we used to watch together, the one from *Lost in Space*? Just like that one, except the nurse doesn't yell out, "Danger, Will Robinson!"

But the bottom line is that Mom and this guy are moving to L.A. It's going to be pretty soon, and that means I'll have to go with them. I won't be near Stanford like I am now. Going to Stanford at least once a month, or something like that, is like a necessity for me right now. For my treatments.

And, the really worse thing about this all is that I won't get to see Aunt Shirley anymore. I love her so much, and I can tell she loves me back. Sometimes I wish that she could have been my mom.

Right after saying that Aunt Shirley's eyes started to tear up. I didn't want to make her do that. But I needed to get this letter done too, so I said, "Come on, Aunt Shirley, don't cry. We've got to finish. Save it for a sad movie, will ya?"

"You're right," she said. She sniffled for a while longer, found a Kleenex®, blew her nose, and we continued.

And, another thing about Aunt Shirley, is all the stuff she's taught me has kept me pretty much as healthy as what the doctors could do. So, it's kind of likely that if I move down there, I'm not going to do very well. I'll probably get a lot worse.

I just don't want to be all alone. Having to be with Mom's new husband at all is worse than being alone. It's like being with a person who's killing you, just by being around them, because they're so rotten. Aunt Shirley tells me that God didn't create evil, and there's no such place as hell. But if that's true, then I guess when Mom's with this guy she just turns into someone who's sort of messed up. Aunt Shirley says Mom's changed a lot since when she got her share of the inheritance from Grandma and Grandpa after they died. And my old nurse, Khadijah, feels the same way about Mom and this guy. She totally gets it, the truth. She came over here and told Aunt Shirley everything. I think Hunt, the fiancé guy, even treated Khadijah differently because he never thought of her as the right kind of people. No offense, but I remember once he said bad stuff about gay people and AIDS before.

You don't have AIDS, do you? I don't think so, because you would have told me. I hope you didn't tell me that in one of the other letters I got that I couldn't read. My insides tells me no. Aunt Shirley taught me to trust my instinct. "It's never wrong," she says. It was her instinct that told me to write to you now. She said it's important for me to tell you exactly how much I want you to come back and be my dad again.

Can you do that for me, Dad? I know you're real smart. And I want you to do this really, really bad. Maybe that place, Amnesty International, can help you get out of jail. Aunt Shirley told me that that's the main thing they do anyway. So, Dad, please come home. I know for sure that San Francisco is way better than San Salvador because it's better than most places I've ever been, ever. It's the perfect place for innovators, too. That's what I'm going to be when I grow up. Maybe you can help me be one.

How does this all sound? I totally hope you want this as much as I do. I'm sure you do, because duh, who wants to be in jail? Nobody.

I also hope you'll send me lots and lots more letters. And more than anything, I hope real bad one of them says, "Miguel, I got out of jail, and I'm coming home real soon to get you. You and I will be a real family, just like we were before." This is the letter I will wait to get from you. This is the one I'll keep inside my head. So that means you *have* to write it.

I can't wait. And, instead of saying "I hope to see you again," I'll say, "I know I'll see you again soon." That's what makes it happen, when you say it out loud that way.

Love,

Miguel

P.S. I don't call myself Miguelito anymore because I'm now more like a young man than a little kid. Just so you know.

"Well, I guess that was enough to say," I told Aunt Shirley.

"Yes, that was plenty. I'm sure he'll love reading it," she said.

"But, Aunt Shirley, can you do me a huge favor? Can you please type it up before you send it off, so it looks professional?"

"Oh, definitely."

"And, Aunt Shirley, thanks again for all the things you do for me. I'm real glad you had this idea to write a letter to Dad. Having him know the truth makes me feel better somehow."

When it got to be nighttime, and just before I was getting ready to go to bed, Aunt Shirley said to me, "Miguel, I'm so sorry I never realized before all you have to go through in life. I should have known these things long ago. I had no idea all you've had to live with."

"Oh my God, I'm so happy you know this now. I'm glad you finally get that just because someone loves you, doesn't mean they're good for you to be around. Do you still think the best place for me to be is with them?"

"Nope. Not any longer. As a matter of fact I just got off the phone with your mother."

"You *what*?"

"I only spoke with her briefly. She was in her hotel room in Paris and there were a few things I needed to say to her now, things that couldn't wait."

"Wow. I can't believe it. Did you talk about...me?"

"Yes, we did. But I also asked her how the ceremony went. I even asked about Hunt. It all seemed to go very well. We had a nice conversation. She'll be back in the city tomorrow as planned. She's coming over here to pick you up at around two."

It was great to hear that the conversation went nice and that the wedding was good too. That meant Mom was going to be in a good mood when she got back.

The minute Mom arrived at Aunt Shirley's I could tell I was right. She was so happy to talk about the wedding and all the fancy people she met when she was in Paris. Hunt, my new step-dad, didn't come back with her though. He flew directly back to L.A. I still didn't know for sure where I was going to end up or how soon. So, while we were in the car driving home, I asked, "Are we going to be moving soon, down to Malibu?"

"Well, *I* am. We haven't decided yet what we're going to do with you," Mom answered.

"What do you mean *do with me*? Are you mad at me, Mom?"

"I'm so furious with you right now. It's a miracle I'm able to drive this car."

"What do you mean, Mom?"

"You made your aunt call me while I was in Paris, didn't you?

Interrupting my honeymoon with Hunt. How horribly inconsiderate. And, to tell me those lies about the way I've treated you. Do you know how that makes me look to her? I've never been so humiliated."

"But, Mom, I didn't make Aunt Shirley call you. She did it by herself. Plus, what's the big deal?"

"I can't believe you'd tell so many lies. Lies about me. Lies about my husband. I love you, Miguel. I've devoted my whole life to you."

"Mom, I told the truth." Almost as fast as I finished that sentence, Mom took her right hand off the steering wheel and raised it in the air, getting ready to slap me in the face. But it just stayed there.

She never did slap me. But what I remembered most from her raising her hand was that it seemed like it was something she's wanted to do forever. Raising her hand, taking a stand, telling her opinion were all things she wanted to do forever, but never did. What really made Mom want to do this? Why hadn't she ever done this before? Who or what was she really mad at?

CHAPTER TWENTY-ONE

The next day my stomach and throat hurt so bad, it was like a bunch of non-stop bee stings inside of me. All I could do was stay in bed and not be around anybody. I took my medicine and did all the things I had seen the doctors do a million times before. That's all I could do to take care of myself. Somehow the hurt made me think about Dad. I thought about how I would have given anything to trade places with him. I'd much rather have gone to a prison in El Salvador than live the life I was living.

My phone began ringing, but there was no way in hell I was going to answer it. Then, at the last minute, something made me pick it up. Before I could even say "hello," the other voice said, "Miguel, what happened? What's going on? Are you all right?" Aunt Shirley asked in a panicky way.

"No. I'm not OK. My stomach hurts real bad, and maybe I should go to the doctors."

"Where's your mother?"

"Didn't you already talk to her?"

"No."

"Didn't you talk to her since I got home last night? How did you know something was wrong with me?"

"I just knew. It doesn't matter...I'm coming right over. Where's your nurse, Mrs. Sternhoffer? Will you be OK until I get there?"

"She's not here. Yeah, I should be OK."

"Great! Miguel, please go to your window for now. Make yourself calm. I'll be there in about thirty minutes."

"But, Aunt Shirley, in the car last night I could tell Mom's changing. I'm real afraid of her now. She's becoming just like Hunt."

"I'm coming right over. Are you OK right now? Did she clean and bandage you this morning?"

"No, she's not even home. I put all the medicines and bandages on by myself."

"I'm leaving now."

I couldn't imagine how Aunt Shirley was going to get across the bay in just thirty minutes. There would have had to be no one else in any of the fast lanes in order for her to make that happen. Whenever Aunt Shirley drove it's just like she wanted to get it over with and out of the way. She always drove way too fast. But I was so happy she was coming. Happy and relieved. If I needed to go to Stanford, she'd definitely take me there for sure. And I wasn't in the mood to get another infection, not for this new wound. That's why E.B. patients die in the first place, not from the wounds, but from the infections that come after. Deep inside my head maybe I really did want to die but just skip the infection part that comes first.

All the time after the phone call I kept looking at the clock. It had become a race to see who would get there first, Aunt Shirley or Mom. Waiting all that time made me real nervous, and that wasn't good either. Out of nowhere I imagined I heard the front door opening when it really wasn't. I imagined that the one who opened that door would be the one who decides if I was going to live or die. Just at the point when I couldn't take it anymore I heard keys jingling outside our door. They jingled longer than normal. They jingled too long for it to be Mom because she knew that sometimes our lock got stuck. So in my head I knew it was going to be Aunt Shirley who opened the door. And I was right.

For someone who looked calm most of the time, Aunt Shirley raced into my room kind of frazzled and nervous, like a total mess. She came running up to me, almost knocking me over, and said, "Miguel, I got here as soon as possible. How are you doing? What's going on?"

"My stomach still kind of hurts real bad. But not as much as right before."

"Right before what?"

"Right before you called me."

Aunt Shirley's look to me changed a little bit, then she asked, "It's your stomach? Let's talk about this while I figure out what to do. Did you eat something that may have irritated it? I'm going to call Dr. de Pascual right now. Do you know his number? Never mind, it's in my bag. I threw it on the couch when I came in. I'll get it."

Aunt Shirley sprinted back into the living room and must have gotten the phone number from her book in one-second flat because I could already hear her speaking on the phone in there. It must not have been a very long conversation because she came into my room real soon after and said, "Everything's going to be fine."

"So, you're going to take me to the hospital?"

"Yes. She told me to give you two of your pills, you know the ones. The ones that start with *Str*, *Str*-something."

"Who's *she*? Well, it doesn't matter. They're in my bathroom."

"Fine. I'll go get them. You stay here. I'll be right back."

Aunt Shirley was still a little bit frantic and must have been throwing things around because I heard lots of crashing noises coming from my bathroom. "I can't find them," she said.

"I'll show you," I said. I left my room and walked into the bathroom. Yikes, it looked like a cyclone or tornado or whatever that thing was in the movie *Twister* just came in and puked all over my bathroom.

"I can't find them. Where are they?" Aunt Shirley asked.

"Well, they were supposed to be right here," I said, while pointing to the place on the counter where all my pills usually were.

"Well, they weren't there. I looked. I put the ones that were there somewhere on the floor."

"Here they are." They were right at the base of the toilet.

"Oh, good. Well, take two of them. Here, let me get you some water. Then let's get you packed and out of here."

When Aunt Shirley gave me the two pills and water everything got a lot more still. Aunt Shirley slowed down and so did I. She patted me on my head and I felt rescued. It was a feeling I'd never forget. Aunt Shirley was meant to come over then. After walking out of the bathroom we both sat in front of my bay window and looked out. It was peaceful. Aunt Shirley was the first one to talk when she asked, "What did you eat last night? Anything different?"

"Um. I guess I ate some rice and some avocado."

"Anything else?"

"For dinner, you mean?"

Aunt Shirley could tell I was keeping something from her so she asked more questions. "No. Tell me everything you've eaten since I saw you yesterday."

"I had some bananas, too."

"Miguel, tell me."

Normally I just wouldn't have told her. But I could tell there was no getting around it this time. "A bay leaf...so it would hurt me."

Aunt Shirley was speechless. Her mouth was open but closed again to make one more question. "Why did you want to do that?"

"Because I'm so bad. It's my fault. I'm the one who made Mom the way she is."

In a real, real serious way Aunt Shirley looked over at me, shaking her head sideways. "No. No, Miguel. You are *not* bad. You—"

"Shirley, what are you doing here?" Mom asked out of nowhere.

"Sharon, oh my God. You startled me. Let me catch my breath," Aunt Shirley said.

"Mickey, why is your bathroom such a mess? Shirley, it's usually much neater than this," Mom said.

"Neater? Sharon, what are you talking about? Your son is in pain. I'm taking him to the hospital immediately. Let's pack your things, Miguel," Aunt Shirley said.

"Mickey, stay where you are. You don't have to go anywhere, dear."

"I've already called the hospital. They're expecting him."

"With whom did you speak? Dr. de Pascual?"

"No, some woman in the Dermatology Department."

"Well I spoke with Dr. de Pascual last evening. He said it sounded as if a trip to the hospital is unnecessary."

"Aunt Shirley, that's not true."

"Mickey, quiet now. Get back into bed, hon," Mom said.

Aunt Shirley then pulled Mom by her arm and into the living room. But they started shouting so loud that I could still hear every word. I never knew Aunt Shirley could get so mad. Maybe it was something she always wanted to do, have this talk with Mom, but never could before.

"Sharon, I just don't understand you anymore. The way you've been neglecting Miguel lately borders on criminal behavior."

"I've always treated Mickey well. He's always given the best of care."

"Stop calling him that. His name is *Miguel*!" Aunt Shirley shouted.

"Shirley, he's *my* son. I'll call him whatever name I want. What we decide for him is best."

"We? Meaning Hunt? Sharon, I need to know right now, right this second, what you plan on doing with Miguel now that you've married that man."

"Why would it be of concern to you? He'll come with us."

"Do you want him with you? Does Hunt want him to be with the two of you? Be honest with me."

"Of course we want him with us. He's my son."

"Please, why don't you admit to me that you'd, he'd, prefer that Miguel live somewhere else? I'd like him to live with me."

"Live with you? I don't want Mi–, my son being exposed to you. Your crazy beliefs. They're not good for him."

"Sharon, I'm just so worried. I think because of this connection you now have to this...man, you're neglecting Miguel to the point where you're endangering his safety, his life."

"You're not a mother. Or I should say you're no longer a mother. How on earth would you know anything about proper parenting? You're the perfect example of what is...an unfit mother."

It became completely silent. I couldn't tell what was happening. I couldn't tell if Aunt Shirley was so mad she couldn't speak, or if Mom was just tired of yelling.

"That's so unfair of you," I heard Aunt Shirley say to Mom in a softer voice.

"Am I supposed to pretend it never happened? Am I supposed to forget how reckless you were? I had to lie for you so the rest of the family wouldn't find out."

"I never asked you to lie."

"What did you expect me to do? Did you think there would have been no consequences if you had told everyone about it? I highly doubt that."

"But I was sixteen. Having a baby at sixteen is not a sin."

"That's not what I'm talking about. I'm talking about—"

"You promised we'd never discuss that again, ever."

"And now, you'd seriously think I'd let you be responsible for my own son? After what you let happen to your own child?"

"Stop it, Sharon. You make it sound as if you're blaming me. It wasn't my fault."

"It certainly *was* your fault. Your horrendous error in judgment for ever becoming involved with such a maligned man. *That* was your fault."

"I was sixteen. How was I to know? You're forgetting that I lost that child, my precious baby girl. Taken away from me, kidnapped. Don't you have a heart? Don't you have any compassion for what I've been through?"

"I should be sympathetic for someone who allows herself to become pregnant with a man, a man who ends up *kidnapping* their own child? And then...*murders* it? No thank you. To be drawn to such a psychopath in the first place is insane."

"I can't believe you're being so cruel. How could you possibly blame me for what he did?"

I couldn't believe what I just heard. Aunt Shirley always told me to only tell the truth. But I finally found out her biggest secret, something she never told me anything about. I felt like I wanted to die for her.

What I couldn't understand though was how Mom was mad at

Aunt Shirley instead of feeling sorry for her. I wanted to run into the living room and hug Aunt Shirley because I could imagine how bad she must have felt. I didn't go in there though because I thought at first Aunt Shirley was probably embarrassed about me overhearing what Mom had just said.

Somehow I could tell that one of them had left the living room to go somewhere else in the apartment. It wasn't like it was over though. More was going to happen, I could just tell. Maybe Mom was going to apologize for being so mean. Maybe Aunt Shirley would just go home and try to forget about what took place. In all the fighting I forgot I was supposed to pack for the hospital. I guess this fight was meant to happen instead.

Out of nowhere someone finally said something in the living room. "I've never been more serious. I'd truly like Miguel to live with me. I so strongly feel that you seem to be out of options. Go ahead and think whatever you want about me and the mistakes you think I've made. But that boy in there needs someone to care for him on a continual basis. I want to take full responsibility of him, and that includes financial responsibility," Aunt Shirley said.

"And how would you be able to do that?" Mom asked.

"Money has always been there when I needed it. Money isn't what Miguel needs most right now anyway. He needs attention and love. More than that, someone who believes in him. Now that you're with Hunt, can you give him this?"

"I have always loved my son." Mom said. But this time something changed in her voice. She wasn't sounding like she was trying to convince anyone.

"What about Hunt? What does he know about E.B.? Does he have the time or the desire to be a stepfather to a child who needs so much?"

"Well, he *is* very busy. His career does mean everything to him. He could learn. He's more than prepared to hire a live-in. Anyway, Mickey requires medical care more than attention right now, more than either one of us is able to provide at the moment. Hunt will make sure Mickey has all he needs."

"I disagree, Sharon. Medicine is not a cure. What I can hopefully give Miguel is help in stimulating his desire to live life, to attain any goal he's able to manufacture for himself. Don't you want to see that for your son?"

"I imagine so. I mean, of course." Then there was a short pause.

"Sharon, I'm hoping you can see this as clearly as I do. You and Hunt can have a perfect life together with or without Mickey in it. What I can help you do is give Mickey a wonderful life. So you won't have to worry. You'll be free to travel, attend functions or events, and give Hunt the attention *he* deserves. It sounds as if he's someone who needs you very much. Your time and attention." This time what Aunt Shirley was saying wasn't the truth, or maybe just a real little part of it was. I could tell what she was doing, but I don't know if Mom could. She was acting. And it was so strange to hear. Aunt Shirley was copying what Mom did best, acting like having a man in her life would be the perfect solution for everything.

"That's so true. Hunt does need me. We're inseparable. It's doubtful he'd be able share me if my focus went elsewhere," Mom said.

"Absolutely. He's such an important man. And behind every successful man there's a woman behind him supporting him." Wow, Aunt Shirley went off the deep end with that one. It's like she was mimicking Mom to her face, just exactly the way Mom would say something. Aunt Shirley was talking total bullshit.

"You're right again. And the image we need to create as a couple needs to be carefully considered as well. What would people think about being seen with my poor son, so...disfigured? It can be very alarming. It's happened to me so many times before, and frankly, I shouldn't impose such a burden on Hunt," Mom said.

"Oh, my, no. What a colossal burden that would be. And, especially in a community like Los Angeles where physical appearance means so much. Poor Hunt would be shunned, chastised by his mere association to such an unfortunate outcast. What a horror that would be."

"I never thought of that. I'd hate to be responsible for placing his career in jeopardy. At this stage, I'm not really sure how Mickey would be able to fit into our new world."

"I'm so glad you now see that for yourself. I'm only thinking of you and your future. Your future with Hunt. I do so want to see this marriage succeed. Why jinx it right off the bat when you needn't?" Aunt Shirley was giving such a great performance. All the drama schools she'd been to sure were coming in handy.

"Well, the points you've brought up are seeming to sound so perfectly clear to me. If you do indeed want to care for Mickey full-time at your home in the East Bay, I might give it some thought. It may all be for the best. Hunt will be so pleased."

"Oh yes, I'm sure he will be. After all, what he thinks is what matters most," Aunt Shirley said, as she got exactly what she wanted.

And so did I. I almost fainted that Mom gave in, and I was finally going to end up with Aunt Shirley. I had never been so happy in my entire life. My biggest wish of all time was about to come true.

CHAPTER TWENTY-TWO

"These are consent forms your aunt must sign," Mom told me.

"What are they for?" I asked.

"This gives Shirley permission to make decisions on your behalf when you're in the hospital. They've got to be signed by her, in order for the doctors to perform surgeries and medical procedures on you. Shirley will now be your decision-maker, your guardian. She's now fully responsible for your life."

"OK. Sure I'll definitely make sure she signs them."

"And make sure she sends them certified to the administrative offices at the Medical Center. They already know they're the reason I've chosen to do this, leaving you with Shirley...so you'll remain close to their facilities."

Everything was going so well. It was turning out better than I ever could have expected. Instead of just being my aunt like she always had been, it's like Aunt Shirley was going to be my new mom for a while. And, it was even getting to be official. There was a ton of papers going back and forth that all needed signing. Even Hunt was being helpful. He thought the whole thing was a great idea. He organized most of all the legal stuff that needed to be done.

But just as quickly as I got excited, I quickly became unexcited. Mom had gone into her room to answer her phone, and when she came back into mine she said, "You don't need to pack up everything just now, hon. Hunt has reconsidered. You *will* be living with us in Malibu."

"What?" I screamed.

"You'll be coming with us. Everything has changed. We'll both be moving down there in three weeks."

"You're joking. What about all the papers that've been signed? You can't just unsign them. Aunt Shirley's expecting me to move into her house."

"Mickey there's no need to raise your voice like that. You won't be living with Shirley after all. You'll be with Hunt and I."

I was so mad. And I got way more mad by the time I asked, "Did Hunt

149

do something? Why do I all of the sudden have to live down there now?"

"It's just easier, dear. Calm down."

"But why did you decide this now? What's the real reason, Mom? Tell me. Why did you do this?"

"Well, Hunt was mistaken about something. Something to do with legal matters. No problem though, dear. Not to worry."

"But how come Hunt gets to decide about legal stuff? He's not a lawyer. What exactly did he make you do this time?"

"Well, Hunt and I both were under the impression that I'd still be the recipient of your trust, should you die before you reach eighteen. But, as it turns out, we were wrong. Hunt's attorney, as well as mine, told us that should I at some point no longer be your primary caregiver and legal guardian, I may lose my claim to that money. Hunt said that we can't let that happen. The money would be tied up in court for years."

"But, Mom, why do you keep expecting me to die before I turn eighteen?"

"Oh, I'm not, dear. Don't get me wrong. I hope you live forever. I'm just thinking practically."

"Mom, but it's like you don't want me to be alive anymore."

"Mickey, oh darling. You're misunderstanding everything."

"Mom, how come you told me Dad will probably never see me again? That he might never be able to leave El Salvador?"

"I don't remember saying that."

"Yes. You did. And you know what Dad told me in his letter? He said he's sure that someone set him up. And I'm positive that Hunt's the one who did it. Did you know about this? Or not?"

"Who have you been talking to? Where are you getting these ideas, Mickey?"

"I should just go tell the police or Amnesty International what's really going on so they can investigate. Then it will be Hunt's turn to stay in jail."

"Mickey, I simply won't stand for this. Hunt adores you. I can't imagine how you're able to come up with this...nonsense. Are you taking drugs? Is that why you're acting this way?"

"If I did take drugs I would have taken bottles and bottles of them so I would have died long ago. Just so I can be with Jorge again."

"Why are you saying these things? What is wrong with you? Haven't you been happy? Haven't I always given you exactly what you've asked for? Now that I'm married to Hunt I can give you even more."

"But that's just money, Mom. Don't you ever think about Jorge anymore? Don't you wish you could just change everything?"

"I never forget about Jorge. I remember him constantly. But I can't change...anything. I can't. I've given you both such a privileged life, and now you're just as ungrateful as he was."

"What's so privileged about having E.B.?"

"Oh, Mickey. I'm so so—" Then like a totally different person Mom said, "I know why you're doing this now. It's because of what Jorge wrote in that letter, those horrible things. Blaming me for his death. How shameful."

"What letter?"

"The letter I found in your room. The one under your mattress. Weren't you wondering where it had gone?"

"You took it?"

"I took if for this very reason, the day you'd turn on me. Hunt told me you'd do this. He said you'd use it against me. Hunt has it now, and he'll make sure you have no shred of evidence to disparage me in a courtroom."

"A courtroom? What are you talking about?"

"My reputation is too important. For years I've imagined you'd do this to me. Turn my misery into your profit. Destroy your own mother's life so you'd be able to advance your own. Shameful."

After being so totally angry, I then became shocked. All I could do was stare at Mom. It was like a mixture of feelings. I had a right to be mad, and I knew that what I was saying about Hunt was somehow the truth. I just knew it. And no one needed to give me evidence. But when Mom started talking about the courtroom-stuff and turning on her, I saw her as a child again. Part of me wanted to help her.

For the first time I thought that Mom might be kind of mentally ill. The things she was saying were so far off base. A courtroom? What the hell?

What I thought about next reminded me of what Aunt Shirley told me over and over, "what you prepare for is what you're going to have in life." I had no idea that Mom, for years, had been preparing for some kind of courtroom trial. And since that's what she kept in her head all that time, she'd definitely get it at some point.

It's a lot like that totally rich lady in Sea Cliff who always told people that her husband was going to kill her, and he'd get away with it 'cause he was some celebrity. She even hid photos of herself in a safe, showing herself with bruises all over, pictures she thought would be used later on as evidence in a trial. All along she was preparing for the husband to kill her. And he did. The lady set it up for herself. She prepared for her own death because that's what she created.

Clint Adams

Well, one thing I've never prepared for was to lose. In my head I was always the winner. Taking some sort of action was always the best thing to do. I knew I had to take another *first step*. I didn't even care if God would give me a break afterwards either. I knew that what I was going to do next would make a huge difference in the rest of my life.

Since I thought that Dad may somehow have gotten my letters after all, I thought I'd write him another one. In my head I knew that that was right. While I was headed back to my room, Mom asked, "Where are you going?"

"I'm going to write another letter to Dad."

"How is the letter going to get to him? He'll probably never even see it."

"Aunt Shirley will mail it for me. She's the one who mailed my letters from before."

"Oh, Mickey. I think you're wasting your time. You're making everything so difficult. I just know you're going to make yourself sick again."

"This is something I've got to do. I've got to tell the truth." I then walked away from Mom, and there was little she could do to stop me from writing Dad's letter. She had no idea how strong I really could be. And I was getting even stronger.

In my room I turned on my computer. I couldn't wait to get started. I didn't even care if Mom heard me dictate what I was getting ready to write. Usually I made sure I was way more quiet if I knew my mom was within hearing-range inside our apartment, but not this time.

Dead Dad,
How are you? I sure do hope you're getting out of jail real soon. You know why?
Things are really, really weird here. Mom and I just had a huge fight. I was supposed to move in with Aunt Shirley because Mom and her new husband are moving to L.A. Then, at the very last minute, they changed their minds. And Mom wanted me to stay with her, because she still thinks I'm going to die soon. It's also a way that they'll get all the money Grandpa and Grandma left for me.
Somehow if I live with Aunt Shirley, they won't get it anymore. What's the big deal about the money anyway? I mean, who gives a shit? So when I found out I couldn't move after all, I got really mad.
When I was talking to Mom I reminded her of something she told me a long time ago. I never told you because I thought it was maybe just a

152

bluff. But maybe it was the truth. What she said was, 'I'm pretty sure you'll never be able to see your father again.' I'm not so sure that's what she said exactly, but since you already felt like you were set up, I'm totally positive that Mom's new husband is the one that did it.

This is none of my business, but was she really pissed when she found out you were gay? She said you're the one who ruined our lives. And that's way wrong. Hunt, the new husband, probably knows all this by the way. And I wouldn't be surprised if he did something illegal to get back at you. Plus, Mom always thinks that the worst thing anyone could do to her is to embarrass her, and that's what she thought you did to her.

Anyway, another thing is whenever I get sick these days, nobody really cares. I've got a different nurse now, Mrs. Sternhoffer. But she just goes through the motions. And what if Hunt and Mom not only believe that I'm not going to survive, what if they really want me to die? That way I'll be out of the way, and they'll get all that money.

Now I'm mad that that money was left for me, because if Grandma and Grandpa would have only left it to someone else, I could have been free by now. Is it true that money is the root of all evil? I guess that maybe it's just evil if evil people are involved. Khadijah even told Aunt Shirley that Hunt and Mom aren't so good to be around. Can you believe it? Khadijah never liked Mom and Hunt at all, and I never really knew it until she told Aunt Shirley everything. The reason I'm telling you all this is so you'll know how really bad everything is here. You could change all this if you really want to get out of prison bad enough. You do, don't you? What if they'd really do anything to get rid of me? You know what I mean? And that makes me kind of scared. And according to Aunt Shirley, that's the worst possible thing to ever be.

Maybe you won't get this letter after all, and I know you won't like what I'm going to write next. But I've thought about it a lot, especially since it looks like I'll absolutely never get to live with Aunt Shirley. And, I don't know if you'll ever get out of jail. So, I think maybe the best thing for me to do is go to heaven. Plus, I miss Jorge a lot of the time.

I know I have to be extra careful, because if this is what I want, and it's in my head, then that's what's really going to happen to me. So, right now it's not really for sure going to happen because I still haven't said out loud that I'm ready to go. But, I'm just telling you so that if you find out from someone else, at least you'll know in this letter that going to heaven is OK with me.

I hope you won't get mad with me 'cause that's where I've gone. Aunt Shirley says that heaven is really the best place to be anyway. It's a place where people go to decide what they want to do next on earth. This will give me a lot of time to think about what I want to do when I'm back. I think next time I'll pick a different life. And I'm way tired of having E.B. So next time I want to be really healthy, or at least have some disease that's not nearly as bad.

I hope you get out of jail though, so you can have more things to do in your life this time around. What do you want to do next? After this one? I'm almost sure the next time you won't plan on going to jail, right? By the way, do you get all this stuff I'm talking about?

I will definitely miss Aunt Shirley the most because I have the feeling she's finished. So, if I go to heaven pretty soon, that means I only have just a couple more visits with her this time in life, before I never see her again, ever. I wonder what people do when they go to heaven for the last time. Where do they go after that, after they've learned everything they have to on earth? Maybe there's some other planet they go to, to learn lessons.

Anyway, I'm glad you were my dad. You're really good to me and Jorge, and we were both lucky you taught us good things. Thanks for telling me about all those awesome TV shows we used to watch together, those were way cool. And thanks for making me feel totally loved, that meant a lot to me. It's too bad though that now you've run out of kids to love. Maybe you'll have some more someday. I mean, you know, adopt them or whatever. Are you going to have a wife that's a man when you get out? Is that how it works?

So, Dad, I love you lots and lots, that's for sure. But, since you love me so much, you probably want me to be happy too, because love and happiness kind of go together. And, I think I'd be a lot happier if I go on to heaven pretty soon. It's like the only thing that makes sense. I've definitely taken the first step lots of times, but I'm not so sure God has ever given me a break. Maybe I'm not supposed to get any.

Maybe He wants me to go to heaven too. Maybe I just need to start all over again. If I do, I'll definitely put in a request to have you in my life next time. That would be good. Would that be good for you? I hope so.

Now it's time for me to say goodbye. I'll sure miss you, Dad. I don't really know what else to say. The last thing for me to say is, maybe I'll see you again. Maybe this time, or maybe the next one. Either way it turns out to be is totally cool with me, as long as I get to see you again sometime.

Get freed soon, OK?

Lots and lots and lots of love,

Miguel

CHAPTER TWENTY-THREE

"Miguelito, don't stop believing! The minute you do, you're toast. You have too much to look forward to in life. No. No way. You're not done yet. Not by a long shot," Aunt Shirley told me over the phone.

"But I'm so tired of it all. Every time it looks like something good is going to happen something bad happens instead," I said.

"Well, of course. If that's what you keep saying out loud, then that's the way it's going to keep happening."

"I don't care about that stuff anymore either. No offense. I don't care what I say out loud, or in a letter, or in my sleep. I just don't care."

"There's no way I'll accept this. You don't care about *anything*? Nothing? What about all those things on your *To Do* list?"

"I erased everything on it. Oh. I take it back. There's just one more thing I care about, one more thing left on my list. Can you mail a letter to Dad for me, just like the way you mailed those last two?"

"Certainly. Is your mother home?"

"No, she's not home now. She didn't tell me where she was going, but I heard her leave a long time ago. Why?"

"I'll come over and get the letter right now. How's that?"

"Oh, that's great. But, are you sure you want to come over? Remember how it was the last time she showed up when you were here?"

"I have such a strong feeling about something. I just know a turning point is right around the corner for you. Can I tell you what's on *my To Do* list?"

"Duh. What? Marry Tom Cruise?"

"When I come over to get your letter, I'm taking you back with me."

"What are you talking about? Mom said 'no'."

"But I say 'yes.' I have the feeling I'm not going to see her. So, can you be all packed and ready to walk out the door in about forty-five minutes?"

"For how long? I mean, where are we going? Am I going to your house? Forever?"

"Until I get sick of looking at you, that's how long."

"Oh, hush. Wait a minute, are you for real?"

"Of course I'm for real. Get going. In just a few minutes you're outta there, babe. I'm totally serious, so get started right now. And whatever you aren't able to pack, we'll buy. OK?"

"Definitely, Aunt Shirley. You are absolutely the coolest."

"I know. Oh, and one more thing real quick. I love you, doll."

"I love you too, Aunt Shirley."

Oh my God, I didn't even have time to let myself get real excited because I had to pack so fast. I hoped Aunt Shirley was right about buying new stuff, 'cause I knew I was going to forget something. My underwear, my socks, my masks and bandages, my medicines, my pictures of Jorge and Dad...and Mom. I needed all this stuff. I guess I didn't care that I was going to miss the last few weeks of school. Maybe I could go to summer school over in Berkeley.

After I finished packing everything, I waited. I waited in the living room, then in my bedroom. And when I was sitting in front of my bay window, thinking that it would be the last time I got to look out it, my phone rang. I sure as hell hoped it wasn't a solicitor, but I answered anyway and said, "Hello."

All I could hear was lots of different loud noises, like traffic and honking. But then I heard, "Miguel, it's Aunt Shirley. Can you hear me?" she screamed.

"Yeah. Barely. Where are you?"

"I'm at a gas station in Emeryville, near the freeway. Something's going on with my car. There's smoke coming out from under the hood. Right now they're trying to figure out what's wrong."

"Well, are you still coming over?"

"Oh, yes, doll. Nothing will stop me from going over there to get you. You just hang tight, and I'll be there before you know it. If I have to I'll just leave my car here, and rent another one."

"Wow. Thanks for doing all this. I can't wait to see you."

"I've got to go. This guy's waving at me to come back. I'll see you soon. Bye, doll."

"Bye, Aunt Shirley."

Lots of times I got really mad at how much I had to wait for things. But when I took a second to totally stop and realize that what was going on was what I'd been waiting for all my life, it all became OK. Aunt Shirley was the one who told me that there's never a reason to rush. Being impatient accomplishes nothing. Everything is meant to happen in its own time. God runs the show, not people. Plus, people are the ones who invented clocks. God never had one back then.

The best thing that was going on while I waited was that Mom still didn't get home. It sure was taking a long time and I was really, really ready to go. The more I waited the more I remembered things I wanted to take with me, like my letter to Dad. Duh. That's like the major reason I needed to see Aunt Shirley anyway, so she'd mail it for me.

A whole hour went by, then another half hour, then another one. If I really wanted to I could have definitely walked down to the BART station and taken the train across the bay. I thought of a million things I could have been doing. That was another thing, *could have* and *should have*. Aunt Shirley said that that's what people think about when they don't acknowledge the plan God made for them. They always think they could have or should have done something to prevent something else from having happened. They didn't get it. Those things were supposed to have happened in the first place...for a reason. They couldn't have prevented anything.

When I was in the kitchen eating some instant flan I thought I heard the phone ringing in my bedroom. When I got there the ringing had stopped. Then I did call-return, but it didn't work. I waited for a little while, and walked away. Then our main phone rang. It had to be Aunt Shirley. I was sure of it. "Aunt Shirley?" I asked.

"Yes. Miguel, how did you know it was me?" Aunt Shirley asked, and then she apologized by saying, "I am so, so sorry. This has been an absolute nightmare. I left my car at the gas station because I couldn't drive it. And now I've called a few car rental places. They're all out of cars because it's Memorial Day weekend."

"How about if I take BART over?" I asked.

"But what about your things? You're taking stuff with you, aren't you?"

"Yeah, you're right. I guess I wouldn't be able to carry them all the way down the hill to BART."

"No, that won't work. Too much to carry. I'll find a car. I'll come up with something. But since I'm running late I decided I don't want to run into your mother. Is there any way you can carry your stuff over to the Fairmont or the Mark Hopkins? I can meet you in the lobby, and that way we won't have any problems."

"Oh, for sure. They're like right next door. Let's meet at the Fairmont. I like the lobby there the best. But, you know what, Aunt Shirley? I just thought of something. Do you think this is meant to be?"

"Why do you say that now, Miguel?"

"Because of all the signs, you're the one who taught me that. It's like this isn't supposed to happen, or you're not supposed to come over here, or something. Something like that."

"Well, that's what I've been thinking all along too. But, I *want* this to happen. I want to help you, Miguel. I want you to be free."

"Definitely. Me too. But maybe it's not supposed to happen this way. Remember that country singer's song? What's her name? Oh, yeah, Tawny Tucker. When she sings, *If it Don't Come Easy, You Gotta Let it Go.* And I don't even like country music too much."

"I never thought I'd ever hear you quote Tanya Tucker, but what she says is right on the money. But, you know what? Now I've got to see you, and bring you back over here. One car rental place I just called said all they have is a minibus, and I'm going to rent it. They're going to pick me up any minute. So let's say I'll meet you in the lobby of the Fairmont in about twenty to thirty minutes."

"Cool. That's fine. Maybe those weren't signs after all, just some kind of bad luck."

"Hey, my determination has overwhelmed me. Look out world...here I come."

"You go, Aunt Shirley!"

"I'll see you in a few, doll."

"OK. Bye, Aunt Shirley."

I guess I didn't realize exactly how much stuff I packed because I could only carry one suitcase and a paper bag. So I decided to leave two of them at home. Oh my God, I couldn't believe it. This was going to be the last time I'd ever be in my home. "Thanks for the great views, Apartment *Thirty-O-One*," I said out loud.

I walked out, bringing my stuff, but the elevator took forever. Actually, one of them was being repaired, so that's always a drag. Eventually, one of the elevators did finally come and while it was going down it stopped on almost every floor. I hated that. And everyone who got on asked, "Are you going on a trip?" Even though it was none of their damn business, I was polite because they probably meant well, and I answered, "I'm going to stay with a friend for a while." I didn't want to tell exactly where I was going, but I never lied.

Since Aunt Shirley was also a friend, I told the truth. The doorman, Al, was a different story though. He just had to know everything. "Where are you off to, Miguel?" he asked.

"To stay with friends," I answered.

"Which friends? Are they picking you up?"

"Well, some friends in the East Bay."

"How are you going to get there? Is your mother going to take you? Where is she right now?"

"I'm not really sure where she is. But I've got to go. They're going to pick me up real soon."

"Why don't they just meet you here? Are they on their way now?"

"Yeah. Right now. I've got to go."

"Well, how about if I give you a hand with those bags?"

"No. I'm fine. Really. They're going to meet me in one of the hotels really soon."

"Which hotel is that? The Sir Francis Drake? The Hyatt Regency? The Hilton? The Sheraton Palace? The Mark Hopkins? The Fairmont?"

"Yeah, the Fairmont. That's where they're meeting me. I've really got to go."

"OK, Mr. Busy Traveler. Have a fine trip. I'll see you when you get back."

"Yeah, Al. Bye."

Wow, that was a close one. I don't think Regis Philbin ever asked that many dumb questions when he was still doing *Millionaire*. I knew I didn't want to get myself too tired so I stopped to take a breath. Then I carried all my junk across Huntington Park to get to the Fairmont. Charlie, the homeless guy, wasn't around, which was kind of good because we probably would have talked for too long. I couldn't wait to get to the Fairmont lobby and sit on one of their cushy, red velvet benches.

And because I really couldn't grip a suitcase handle, I had to use these burlap-like straps instead to carry it. Ouch. That hurt even more with all the extra pressure on the skin on my shoulders. By the time I got near the Fairmont, my dogs were barking.

Once I got into the hotel I felt just like I was going on some vacation. All the lobby was full of people checking in, or leaving to go out to do something fun. I could tell this was going to be some sort of new beginning for me. I thought a long time about wanting to go up the glass elevator to the top floor where the restaurant twirls, but I didn't know what to do with my luggage. Relaxing on the bench was fine with me. So that's what I did the whole time I waited.

I never got to see James Brolin or Connie Sellecca because they stopped making *Hotel* a really long time ago. Pretty soon I began to feel like I had been sitting in the hotel lobby all afternoon. I looked at my left wrist to see what time it was and I was totally shocked to see that I was wearing my watch that doesn't tell time, the one Aunt Shirley had given me when I was in the hospital. I hadn't taken it off since she put in on me the day before. I still didn't know what time it was, but wearing that watch made me think about my aunt. Where was she? The thirty-or-so minutes she told me she was going to be there became more like a couple of hours at least. It was all turning out to be like the total weirdest day. I also wondered if my mom had gotten home yet.

Then, I looked directly at the entrance of the hotel, right over to the people coming inside. And the second before it happened I knew exactly who was going to walk through the doors next. "Mickey, oh my heavens. I'm so glad to see you. I had no idea where you were," Mom said, while racing towards me with smeared make up running down her face.

"Mom, what are you doing here? Did Al tell you where I was?" I asked.

"That doesn't matter. Mickey, oh you're all right. Thank God."

Quickly I became worried when I knew to ask, "Where's Aunt Shirley?"

Mom sat down next to me on the velvet bench, and said "I have something to tell you, sweetie. I just received a call. From someone at Kaiser Hospital in Oakland. Shirley's there. She was in an accident on the Bay Bridge." Mom then burst into tears at the very same time I went into shock.

"But she's OK, right? Right, Mom?"

"Her head. There was an injury to her head. I can't remember everything. Something ruptured. One of her legs is broken. Her left lung was punctured. And she's unconscious. Perhaps a coma."

"But she's going to be OK. Right?"

"It just happened. They're getting ready to operate on her right now."

"But, I mean, she's not going to die. She's not going to do that, right?"

"They think she may be all right. As long as she doesn't go into cardiac arrest."

Something made me look at my watch. "This is how you'll know you'll always be around. Time doesn't exist in the spiritual world," Aunt Shirley had told me. After I looked at that I had to close my eyes real tight and pretend this wasn't happening. I wanted so much for Aunt Shirley not to leave. This was probably the last time I'd ever get to see her, and I never got to say "goodbye."

This couldn't be happening, I thought. Somehow I ended up in my apartment, and I never remembered walking over there. "Mom, can we please go over there to be with her?"

"Yes. We're going to leave in just a minute. I had to find you first. Al told me right away. I won't even ask you what you were doing there."

"Thanks, Mom. Let's go."

"I've got to clean up first. My face is a mess, I look awful," Mom said, while running off to the bathroom.

"Mom, you look fine," I yelled out.

When Mom came back she looked just the same. We went down the elevator to our car. We drove off, headed for Kaiser Hospital, but while we were on the Bay Bridge Mom started crying so hard. "Shirley can't die. She just can't. This can't happen now."

"Mom. It's OK. Aunt Shirley's going to be fine."

"Oh my God, no. This is wrong. It can't happen this way. I've got to tell her first."

"What is it, Mom?"

"I'm so sorry. I ruined her life."

"Mom, what are you talking about? What do you have to tell her first?"

"The truth about her baby."

CHAPTER TWENTY-FOUR

Aunt Shirley didn't die, thank God. Almost three weeks went by and she still stayed in her coma at the hospital. I was also in one myself...a hospital, not a coma. Somehow the skin on my insides, my lymph nodes or something, became infected and made my immune system do weird things. I got real sick. They gave me lots of medicines to take so I didn't get to be awake too much of the time.

When I first got to the hospital though, and thought I was going to die, I did one last thing. I waited until it was late at night when everyone thought I was asleep. I couldn't write a letter because I didn't have my computer and I knew there was nowhere to send it. So, I spoke out loud in kind of a quiet voice, but it was still like a letter, just an out-loud one. With no doctors or nurses around me to hear, I started.

"Dear God,

I hope You're listening to me because I have something real important to say. But first You've got to pretend that I'm Aunt Shirley right now. She's at Kaiser Hospital in Oakland, and she's been in a coma for a while. I don't know when she's going to get out of it, and I don't think people can talk when they're in one, so that's why I'm doing it for her. Aunt Shirley told me that what people say out loud is what's going to end up happening to them later on. So here I go. Remember, I'm talking like Aunt Shirley now.

Hi God, I'm Shirley Kirkland. There's lots of things I want You to know. I'm going to get out of this hospital real soon so I can finish my dissertation papers at school. Then after I do that I'm going to have it accepted so I can graduate and then be Dr. Shirley Kirkland, even though I know I can't work in a hospital or write prescriptions.

I'm not mad because I'm in a coma right now. I just know that You made it happen because that's what was supposed to happen, so that's OK. But You need to know that I'm going to get out of here, be

163

real healthy, and never go back to the hospital. I'm going to live in my beautiful home in the Berkeley hills again, the one that looks at the bay. Thanks for my home by the way. I'm thankful for all the good things You've done for me. But, You know what? I'm not done yet. There's lots more things I have to do.

Anyway, the main thing is that I'll be getting out of here, and I'm not going to die yet. It's way too early. Plus, I really, really want to live. And I really, really want lots of other things. And, how could I get them if I'm not alive? That doesn't make sense. You know what I mean? And, another thing, if this is the last time I'm supposed to live on earth, then I better make it a good one. And, I definitely want to see Miguel again. He's in the hospital at Stanford right now, but he's not in a coma. He's a real good boy. If I go, then that means he'll be alone, and he's my best friend. He's got his mom, but she's gone a lot. So I'm not sure she really counts. She's not very...evolved yet. Yeah, not evolved. Do You know what that means? It means a person who probably doesn't really get why they're here on earth living the life You gave them, all the lessons You wrote down for them to learn. They've got a long way to go.

And, You know what else, God? This is a biggie. I've got to teach a lot more people about all the stuff I know. I haven't worked this hard to become as spiritually advanced as I am, just so I can keep everything I've learned to myself. I mean come on, get real. I'm going to teach everyone I meet. Little by little these people might know better about what You have planned for them all. Wouldn't that be cool?

I sure think so. A lot of the world is so f—, I mean, messed up, and I think everybody could use a huge break. Don't You? Don't You think it's about time the rest of the world gets it? Thank You for giving me so much to learn. I appreciate all the lessons I've had. But, I know for sure that I'm supposed to be around a lot longer, so I'm just going to snap out of this.

I guess that's all I have to say for now. I hope I wasn't too bossy. A lot of the time I'm pretty mellow, but sometimes you've gotta be extra firm so people will listen. So, I'll be talking to You again real soon, right after I wake up from this coma. That's another thing, I know how You like hearing thank You, so I've got to be awake again to tell You that. It's kind of like if You scratch my back, I'll scratch Yours. Got it?

Anyway, I love You, God. Have a good day, or night, or whatever it is there. I don't really know what time zone it is in heaven.

Thanks, again, God.

Love,

Shirley Kirkland"

Whew, that felt so much better to have said all that. I hope that made sure that Aunt Shirley would be all right. It couldn't hurt. After I finished talking like her I was going to tell God what *I* was going to make happen, but I still hadn't made up my mind. I guess I'd have to sleep on it, so that's what I did. I slept so well that I didn't want to wake up. I was so relaxed, and I guess part of me didn't have to worry about Aunt Shirley anymore since I talked to God for her. I wasn't positively sure if it would work that way, but what the hell, I did my best.

In the morning, right after the nurses dressed me up in fresh bandages, and I was alone again, Dr. de Pascual came in and asked, "Hi Miguel, can we talk?"

"Who are you? Joan Rivers?" I asked him back.

"No. Not today."

"That's a good one."

"So, you're doing OK, Miguel?"

"So-so. I'm really tired most of the time. And I really just like sleeping mostly these days."

"How are your spirits?"

"I'm not sure. I'll have to ask them when I get a chance."

"You know what I mean. How's your attitude about...things?"

"I'm OK. A lot of the time I really don't care anymore. I guess I'm getting myself ready to take whatever God throws at me next."

"Oh, I see. Well, it's interesting you say that. I was here at the hospital last night, performing an emergency surgery, and I stopped by your room. The lights were off. I just wanted to observe you, and when I peeked in I heard your voice. I didn't interrupt because you were praying. And, anyway, I know your Aunt Shirley is still over at Kaiser, and normally she'd be right here with you. So, if there's anything you'd like to talk about, I'd like you to tell me."

"Thanks, Lefty. Do you believe the things Aunt Shirley talks about?"

"I'm not really sure. I just know they seem to work for you, and that's what's most important."

"Well, I wasn't *praying* last night. It's actually kind of embarrassing that you heard me because most people don't understand, but I was

165

definitely *not* praying."

"Oh, I'm sorry. I thought you believed in God."

"I do, definitely. But praying is for old-fashioned people. When people pray, most of the time they're always asking for things, they're always asking God for things. Or asking Him to do things and it just doesn't work that way. We are the only ones who can make things happen in our lives. God wants to see us take the first step. God wants us to believe in ourselves just as much as we believe in Him. It's all about believing in ourselves. Everyone on earth has the power to make anything happen, themselves. And when we get this, it makes God real happy. Do *you* get it?"

"Yes. I've got to admit that I'm not the most religious person. But what you say certainly makes sense."

"That's another thing. What I'm telling you is not religious. Religions were created by man, not by God. You don't need to be religious at all to believe in God. And, the same goes for the bible, it's a man-made thing. God didn't write it, Jesus didn't write it, different men wrote it. The bible's mostly just for old-fashioned people who need some sort of evidence, like a book they can believe in. I don't need any, I've got God. For me, personally, I'd rather listen directly to You-know-who instead of reading somebody else's words in some book."

"My goodness, you certainly do have a unique approach to life."

"Maybe."

"So then, based upon what you just told me, you have the ability to get well if *you* make yourself well. That would make God happy?"

"Absolutely. God would say, 'You go, Miguel!' That's what makes Him the happiest. When we realize that we have the ability to do anything. He loves it when, instead of wishing and dreaming for things, or relying on someone else or Him to get things done, we do them ourselves. He didn't put us here on earth so we would have to rely on other people for our happiness."

"You learned all this from your Aunt Shirley?"

"Totally. Aunt Shirley and Mr. Ramirez are the smartest people I've ever met."

"Mr. Ramirez. Wasn't he one of your teachers?"

"Now he's my principal at school, and before that he was my teacher. But, more than all that, he's my friend. He always has the right answer for everything. He's the one who taught me that my Dad is OK, you know, still a good person."

"Yes, your mother has told us about your father."

"Oh, you have to take everything she says with a grain of salt. She has different feelings about Dad than I do. Some of the time she even says stuff just for effect, too. And I know she gives this hospital lots of money. So since you're probably biased, you don't need to believe me if you don't want to."

"No, Miguel. I believe you. You're probably the most honest person I have even known, child or adult. That's a terrific quality."

"Thanks, Doc."

"How do *you* feel about your father? You must miss him."

"Totally. I miss him a lot. It's totally unfair that he's in...El Salvador."

"I know where he is."

"You do? Mom told you that part?"

"Well, that's not important. But, I'm sure he misses you a lot too."

"I guess so. Sometimes he writes me nice letters, and he says he'll always love me. But, the bad thing is that I doubt if he's ever gotten any of the letters I wrote to him. I don't like that."

"I bet there's a lot you'd like to tell him."

"Oh, for sure. Well, the main thing is I would like to tell him goodbye, you know, if that's what I'm meant to do, die. I wouldn't want to leave without telling him that I liked that he was my dad and I was his son. It can't work that way. I need to tell him thanks."

"Miguel, why are you thinking about this now? This talk about *leaving*?"

"Because things are just so bad. And it's like, the longer things stay the way they are, the surer I am that I want to die. And now I don't have Aunt Shirley anymore. I don't know if I'll ever see Dad again. Mom fired Khadijah. What's the point? There used to be tons of things I wanted to do, all those things on my *To Do* list, but I'm just tired of waiting around to do them. I was kind of waiting for a miracle, but it never came. So, screw it. You know what I mean?"

"Your mother fired Khadijah?"

"Yeah. Because Khadijah wouldn't move to L.A."

"What does L.A. have to do with this?"

"You don't know? Mom married this guy and they're moving to L.A. When Mom moves down there for good, I have to go with her, to live with them."

"I knew nothing of this. But, wait a minute. This will affect your commitment to the work we're doing here together, the gene therapy. When were these plans made? When will you be leaving?"

167

Clint Adams

Dr. de Pascual had the same look on his face that Aunt Shirley got when she first got the truth about what my life's really like. Once you realize the truth, you can't go back to faking it.

A few more days went by, and I could tell that Dr. de Pascual seemed more protective of me, especially since he knew that Mom had been to the hospital only once to visit. But that was usual for her. And, I was really grateful she didn't visit more often, because she might have brought Hunt with her. Plus I didn't feel like being around any extra fear.

This time at the hospital the circumstances were getting to be way different. The infections to my lymph nodes were not healing the way the doctors thought. The worst that had happened before was that they would do some kind of surgery, and I'd eventually get better. This time they couldn't do any surgery because it was all over my lymphatic system. For the very first time I could tell the doctors thought that I was probably going to die.

Like I told Lefty before, I didn't really care what God had planned for me. Maybe it was the perfect time for me to leave, and just start up again when I felt like it later on. Sometimes I could barely talk to the nurses because I was so tired. But I still was very careful about the words I used. I mostly asked questions about Aunt Shirley to anyone who might know something. Her condition hadn't changed. But, if I was going to die, I still definitely wanted to say "goodbye" to her, and somehow say "goodbye" to Dad too. The best thing about it all was that I was going to get to be with Jorge again.

More days went by, and I remembered how Aunt Shirley always said that everyone should be self-sufficient. But sometimes I got pretty lonely because I wasn't getting hardly any visitors. But out of nowhere Dr. de Pascual came into my room and introduced me to a man I didn't know. After we talked about stuff that didn't really matter, Dr. de Pascual left the room, and the man stayed and told me why he was there.

His name was David Schwartz, an attorney from San Francisco. He said, "What I have to tell you is very important. Dr. de Pascual wanted me to remind you that if you feel yourself getting too excited, let me know, and we'll do this another time. OK?"

I nodded yes and didn't talk because I was still a little bit suspicious.

"I've been retained to represent your father, to act on his behalf here. He's in the process of pursuing your full and unconditional custody."

This time, instead of being suspicious, I was totally shocked and asked,

"Where is he?"

"Your father should be in Mexico City any moment. He was just released from prison. He won't be returning there. The reason he's not here right now, to be with you, is that complications have come up regarding his entry back into this country. He received some letters from you which made him very concerned. And as soon as he was able, he retained my services to pursue a hearing before a judge. Somehow he and I were able to correspond twice while he was in prison, and he did apparently receive the paperwork I sent him, paperwork I've since received back, signed. This all got the legal-ball rolling, so to speak. Do you understand what I've just said?"

"I can't believe this. I mean, yeah," I told him.

"He was incredibly concerned about you. And, not knowing exactly when he'd be able to be here in person, he wanted me to speak with you before you hear this from anyone else. Several people are being subpoenaed now, in order to provide depositions for a judicial review. A court date will be known shortly."

"Are you for real? Wow. Well, what am *I* supposed to do?"

"Nothing. Your doctor explained to me that you should not participate in any way. You can't be exposed to any more stress. Everything should be fine. I'm just hoping that you'll be able to speak with your father when he calls you."

"He's going to call me?"

"Oh, yes. As soon as he's in Mexico. He wanted to wait and call you from there, after he's safely out of El Salvador. He's going to do everything he can to get you back."

CHAPTER TWENTY-FIVE

On a day when my energy was real, real low Mom came to see me. It was so strange because she already visited me. For her, visiting me more than once when I was in the hospital had hardly ever happened before. She said it was too painful for her. I was too tired to say much, but getting a visitor, even if Hunt was with her, made me feel a little bit better.

"This is a record stay for you. Isn't it, dear?" Mom said.

"I haven't ever been here this long. If that's what you mean," I said back.

"Hey there, sport," Hunt said.

"They told me you won't be having surgery this time. That's a relief. You already know that, I suppose. You're going to be fine, hon," Mom said.

"We'll see. Is it true that Dad's suing you?"

Instead of looking surprised at what I asked, Mom just acted like she was. Then she looked at Hunt to see his face, and she said to me, "Well, what on earth? Where did you hear this?"

"A man came in. He's an attorney, Dad's attorney. Dad got out of jail."

"Mickey, you're not serious. Suing me? He's out of...there? I'll be surprised if he'll be able to get out of El Salvador though," Mom said, as she looked back over to Hunt.

"He already did. The guy told me Dad's in Mexico, or he definitely should be there by now."

"What the...this wasn't...," Hunt started to say, but never finished his sentence.

Because I was so tired every single minute, I had a hard time figuring out what exactly was going on. But it probably wasn't good. "You didn't get any papers?" I asked my mom.

"No. Not at all." Mom wasn't telling the truth. I could tell. She only said that because Hunt was right there.

I was about to ask them when they'd be leaving but then someone knocked on my door. It was Dr. de Pascual. He had kind of been hanging around me all that day, and I really didn't know why. "I think Miguel needs time to rest now," he said.

"Well, how's his condition? Is it improving? Doctor, he doesn't look well at all," Hunt said.

"His condition is unchanged. Perhaps we can talk outside. Miguel really does need his rest."

"No. I...I want to spend more time with my son. I rarely get the chance to see him. He means everything to me." Then the weirdest thing happened, Mom started crying. She started crying real hard, something I'd never seen her do at the hospital before. "All I care about is my son. He always comes first in my life," she said right before she turned her face away so I couldn't see it. Mom was being for real. She really did care.

"Sharon, we're doing all we can. Everyone here cares about Miguel so much. We all want to see him improve."

"Oh, I just can't stand it. It hurts me to see him like this. When it seems as if there's so little that can be done. Just look at him, look at all the pain he's in," Mom said.

"I know. I'm so sorry, Sharon."

"It's killing me," Mom said.

"Doctor de Pasqua, maybe it's only best, I mean, the most humane thing possible, to end the pain he's in. So he won't have to suffer any longer. Look at what this is doing to Sharon," Hunt whispered to Lefty.

"What are you saying?"

"I'm really thinking of her. Between you and me, doctor, if he doesn't take a turn for the better real soon, you certainly have our permission to...pull the plug or...whatever."

Almost before Hunt could finish what he was saying, Dr. de Pascual got behind Hunt and pushed him out of my room, along with my mother. "Let's talk outside," I heard Dr. de Pascual say as he closed the door behind them. The rest I couldn't hear, and I had no idea where any of them went after that. I just pretended that Hunt and Mom had never been in my room in the first place. Then I became way too tired and fell asleep just a few minutes later.

It was going to be easy for me to sleep because what I heard didn't affect me, just like nothing else did. Caring about nothing was normal for me at that point. It actually made me want to go a little more than ever before. I knew I should have felt so excited that Dad got out of jail, that he wanted to have custody of me, but I really didn't care anymore. Getting excited would have taken up too much energy. I figured it would never really happen anyway. I've had way too long to wait. And every time I waited for something good to happen, it never did. There was always some new obstacle. I knew for sure that in life there were more obstacles than good things that happened. So the only solution, I thought, was to prepare to leave, and come back another time if I wanted to.

Just before I fell asleep I thought about what it would be like to not wake up. Would it be like the people who float over their bodies in the movies? Was there really some white light? Or, was that just in the movies too? If I died in the middle of the night, would I have to wake up to go to heaven? Or, could I just go there while I'm still sleeping? I think that would be the best thing to do. That way I could have a good night sleep, then wake up already in heaven. That's what I wanted to do.

Soon after being asleep though, Jorge had come up to me in my dream. Somehow we were at the place we were at a long time ago, Playa del Carmen, Mexico. The place I found on the Internet. It was exactly the same as before, except this time we were walking in the other direction down the beach, and Jorge looked a lot different. He looked really clean, like he just got a fresh haircut. All the curly parts were gone. Jorge even seemed taller, really relaxed, and sounded kind of calm when he had asked, "Do we have anything from Haiti yet?"

"No, not Haiti," I answered.

"Well, we've got to find something from there. We have to find something from every country, or else it doesn't count. It's all or nothing."

"That's always been the way you do everything."

"What? The way I do what?"

"Jorge, dude, for you everything has to be all or nothing. Everything has to be done all the way, or none of it counts. You're never satisfied with what you've done. You're never satisfied with anything."

"I don't see what's wrong with that. What's the big deal?"

"I kind of think that that's a waste of time. I mean, you've got to be satisfied with *something*."

"It's definitely not a waste of time. Why settle for a half-assed anything? What's the point of living if you don't have high expectations. Everyone alive should only have the highest expectations."

"Yeah, maybe you're right. Hey, here's something. It looks like some kind of spray deodorant. It's from the Cayman Islands. That's a new one, right?"

"I'm not done yet. I'm telling you this for a reason, so you'd better listen. You're not trying hard enough, sometimes you give up too easily, you've settled. Anytime you settle, you're not really totally alive. Settling is for losers. Miguel, you're not a loser."

"So, I'm a loser. Whatever."

"And, that makes fear the winner. All because you didn't believe hard enough, you're going to end up letting fear kill you."

"That's exactly what you told me in your letter, that fear killed you. All those fears you learned."

"Yes, absolutely. I should have believed even harder. It got down to the last minute, and fear won. Fear won because I gave up. I got to a point where I didn't care anymore. I didn't care about anything or anybody."

"That's how I am right now. I'm actually kind of ready to go to heaven pretty soon."

"Well, if that's what you're preparing for in your mind, that's what's going to happen. But if I see you in heaven any time soon, I'll be so ashamed of you. It means you haven't learned any of your lessons. You will have dismissed all that Aunt Shirley has taught you. You have only one obstacle before you, fear. And you have a God-given miracle of an opportunity coming to you, Dad. Which do you choose to accept?"

"Yeah, that's right. I know Dad got out of jail. But if I get too excited, and the court thing never happens, or I still have to end up living with the guy Mom married, then I really will want to die, big time."

"Why think that it's not going to work out? If that's what you're preparing for yourself, then you'll surely never see Dad again."

"You sure are talking fancy. What's up with that?"

"Miguel, this is a major moment in your life, a huge opportunity. Don't you know why all this is happening? Every time a bad situation comes up, something unexpected, it immediately creates an opportunity for you...to learn your next lesson. God has given you this great opportunity, this great lesson. The rest is up to you. Then, it all comes down to choices you make in your mind, the impression you leave there. What you prepare for now is what you will have. It's that simple."

"Can we keep looking for garbage, *pleeeeze*?"

"OK. But remember that everything is your choice."

"Yeah. I got it."

"Let's have a Coke. You want one?"

"Yeah, that's a great idea. I know where there's a bar, just around that point. Let's go."

Jorge and I walked to the point with palm trees on it. Their branches were blowing softly in the wind. Windsurfers were in the sea, and the fish were jumping out of their way. It was such a perfect time. Coming towards us was a huge cruise ship, full of tourists who'd eventually get out to go to the ruins at Chichen-Itza and Tulum. I remembered how much I always wanted to go on a cruise ship. I guess I could only do that if I wanted to stay alive. I figured I better decide pretty soon.

"Is that the place we're going to?" Jorge asked, pointing to the bar.

"Yeah. I know they'll have Cokes for us. Ice cold," I said.

We walked up to the bar where no one else was, except for the bartender.

"Dos Cokas, por favor," Jorge said to him.

"Look at this," I told Jorge while showing him a newspaper I found on my seat.

"It's a paper from Cancún."

"I don't speak too much Spanish. What does this say?" I asked, while pointing to an article on the front page.

The bartender gave us the two Cokes, and I said, "Gracias," because I knew how to say it. Pretty much the only other words I know how to say are swear-ones.

"'*El Padrastro Peligroso*.' That's the title, '*The Dangerous Stepfather*.' Let me read it," Jorge said.

"Here." I gave him the newspaper to read, and as he looked it over he glanced at me in between.

"Are you positive you want to know what it says?" he asked, after he finished reading the title.

"Yeah, sure. Why not?"

"Well...it's about a crazy stepfather who got tired of taking care of his new stepson, Miguelito. It seems he always wanted him dead. So, one day, he whacked his stepson with a metal baseball bat. And after being beaten with the bat, Miguelito, became temporarily unconscious, but not dead. Then the stepfather took the boy to a deserted area and placed him in a garbage dumpster, a dumpster that he was able to close but not lock up after he put the boy in there. That's where they found him, dead. It wasn't being hit that killed the boy, being trapped in the dumpster is what did it. Miguelito didn't try hard enough to get out. They still aren't able to tell everything because the body was so badly ravaged by the hungry rats that crawled around inside."

I couldn't speak. I thought he must have been joking about the name. But then he showed me the paper, and there it was, the name, my name,

Miguelito. I felt like I had to vomit.

Even though I looked like I was going to puke, Jorge continued by saying, "There's one more thing to add to this story I'm telling you, something you're supposed to know about. Make sure Hunt can't get into your hospital room at night while you're asleep."

Right after Jorge said that, right at that moment I woke up, my dream was over, and Jorge was gone. In the complete darkness of my hospital room I stared at nothing, with my eyes wide-open. I didn't get much sleep the rest of the night. Dreaming about Jorge was usually such a good thing. I always felt better knowing that I got to see him again, and we got to do something fun. This time was different. Was that why I had the dream? So Jorge could tell me that story?

Aunt Shirley used to say that dreams are kind of a way God's able to talk to us. After all, He's not a human person, so He might not even be able to speak English. Without much wondering, I could tell that this dream meant something. Before I could hear any noise in the halls of the hospital, and before my morning nurse came in to change my bandages, Dr. de Pascual was right in front of me. He had a very serious look on his face. "Miguel, I didn't think you'd be awake this early." he said.

"Well, if you didn't think I'd be awake, then why did you come here to see me? Just kidding," I said.

"I actually came into your room after your mother was here last night, but you were already asleep. And, it was so important that I spoke with you. How about if we talk for a bit right now?"

"Sure. I'm still kind of tired. So why don't *you* do most of the talking."

"OK, I will. I don't know for certain if you heard what your stepfather told me last night, but what he said made me quite upset. And I thought you and I should talk about it. I actually asked him, well, the both of them, not to visit you for a while. It—"

"You did? Oh, that's perfect."

"Why is that perfect? I know you and your mother have had differences of opinion about Hunt, but...so you aren't upset at what I told them?"

"No. No way. It's totally perfect. The timing's just right, too."

"Good. I'm glad you're pleased."

"And not just me. Jorge and I are both pleased. I had a dream about him last night. But the bottom line of the dream had to do with Hunt, the dangerous stepfather. He told me I should make sure that Hunt couldn't get into my room here after I'm asleep. Jorge told me that right after he told me

175

a story about a stepfather who kills his stepson with a baseball bat in Mexico. It was way gross."

"My goodness. How alarming. That dream certainly had a potent story to it."

"I know. Do you believe that dreams tell a message? From God?"

"Well...maybe I do. Yes, I guess that's where they come from."

"Oh, this is such a good thing. Aunt Shirley would be so happy. She'd be happy because you're getting to be less scientific about the way you see life, and more like the way she is."

"Yes. Your Aunt Shirley. I miss not seeing her here. She makes you very happy, I can tell. I hope she's improving. But getting back to your dream, your message, I want you to know that I've done something more. Regarding your protection while you're here. I told the staff last night that you are to have no visitors whatsoever from this point on, ever. I'll tell the day-staff the same, as well as hospital security."

"None? But, Lefty. I like it when I get visitors. Why did you do that?"

"Jorge and I somehow must have been in sync last night. I did it solely because of your stepfather. But, if he found out I barred only him from visitations, I'd be in big trouble. So, this keeps him at a distance...while you're sleeping. Just as Jorge told you."

"Thanks a lot, Lefty. That's way cool."

"But, if there is anyone else you'd like to visit with, someone other than your mom and Hunt, let me know, and I'll make sure they get in to see you."

Dr. de Pascual made me feel so good. Not only because he was taking care of me so well, but because he became another one who learned to believe the truth about what my life was really like. Maybe the truth would be the thing that would set me free after all.

CHAPTER TWENTY-SIX

"For some reason I haven't gotten a call from your father yet,"
Dad's attorney told me.

"But he's OK. Right?" I asked.

"Oh, I'm sure."

"No. Wait a minute. Please don't say 'I'm sure' if you're not. I only let myself listen to the truth these days."

"Truthfully then, your father most likely is fine. Very recently I received correspondence from him regarding the upcoming hearing."

"You did? So what's going on with that?"

"As we discussed before, you won't be involved. But your father did ask me to make this call to you to keep you informed. He said you always like to know what's going on. 'You relish knowledge,' he said."

"Definitely."

"The court date is scheduled to be the fifth of June in one of the smaller rooms in the Hall of Justice."

"Is the person who loses forced to go to jail?"

"Oh, absolutely not. It's not a trial. It's similar to a custody hearing. It's called a law-in-motion hearing. The outcome will determine who will be awarded legal custody of you. The judge will review all the material presented and make a decision. That's what people who know you, your mother, and your father will provide, sworn depositions for the court. The judge then analyzes them, considers the pleadings, and decides."

"There's no jury? In the movies the jury's the one who decides."

"But like I said, this isn't a trial. It's a hearing that will take place in a courtroom, but it's not a trial. Absolutely no one will be punished or sent to jail."

"Well, that's cool."

"I know this can all sound so confusing. But it will go quickly. And the judge assigned to this hearing is more than fair."

"So, do you really think that Dad is going to win?"

"I will do my best to see that he does. Your mother does have a very influential attorney representing her though. He's rather well-known."

"Big deal. If the judge knows the truth, then he won't vote for Mom's side."

"*She*. The judge is a woman. And you'd be amazed at how powerful a high-priced attorney can be in relation to the judicial system."

"I've already learned that money is too powerful period. In any kind of system."

"Miguel, you're pretty smart. Wise for your age."

"I'm not smart enough to know the answer to one thing though. How did money ever get to be more important than people anyway? I don't get it. Do you know the answer?"

"Good question. Maybe it's always been that way. Who knows? I'm just happy that your father has the resources to proceed with legal action. He's very forceful. He's one of the most determined people I've ever known, especially where injustice is concerned. Your father had no idea how much you were being neglected. It's a good thing you wrote those letters to him."

The conversation with Dad's attorney was good because I definitely did like to know what's going on. Not knowing what was going on with Aunt Shirley was bothering me though. I thought about her all the time. I didn't know much about comas, only stuff I had seen in the movie *Coma* with Michael Douglas. It was totally gross because they kept all the people who had a coma just hanging around like inside a meat locker, and then they sold their body parts all over the place to strangers.

When Mom came to visit me in the hospital before she wasn't allowed to, she told me about Aunt Shirley. But she didn't really tell me how she was doing. She just told me technical stuff I couldn't understand. The good part of what Mom said was that Aunt Shirley's leg and lung were completely healed. So she'd be just like new whenever she woke up.

Another good thing was that Aunt Shirley could spend lots of time in her coma thinking about what she wanted to do next. And she didn't even have to go all the way to heaven to figure that out. She'd still be the same person when she woke up. That's way different from when you go to heaven, because you always have to come back to earth being somebody else, a new person. Your soul is always the same, but all the rest has to be different. Those are the rules.

Eleven O'clock was coming up and I knew that Khadijah was going to call me. She found out I couldn't have visitors anymore, so she was planning to call instead. In my room they put a speaker phone in, and that way I didn't have to hold onto anything. All I had to do was press a button once, and that was that. At first, when I started using it, the person on the other end sounded kind of weird. But I got used to it.

About one minute before eleven the phone rang. No one else was in my room so I had tons of privacy. I pressed the button and said, "Hello." It sounded real staticky on the other side, and there were tons of loud noises. I thought maybe Khadijah didn't hear me because she didn't say anything. "Khadijah, can you hear me? Are you there?" I asked. Nobody still said anything, so I was just going to hang up. That's what I always do whenever I get bad modem connections too. Maybe the next one would be better.

Just before I pressed the button to end the call, I heard, "Miguel? Are you there? I can't hear you," the voice said.

Some kind of delayed echo was going on. So it was like I was talking to myself. "Dad?" I asked.

"Yes, Miguelito. This is your father." With the echo I had time to wait for it to sink in that I was actually talking to my dad. I couldn't believe it. This was like a major miracle. All this talk about him getting out of jail, and trying to get custody of me, never seemed real before. I never accepted it, but hearing his voice on the phone changed all that.

"Dad, I can't believe it. I never knew if I'd ever hear from you again." Somehow, as if by magic, or You-know-who, the phone connection instantly got way better. And I could hear Dad perfectly.

"Oh, that's an improvement. Can you hear me OK? How are you?" Dad asked.

"I'm OK. Oh my God. It's still hard to believe that I'm actually talking to you. Where are you?"

"I've been wanting to call you for the longest time. I was finally able to get into Mexico. Right now I'm in a little town near Cancún called Playa del Carmen."

"You're joking, right? Playa del Carmen?"

"Yes. I'm scheduled to arrive in the U.S. via Miami, rather than L.A. or San Francisco. I'm hoping to get out tomorrow. I know I'm taking the long way to get to you, but it's the only way I can do it."

"But, Playa del Carmen?"

"Yes. You see, Cancún is the closest Mexican city to Miami. And as soon as I arrived, Cancún was full up, so that's how I ended up here."

"But, you won't believe this, Dad. Whenever I dream about Jorge, we're always in Playa del Carmen. This is awesome."

"Are you kidding? I didn't know you and Jorge were ever here. Did you two come with your mother?"

"No. I found out about it on the Internet."

"Well, this must be some kind of miracle. But, hey, before we say anymore, I want to know how you're doing."

"Um, OK. I just have to be extra careful. They can't do surgery on the skin on my lymph nodes, so they just kind of have to heal on their own."

"And are they?"

"Maybe. The doctor said the thing that needs healing the most is my attitude."

"I can't imagine why he'd say that. You're always so hopeful. You know you're going to be fine, don't you?"

"If you got all the letters I wrote to you, you should know how bad it is up here. Not just with me, but Aunt Shirley's in the hospital, unconscious. She was in an accident."

"What?"

"Yeah, and the worst part is they don't know when she's going to get better. So, I don't want to talk about her right now. Are you coming to San Francisco soon?"

"Absolutely. As soon as I arrive in the U.S. I'm taking a flight from Miami to the Bay Area. I can't wait to see you."

"I can't wait to see you too, Dad. So, you can get back into the U.S. no problem?"

"That's actually what's causing the hold up. Since I have dual citizenship I was able to enter El Salvador with my Salvadorian passport. But while I was in jail they confiscated my American passport. I was able to enter Mexico with the Salvadorian, but getting back into the U.S. is a different matter. It should all be resolved by tomorrow morning."

"This is like a dream, Dad. Seeing you up here again will be like all the things I ever wanted rolled into one. Do you really think you can win a lawsuit over Mom to get me back?"

"It's not a lawsuit, Miguel. I'm not fighting with your mother. That's what you want, to live with me again, isn't it? In your letters you seemed more than ready for a change. That's still the case? You want to move in with me, don't you?"

"Oh my God, yes. Yes. Yes. I was ready a long time ago. I've been waiting for this for like a million years. Where are we going to live? We don't have to move to L.A., do we? Did you know I even dreamed I was going to live with Roseanne? Oh my God, I can't believe this is happening."

"Who's Roseanne?"

"Never mind. So, when are you getting here exactly? When am I going to get to see you?"

"The day after tomorrow, son. Oh, Miguel, I've got to tell you something. I've felt so guilty. I've got to apologize now for not being there for you these past two years. It was awful being away from you. And when I got your letters, when I heard...the truth, I felt like dying."

"Hey, Dad. Forget about it. Whatever."

"No. I want you to know that I am so sorry. Somehow I thought you were being treated like a king. I had no idea about everything else, your mom's new husband. She does love you, you know. She's always done her absolute best for you. She'll always love you, Miguelito, and what happens next won't ever change that."

It was strange to hear Dad say this stuff. After all, he was suing Mom, but he still had all these good things to say about her. "I hope you're right, Dad. Sometimes Mom's hard to figure out."

"You just need to show her some compassion, that's all. Compassion."

The c-word. I hadn't heard anything about the c-word since Aunt Shirley told me about it a long time ago. Why was I supposed to show Mom compassion again? No one ever told me. What came into my head next was what she had said to me as we were driving across the Bay Bridge to get to Kaiser Hospital in Oakland. Without thinking beforehand, these words came out of me, "Dad, did you know Aunt Shirley used to have a baby?" All I could hear was the static, nothing else. Then I realized what I had just said. But it didn't stop me from asking again. "Did you know she used to have a daughter when she was sixteen?"

"Miguel, who told you this? Why are you asking me about this now?"

"I don't know, Dad. When you said the word compassion, this is what came into my head. I need to know the truth."

"Well, we'll certainly talk about this when I get back on Wednesday. How's that?"

"Dad, I need to know right now. My insides tells me that. If I don't find out now I'll explode."

Through all the noises in the background I could hear Dad take a deep breath. He knew I meant business. "Yes, your mother told me about Shirley."

"Her baby. What's the truth about Aunt Shirley's baby?"

"The truth? Yes, she did have a baby when she was sixteen."

"No. The rest of it. I know what the guy did to the baby, but what's the rest of it? The rest of the truth."

Dad waited a little bit and said, "Miguel, that's all. It's a horrible thing. Let's not talk about this anymore."

"No. I need to know about Mom. What did she have to do with it all?" My insides were burning because I needed to know all the truth so I could understand more. In order for me to have compassion I had to know everything. "What happened is what made Mom the way she is, right? Afraid?"

Dad was speechless. And somehow I had no explanation for the things I was saying, I just said them. A full minute went by. All I heard was static, but then Dad said, "Your mother always felt responsible. She gave the baby to Gilbert, the man Shirley had the baby with. Your mother was taking care of her one day, and Gilbert said he was going to take the baby to be baptized. He didn't...you know the rest, don't you?"

"And Mom's felt guilty ever since."

"Yes. She went against Shirley's wishes. She encouraged Gilbert to go. She had no idea what he was really going to do. I imagine this is what caused her to be overprotective of you and Jorge. Afraid."

"Oh my God. Poor Mom. She never did anything wrong. It wasn't her fault."

Somehow Dad and I were on the phone for so long that I blocked out for a while what he told me about Mom. I never wanted to hang up, but it was time. "I'm going to give you a very happy life. I love you so much, Miguelito."

"I love you too, Dad. Are you going to call me again before you get here?"

"Are you kidding? You're going to get sick of hearing from me. What do you want me to bring you from here? A hammock for lounging around? A miniature Mayan pyramid? A glass dolphin?"

"Garbage. That's what I want. Garbage from the beach. The best souvenir you could ever bring me is some garbage from Playa del Carmen, because that's where it all collects. You see, it's on the edge of the Caribbean, but it's not an island. So it's like all the garbage gets trapped there on the shore. It can't float away to anywhere else."

"What are you talking about? Garbage from the beach? What's the joke?"

"When I had my dreams about Playa del Carmen, Jorge and I would find garbage on the beach there. And the coolest part about the garbage is that it's from all different countries in the Caribbean. It's not like piled all over the place. You've got to go looking for it, like in the dried seaweed on top of the sand."

"I really just got here. I haven't even been to the beach yet. I don't really think there's any garbage on it though. This is a tourist town. I'm almost sure I'm not going to find any garbage on the beach here."

"Well, can you do it for me, Dad? Bring me back things that come from the most faraway places. I know you're going to find stuff there. Go for long walks, and you'll definitely find bottles and cans and all kinds of junk that's made of plastic, things that float."

"You really want me to do this?"

"Oh, yes. Because it will make it all real. Playa del Carmen is the place where my dreams actually became real, and now I'll have proof. It's the place where you called me from. It's the place where I got to be with Jorge again."

"Well then. That's what I'll bring you. I'll bring you garbage from every country in the Caribbean. U.S. Customs is going to have a field day with me when I arrive in Miami...a Salvadorian ex-con with no passport, transporting foreign trash."

"Hey, I'm pretty sure they must have seen just about everything by now. They won't care."

Before Dad hung up he promised he'd see me in no less than forty-eight hours. I had never been so excited about anything in my life. But it was about way more than seeing Dad again, it was like I was getting the chance to start all over in life. And kind of for Dad too. Not another second could go by before I did something though. What I had to do seemed long overdue, but better late than never.

"Dear God,

It's me, Miguel Estes, formerly the kid known as Miguelito. Remember me? I'm not pretending to be Aunt Shirley this time. I'll talk to You about her again later, and about Mom too. But for now I have to tell You thank You, thank You, thank You, thank You, thank You, thank You, thank You. I told You seven times because that's my lucky number.

And, if You don't know already, I'm saying thank You for getting Dad back into my life. It's a total miracle. Thanks for getting him out of jail, and for getting him out of El Salvador. I'm way grateful to You for this. So thanks again, times seven.

Another thing is, I'm really sure about something, something I wasn't so sure about before now. So, here's that part.

I want, I mean, I'm going to live. That's what I've decided. I'm going to make that happen. I'm going to get better real soon. There's too many things I need to do. As soon as I'm done talking to You I'm going to make sure my *To Do* list is crammed full of stuff. And more than that I'm going to make myself well, and get the hell out of the hospital. The speaker phone is really the only part I like about being here anyway. The rest of it really bites. No offense.

Dad is going to win the hearing and we're going to be a family again, just like before. And, if there really is garbage on the beach in Playa del Carmen, like there was in my dreams, Dad will definitely bring some back. And that will remind us both of Jorge all the time.

So how does that sound? I just wanted You to know that I'm going to do my part, You know, take the first step. The minute I see Lefty again, my doctor, I'm going to tell him I'm out of here. I mean enough is enough. My infections are going to go away, and I will be healthy enough to leave really, really soon. This is what I'm going to do. And, if You feel like giving me a break after this, that's fine too.

Oh God, there's one more thing. Since Aunt Shirley hasn't decided when to wake up from her coma yet, can You make sure that she's OK. She always said to me that You talk to people through their dreams. So since she doesn't know what's going on with everything right now, can You please make her have a dream that's kind of a news update. And tell her that I love her, and I will see her real soon.

Thanks, again, God. You're doing a great job. I mean really. You go, God! I'll talk to You again any day now when I'm back in the real world.

Love,

Miguel

P.S. Can you make sure Mom knows that I love her too."

CHAPTER TWENTY-SEVEN

A few weeks had passed and my health improved a whole bunch. But the excitement I felt the day before I was scheduled to get out of the hospital didn't last too long. My attitude changed right when Dr. de Pascual, Dad, and Dad's attorney all came into my hospital room at the same time. All three of them had the same look on their faces, like they didn't want to have to tell me something.

I just figured, what the hell. Nothing could be that bad because my dad was back. "Miguel, I've brought David in with me to explain something to you. And Dr. de Pascual is here to advise us about your health," Dad said.

"Who died? I mean, you all look like you just got done watching the ending from *Terms of Endearment* or something. What's up?" I asked.

"Well, Miguel, there appears to be a major standstill in the proceedings. The judge, for a second time, announced that she needs more time to re-consider the pleadings. We've done all we can, and after reviewing depositions from several people, the judge still isn't able to find anything conclusive that would make her decide in favor of your father. Your mother and the people who know her have given very, very strong depositions leaning in her direction," Dad's attorney said.

"And, the judge seems to be regarding all the evidence presented against Hunt Manly as being circumstantial. Do you understand what we're telling you?" Dad asked.

"Yeah. I remember *L.A. Law*," I said.

"What we're telling you is that, right now, it could go either way. With no conclusive evidence being provided for either side, the judge is finding it very difficult to give this case the validity it deserves. But there is one solution," the attorney said.

"And, before you hear what that is, I'd like you to tell your father and Mr. Schwartz exactly how you're feeling. Tell them a little about what you and I have discussed, what you need to do in order for you to maintain your good health," Lefty told me.

"Um. Well, you said that I should stay home for the first few weeks after I get out of here tomorrow. I've got to take that new kind of medicine you're giving me. And, I'm supposed to be avoiding stressful situations. Is that right? Isn't that what you said?" I asked.

"You're absolutely right. Yes, that's what I said."

"But you wouldn't be letting Miguel leave tomorrow if you felt he wasn't healthy enough to leave. Would you, Doctor? Miguel, the main reason we're here right now is because the judge would like to speak with you. She specified that she'd rather meet you than get a deposition from you, that means you being interviewed by someone else. David told the judge all about you. She's rather progressive. She's been known to voice her instincts in matters similar to this. It would have to be tomorrow, but it would only be for no more than two hours. This is something I'm not asking you to do. Dr. de Pascual knows how crucial this is. But if any part of you doesn't want to participate, you don't have to."

"I only have to meet with her for two hours? And then, can we do something fun after?" I asked.

"Not too fun," Lefty reminded me.

"Well, yes. I'm hoping so. But, don't forget, for right now, you still belong to your mother. If I don't gain some sort of custody, it's up to her if I'll be allowed to see you at all."

My decision to meet with the judge was like a major no-brainer. Duh. I mean, why not? "Yeah, I want to talk to her. No problem," I said.

What the three of them were feeling, being afraid to ask me to talk to the judge, was the total opposite of what I felt. It was my big chance. It was my turn. And, for the record, being afraid of anything is for wimps.

Before long it was the next morning, and it was my time to go home. Saying "goodbye" to everybody at the hospital was kind of sad because it got to be like home for me. One of the nurses, Irina, was even coming back with me to my house to live for two or three weeks. Maybe it was kind of a way for the nurse to protect me too if Hunt was around. That made me feel safer.

Just as Irina and I both were getting ready to leave in a cab, Mom showed up to pick us up in her car. She drove all by herself, no one else was with her. Somehow she looked like a different person. Something was definitely new about her, but I didn't know for sure what that was. Sounding just like Jorge in my dream, Mom's voice was calmer than normal when she asked, "How are you doing, Miguel?"

"What did you say, Mom?" I asked back.

"I just wanted to know how you're doing. Are you feeling OK? You must be happy about being well enough to leave."

"No. I'm fine. But you called me Miguel. You haven't done that in a real long time." I was completely shocked. It meant a lot to me that she called me Miguel. It meant to me that maybe she finally accepted me, and accepted what I am, what she created. Maybe she accepted that I was Dad's child too, that I was half-Latino. Whatever the reason, I was glad.

Irina got into the back seat and let Mom and I do most of the talking. "I understand you're meeting the judge later today. I'll take you there," Mom said.

"Don't you have to be there too, anyway?" I asked.

"No. I'll be there on the day the decision is reached. She only wants to see you today." Then Mom looked at me in a real honest way. "I'm sorry you have to go through this," she said, while her hands were kind of shaking on the steering wheel.

"Well, maybe it's what's meant to be. Maybe this is like some kind of lesson for everybody."

"Isn't that funny? That's how I see it now, too. All this time Shirley must have been right. Life certainly is full of lessons. They're not good, they're not bad, they're all just steps we must take to make it through life."

"Yes. That's right, Mom."

"And my lesson right now is a difficult one. But one I should have learned quite some time ago." Mom was getting kind of choked up before she said more. It was like it was really hard for her to talk. I didn't know what to believe. Was this all for real? Was Mom telling me all this in front of the nurse so there would be a witness? My instinct told me "no." Mom was telling the truth.

"Mom, it's OK. You don't need to talk about this if you don't want to," I said.

"You really are incredible, Miguel. Such a fine, upstanding young man. And I'm so sorry I never gave you the credit you deserved. You and Jorge were such excellent children. I never should have worried about either one of you. Instead, I should have believed in you."

When I looked over at Mom, after she told me this stuff, it was like I was seeing someone else. It's not like I wanted things to stay the way they were, because I still wanted to live with Dad. But, a lot of me felt sad. I thought it was so strange that it took all this for her to understand about lessons and believing. It seemed like in the movies, like what people said right before they died.

"That's nice you told me this, Mom. It means a lot to me."

"Well, I wish you so much happiness with your father. I'm going to miss you, my boy."

I totally didn't know what to say after Mom said that. Irina, in the back seat started to cry, and then I did too. Nothing more needed to be said.

It was good to be home again. The view from my bay window never looked better. Was it one of the last times I'd do this? Or would I end up staying? Soon I'd know. Before anything else though I had to check my e-mail. As I was about to do that though I saw something sticking out of the top drawer of my computer desk. The piece I could see looked familiar to me. Something I hadn't seen in months. I opened the drawer and couldn't believe my eyes. It was the letter Jorge wrote just before he died. I took it out, and began to read.

Dear Miguel,

When I'm gone I don't want you to waste time missing me, instead I want you to remember all the important ideas we shared. Everything I told you was said for a reason. I wasn't meant to stay here, but you are.

Even though I'm going to heaven, I will always love you. And don't forget, any time you want to tell me something, please know that I'm listening. But now it's your turn to listen.

You have learned so much in your life. You already know more than most people do about why we're here. But in order for you to survive you must be completely free of all fear. God didn't create people to live in fear. Fear is a belief in evil, not a belief in goodness.

And, opposite of what the doctors have said, E.B. is not what's killing me, it's Mom. Her fears have destroyed my spirit. I feel like I've been around her fears for too long to do anything about them now. I've become too weak to make myself well one more time. I want to go, but I don't want you to. You must continue.

You must get away from Mom. I know you love her because she's your mother, but you must get away. Her fears are lethal. All the faith and hope in the world will not work unless you are away from her and her fears completely. You must do whatever it takes, because for you, it means the difference between life and death.

I want you to keep this letter with you always. You must keep it near you until the day you are free. This letter contains all I have left to teach you, so please know how important it is to me that you understand what it says.

I will be gone soon, but I'll be around you forever. I thank God every day for giving me my dear brother, Miguelito.

I'll love you always,
Jorge

Re-reading Jorge's letter made my body numb. I kept it pressed between my two, cold hands for a very long time before I tore it up. If Jorge had lived longer he would have known he was wrong. In my dreams Jorge knew better. I'm sure he learned in heaven what he never had enough time to learn on earth. If I had never learned fear, I never would have learned to have faith...in myself. All this my time Mom had been my hardest lesson and my greatest opportunity. Thank You, God.

Just like I was supposed to, I went to the Hall of Justice the next day. Mom drove me there and she was exactly the same way she was before. Any doubts I may have had about Mom disappeared as soon as she said, "Make sure to tell the judge everything. Be totally honest. You can't go wrong when you speak the truth."

"Thanks, Mom. I'll do that. You know what the first thing is I'm going to tell her?"

"No. What?"

"I'm going to tell her that I've got the best mom ever. I picked just the right one. And now I've got my dad back too, and he's the best dad. God gave me the best life there is, I'm definitely the luckiest boy."

Mom couldn't speak a word. But I still felt like talking so I said, "Thank you for picking me to be your son. Thank you for everything you've ever done for me. Thanks for giving me Jorge. Thank you for making me understand what life is about, why I'm here. Thank you for giving me a purpose. Because of you I got to learn the difference between fear and faith. That's the biggest lesson of them all, and I learned it. Thank you, thank you, thank you, thank you, thank you, thank you, thank you. Remember? Seven's my lucky number."

Mom and I went up the steps of the Hall of Justice, and we found out where I had to go to see the judge. Then Mom went back to her car to wait in the parking lot.

Some guys made me go through a metal detector, but they didn't find anything on me. Right before I went into the judge's office, or chambers, or whatever, I then forgot what judges are called. I thought it was supposed to be *your honor*, but we weren't in a courtroom. Her door was open and she said, "Hi, you must be Miguel Estes. I am Judge Watkins."

"Hi, Judge Watkins," I said.

"You may call me Wyomia if you prefer."

"OK, thanks, Wyominga."

"No. It's not like the state. It's Wyomi-a."

"Got it, judge, I mean your honor. Or whatever." I totally messed that one up, but she didn't care. Anybody who has a different kind of name like that probably expects mistakes I guess.

"So, you know why you're here. Is that right?"

"Yes, I do. What I wasn't sure about was if you wanted to see me with anyone else in the room here, or not."

"No. No one else. I assume you have no attorney. There's no need for you to have one. And I specifically requested for your mother's and your father's attorneys not to be present at this time. This is a bit different. Normally, I spend most of my time reviewing on paper what other people have said, depositions. But, in this case, I wanted to meet you in person, and...chat."

"But without computers, right?"

"No, we won't be chatting on the computers. Oh my. Times certainly have changed. I go back to the days when chatting could only be done with our mouths. But, anyway, I'd like you to answer a few questions for me. May we begin?"

"Oh, sure."

"Tell me how you felt about your father before he left the country a while ago."

"I loved him, he's my Dad."

"What kind of relationship did you have?"

"Well we did lots of stuff together. And, Jorge was with us too. He's my brother, but he's dead now."

"Oh, I'm sorry about that. But your father, you enjoyed the time you spent with him before he left?"

"Oh, totally. It was great. And sometimes we went to places that were in other countries. Mom would go with us too. We all had a good time."

"Do you recall how you felt when your mother and father divorced?"

"Um. It was kind of bad I guess. But, I got over it."

"And how do you feel about your mother now?"

"Right now?"

"Yes, these days."

"Um, well. You want to know the bottom line?"

"Sure. What's the bottom line?"

"I know that Mom loves me lots. And, she definitely did her best, and that's totally cool. She gave me tons of lessons to learn. I used to be really afraid, like Mom. But somehow I totally like the way I turned out. I'm not so messed up, and I think I'm a good person. So, I'm glad I got to live with my mom all this time because I got to turn out this way. That's definitely OK with me. But for now...this is the bottom line part. For now, I think I need a big change. I'd like to be with a parent who believes in me *all* the time, and makes me feel good about what I'm doing. I want to be with a parent who believes in me no matter what I want to do. If I say I want to become a doctor someday and discover a cure for E.B., then I want my parent to say, 'Yes. You do that. You can do it, Miguel. You can do anything. You go!' I need to hear that, especially since I'm going to be a grownup soon. So, the rest of the bottom line is that I already learned everything I was supposed to from Mom. And now it's my turn to learn something new from Dad. No offense to Mom, but I kind of need to move on."

"So, you'd like to be with someone who cares about you? Someone who cares enough that they'll help you create a future for yourself?"

"Oh, totally. That's the main point. I guess I forgot that part when I was talking about the bottom line. But, the bottom, bottom line is that I want to be able to *have* a future, and I need to be alive to do that. I don't know if you know it, but most of the kids who have the kind of E.B. I have don't live too long. Most of them don't ever get to be twenty. I want to believe I'll be way over twenty, you know, so I can become a doctor, and do all the stuff on my *To Do* list."

"I can certainly understand."

"But you know what, Wyomeeea? What you *might not* understand is that for me to live longer I can't be afraid anymore. All my life Mom's been this way. Mom's afraid all the time. Maybe she'll change, maybe she won't. But I had to."

"And, what is your father's...philosophy?"

"He believes anything is possible. Go for it, and it will happen. He's very determined."

"Do you love your mother?"

I waited half a minute, and said, "Yes, I do, definitely. I think kids need their moms. But then when the kids are old enough to realize what's best for them, what they need even more *for themselves*, then they need to take the first step and make changes happen. That's what I want to do right now, more than anything, is make a change."

"If you were to live with your father, would you miss all that your mother is able to provide for you?"

"Oh, I'd definitely miss Mom. But that's the thing. Mom does tons of good stuff for me. She's been awesome. But right now I need even more. I need to have only faith."

"No. I mean the resources she has. Your father doesn't have those same resources."

"You mean money. That's what you mean. Lots of money doesn't mean jack to me. No offense. Money has paid for all my medical stuff that keeps me alive. But money doesn't give me a future. Money doesn't give me a reason to live. I think that's kind of crazy."

"In the depositions I've reviewed, I've read much about your aunt, your mother's sister. Shirley Kirkland. Her name was mentioned often. I understand that you have always wanted to live with her, before she was involved in the accident. Do you still wish you could be living with her?"

"Um, well that would have been cool. But look at how everything worked out. It was *all* meant to be. It was all part of the plan. You know, God's plan, if you believe in God. All of it. It was like from some sort of script. With the letters, and Aunt Shirley knowing where to mail them, Amnesty International, the way Mom was afraid, Dad coming home, and even Aunt Shirley being in an accident. Even car accidents aren't accidents. If she hadn't been in one, I'd be living with her right now, when all along, I was probably meant to be living with Dad. Well, you know, if that's what you decide. I miss Aunt Shirley a whole lot, but maybe being in a coma is not such a bad thing. She may be having a totally better time than all of us put together. Maybe the coma was always part of her plan."

"It certainly does sounds like you're extremely fond of her."

"Aunt Shirley? She's my hero, and she always will be. She taught me not to be afraid. She taught me to believe."

Even though I told the judge that maybe Aunt Shirley's being in a coma wasn't too bad, I still didn't want her to be in one. I missed her so much. She would have been so proud of me, knowing that I had been preparing for all of this, in my head, all along.

CHAPTER TWENTY-EIGHT

"No matter what the outcome is, I will always, always be here for you. I'll make sure of that," Dad told me while we were all waiting to go inside the courtroom.

"I know that, Dad. Thanks," I said.

There were only a few minutes left before everyone was going to know the judge's decision. The attorneys were there, Mom and Dad, some court people, and some extras. It wasn't like the O.J. trial at all. And it definitely wasn't going to be on Court TV either. But tension was still there when we all went in. It showed on Dad's face more than anyone else's. That meant to me that he wanted this all the most, maybe even more than I did.

All the people inside the courtroom kind of had to wait their turn. But then some court woman yelled out, "Estes vs. Kirkland-Estes-Manly," and we moved up to the front. I waved hi to the judge when I got there, but I wasn't supposed to do that. I was just being friendly. Another thing I learned is that lawyers are called counselors too, so it's like they do two jobs at once.

The attorneys and the judge said a lot of legal stuff back and forth, but then it got to be the time when the judge was going to say her decision. It got real quiet, even the people behind us who were waiting their turn wanted to hear.

While I was sitting next to Mom she kind of grinned to me, right before the judge talked. It looked like her grin was saying that she was happy for me, like I was getting something I've always wanted. I was glad Mom did that.

"It is the decision of this court, here in the City and County of San Francisco, that Joaquin Estes from this time on will become the sole, legal guardian of the child sitting before us, Miguel Jesus Estes."

The judge said more, but I don't know if I heard anything else. Nobody screamed or gasped, and the only thing I noticed was Dad standing across from me, crying. He looked kind of like the people on TV who are surprised when they're not eliminated on *American Idol*, those ones who've got tears of joy. I don't know if he was allowed to or not, but Dad came right over to me and hugged me. He cried all the way through.

"Congratulations, Joaquin," Mom said to him. She still looked the way she did when she grinned to me. Dad got his way too, and maybe Mom was happy for him. When I saw them both together I could tell that it was their time to move on, too. They looked like all the guilt they had felt was gone, and they were as free as I was. Dad didn't have to feel guilty for not being there for me anymore, and Mom didn't have to feel guilty for thinking she made me have E.B. It was like God not only gave me one, but gave *everybody* a break all at the same time.

Pretty soon we all had to get out of the front area so the next people could have their turn. I wanted to watch, but instead we all walked outside the courtroom. That was where I felt for the first time that I was given a new life. Right there, in front of the Hall of Justice, a place where lots of people were sent to jail, it was my turn to be set free.

Out of nowhere Dad walked over to Mom and her lawyer and said something, I didn't know what. They both looked happy, so I guess nobody said anything mean. And, when he came back over to me Dad asked, "Miguel, how are you feeling?"

"Fine, Dad. I'm fine."

"Well, how'd you like to do something real fun? Like go on a ferry ride? Or drive up to Stinson Beach?"

"Oh, cool. If we go there, can we see the *Basic Instinct* house?"

"Don't you remember, I showed you that one already. That house is really in Carmel. They just called it Stinson Beach so she'd be closer to the city."

"Yeah, that's right. I forgot. That's like *Pacific Heights*. Their house wasn't really in Pacific Heights at all, it was on Potrero Hill."

"Right again. I'm going to make sure the next place we live has a huge satellite dish so you can watch whatever movie or TV show you want."

"Dad! That would be heck'a cool. A satellite. Oh my God. This is going to be so great."

I just didn't think that life could get better than that. Being with my dad again, plus I get to watch 150 channels if I wanted to. Without a doubt I needed to thank God ASAP. There were actually a few things I wanted to say, so what I needed to do most was find a place to talk in private.

Dad and I got into his rental car to drive to my house first so I could change clothes before we did something fun. I loved being with him again. And since he hadn't been in the city for a while, I played tour guide. As we drove south on Market Street, I pointed to my right and said, "Dad, look over there. That's the Carl's Jr. where a homeless guy in front of it was dead for two whole days before anyone realized he was dead. Can you believe it?"

I liked showing Dad things that the real tour guides didn't usually tell. As soon as Dad and I got to my house I went into my bedroom. But instead of spending all my time changing, I sat down in front of my bay window and said,

"Dear God,

Thanks a lot for making this miracle happen. I guess deep down I knew this was all going to work out the way it did. I guess preparing for something, even if it is planted way, way, way deep down in your brain, still is going to happen. I never knew it would take this long though. But, just like Aunt Shirley said, 'You're the only one who's got the right schedule,' and 'Even though You don't wear a watch, You're timing's perfect.' That's way cool by the way.

Thanks a lot also for making the judge decide the right decision. I liked her. I would like to thank her too someday. And next time I'll make sure not to call her Wyominga. It really seemed like what happened in the courtroom, for all of us, was meant to be. It was like the final chapter and a new chapter all at the same time. Is that how You always do it? Are things meant to be for lots of people in a bunch, and not just for people one at a time? I don't really know how that works. But thanks for doing what You did. I guess I don't need to know more than that.

At least not now. Someday I'd like to have all the answers though, just like Aunt Shirley.

The only thing that was sad about today was that she wasn't there, and we never get to talk anymore. She's OK, isn't she? When Valene Ewing was in coma on *Knots Landing*, it didn't last anywhere near as long as Aunt Shirley's, and Valene's was even part of the end-of-the-season cliffhanger. Is that because it's just an hour show, and things have to go a lot faster on TV?

Well, anyway, I was thinking. Remember when I heard Mom and Aunt Shirley talking about what happened to her, and that bad guy she was with, and the little baby Aunt Shirley had when she was real young? I'm assuming You know, because from what I've heard, You know everything. But the point is, her life can't end until that part is fixed up, You know, it's unfinished business. It's a terrible thing that

that guy took her little baby away and then killed it.

Aunt Shirley, in this life, needs to learn to trust somebody again. That's a really huge lesson, right? I'm pretty sure that this is definitely one thing she needs to learn before her life is done. Right?

Aunt Shirley is also such a great teacher. I know she has lots more to teach other people. You know, like God only created good, not evil, hell, devils and rotten stuff like that. And if God created everything, why would He have wasted His time creating something like a devil? Oops, I forgot. Sorry for talking about You in the third person. For a second there I forgot that *You* are the one who made the whole world.

But, just like I asked the judge, do You want to know the bottom line? I'm sure You do. Aunt Shirley needs to wake up from her coma. You're the only one who can schedule when this is going to happen, but she definitely needs to wake up sometime. I'm not being greedy either because this would mostly be for her, not for me. I miss her all the time, but my life goes on. Hers is on hold. Waking up and learning to trust someone by maybe having a relationship or something would make her life here complete. All her lessons would be learned.

And, is that really why we're all here? Is life just like a big, huge school that's not just for kids? Since I'm thirteen now, and I'm older, I know this is true, and I like it this way. I like whatever You've got for me. Surprises are the best. I used to be more anal and had to plan things out all the way, but now surprises are what make life more fun.

I've got to go pretty soon. But thanks again for all the miracles You've done for me. I want You to know how grateful I am, and I definitely don't take You for granted. So, if You want to do more for me, that I'd be even more grateful for, that's OK too. I can't wait to see what happens next.

Um, and I want to say this too. Thank You for giving me my mom, because without her my life never would have gone this way. It would have been way, way more boring, and way too easy I bet. Living with her was always an adventure, but look how I came out of it. Not so shabby after all. And I guess the biggest thing is that I thank her. Somehow the way she raised me was the best possible way. And now, that's hell'a, I mean, heck'a cool with me.

And by the way, maybe You could cut Mom some slack with her own lessons. They're really hard for her. And if You can't, just tell her that she's OK in my book.

So, thanks a lot. This is a dream come true. But I guess the way it worked out, was that I made my own dream happen. Because deep down I always knew I could. But, don't forget, I'm not done by a long shot. Look out for me taking a whole bunch more first steps.

Until then, goodbye and thank You a lot, God. Later, Dude.

Love,

Miguel"

Talking to God seemed to go by so fast. I had plenty of time leftover to change clothes *and* catch my breath. "Dad, where are we going again?" I yelled out from my bedroom.

"I'm still not sure. Let's just get into the car and be spontaneous," he said.

"You mean, sperm of the moment?"

"*Sperm* of the moment?"

"Duh. Don't you get it? That's what Archie Bunker calls it." I could tell that Dad and I were definitely going to have to catch up on Nick-at-Nite and TV Land so he wouldn't be so clueless. "OK, Dad, I'm ready," I said.

"Well then, let's hit it," he said.

"That's what Aunt Shirley says, 'Let's hit it'." After I said that I ran back into my room to get something, the watch Aunt Shirley gave me. The one that doesn't tell time. It took me over a minute, but I put in on all by myself.

From the living room Dad yelled to me, "You can have soup, can't you? If it's not too hot?"

"Yeah, why?" I said, as I walked back in.

"Let's drive up the coast to Bodega Bay, where we can order two jumbo-sized bowls of clam chowder. How would that be?"

"No way. Awesome. That's where *The Birds* was. That real old movie from the 60's."

"That's why I'm taking you there. Because I know how much you like to see where movies were filmed. We'll have lunch at The Tides restaurant. That's where they shot a lot of it. I tell you what though, sometimes I worry about you, Miguel. Sometimes I think you like television and movies more than real life."

"What's wrong with that?"

"Nothing, I guess."

"I think a lot of the time I like made-up people better than real ones. And since I don't have a whole lot of friends, I like to pretend the ones on TV are people I know."

Dad had a confused look on his face, so I could tell he still didn't quite get it. He didn't understand that what kept me alive most was my imagination. It had always given me a million different ways to get away from the things that were bad. TV people didn't ever hurt me. They never kept reminding me that I was going to die. And, for most of them, they never seemed to think that money was more important than people, except for the totally rich people on *Dynasty*, and Mr. Drysdale and George Jefferson of course.

As Dad and I got back into his car both of us still were pretty happy, and it lasted that way for a real long time. Then I asked, "Are you ever going to figure out how you got put in prison?"

"Gee. I'm not sure, Miguel."

"Do you think that guy Hunt had something to do with it?"

"I don't really know. I do know one thing though. David, my attorney, feels certain that your mom had done something to help me get out."

"Mom? No kidding?"

"But for the moment I'm not going to pursue it. The past is the past, it would be a waste of time. I got what I wanted. I'd rather spend time being with my son."

Then, what happened as we tried driving over the Golden Gate Bridge seemed meant to be. A huge crowd had gathered on the walkway of the bay-side of the bridge. Traffic was just about completely stopped from cars slowing down to see what was going on. Since I was on the passenger side Dad rolled down my window. "What's going on?" he yelled across me.

"Someone jumped off, a boy. No one has gotten to him yet. It looks like he may still be alive," a tourist yelled back.

In the background of all the tourists was the most beautiful sight I'd ever seen in all the world. The San Francisco Bay, the city, the Bay Bridge, the East Bay, Angel Island, Alcatraz, and Marin County. These were places I got to look at every day, places these tourists probably always read about, but places I thought that that boy might never see again. I thought about him for the rest of the day.

I thought about the many times I wanted to die, but didn't. I thought about how many times I wanted to give up. But then I tried to imagine what that boy's life was like. Maybe he stopped believing. Maybe he stopped believing that something better would happen for him. Aunt Shirley always said that suicide was just another way to die, and that man made up the part about it being a sin and that the person would go straight to hell. I always remembered that hell never existed in the first place, because God doesn't punish people. People do that to themselves.

What seemed like a sin to me was that that boy probably didn't have any faith. When Dad and I got to Bodega Bay I found a place to be by myself, and I told God all about that boy, a boy I didn't even know. I talked out loud so it would matter, and as I did that I realized something very important. Maybe if I could have taught him about faith and believing, just like the way Aunt Shirley taught me, he never would have jumped off the bridge.

Before I finished talking to God again I looked down at my watch. It reminded me of the two questions I always used to ask Aunt Shirley, "What is my reward going to be for suffering so long? What am I going to get for all the lessons I decided to learn?"

"Your reward will be your ability to help others. Your reward is not what you will be given, it's what you will be able to give back. You will always have E.B., you might always struggle, but soon you'll have something miraculous to share with others...this is your reward," Aunt Shirley had answered.

Right then, I knew that this would be the best way I could thank God for all the miracles He had given me.

On the news two days later they talked about that boy. They thought he must have jumped off the bridge because he was dying from AIDS and was tired of living with all the pain. Even though tons of people over the years have jumped off the Golden Gate Bridge, this boy was one of the very few to survive, even though he did get pretty messed up. He was probably someone who totally needed to talk to someone else. Instead of talking, they arrested him, because jumping off the bridge is a crime. His name was Miguelito, the same name as the name of the boy who used to be me.

It took a while, but I eventually found out where I could find him, and I ended up writing him a letter. A few weeks after that he wrote back, and we've been friends ever since. I taught him so many new things, and it made me feel real good to help someone who was just like me.

Miguelito learned that only he could make himself well. He spoke only positive words out loud. He prepared a great future for himself. But making up his *To Do* list was his favorite. Miguelito kept his list near him all the time, and he always made sure it was full.